THE SILENCE OF SNOW

Ginny Vere Nicoll

❄

Feel Good Books

Ginny Vere Nicoll

Published by Feel Good Books

www.feelgoodbooksonline.com

ginny@verenicoll.co.uk

© 2021 Ginny Vere Nicoll

First edition

ISBN: 978-0-9563366-5-1

Cover design by Tamara Hickie
(tamara@studiohickie.com)
from an original watercolour painting
by Ginny Vere Nicoll

Songs:
Tobiah Thomas
www.tobiahuk.com

Printed and bound by
KerryType Ltd, Midhurst, West Sussex, GU29 9PX

This book is a work of fiction.
Names, characters, places and incidents are either a
product of the author's imagination or are used fictitiously.
Any resemblance to actual people, living or dead,
events or locales, is entirely coincidental.

Acknowledgements

I TOOK a short trip to Estonia one winter, when the snow lay thickly on the ground. The old part of Talinn was special. The people were helpful and friendly, yet I did sense a definite atmosphere of unease caused by their Eastern neighbour! This encouraged the idea of a novel set partly in their country.

I love being in the Swiss Alps where I feel safe, well looked after and secure. For me, the mountains have been a haven of peace, for quiet moments, for happiness and thought, but also for recovery from turbulent times. Hence the 'safe house' in the mountains! So once more, Switzerland must be included. Nearer home, my mother's family and I have a special affinity with the Scottish Highlands. Travelling around to research the more remote areas was the greatest of fun. I would like to thank all the people who have helped me from these three completely different, yet stunningly beautiful, parts of the world.

A big thank you to Mark, my husband, who during these last two difficult years of Covid lockdowns has spent endless hours editing, giving me encouragement and advice. He always wanted to be in publishing – not the law! I'd like to thank our daughter, Tamara Hickie, for once more understanding exactly how I hope to present my story on the cover; also to her husband James for his part in looking after my website and for his fun authorial photoshoots! Thank you to my printer, Darren, Sue especially and the KerryType team in Midhurst, for their patience and high standard of work, once more, in creating 'The Silence Of Snow'. Also to Tobiah for all her lovely haunting songs based on my novels. Another big thank you again to Tim O'Kelly and his group of upbeat and helpful ladies in One Tree Books, Petersfield, for letting me have my seventh launch in his lovely bookshop.

Lastly, a thank you to everyone else who has supported me and to my loyal readers: perhaps you might recognise characters from my previous books, some of whom I feel are almost family! If you are kind enough to read my novels, I hope that you really enjoy another adventure set in the lovely locations I have chosen for The Silence Of Snow.

Dedication

I would like to dedicate this novel to my nearest and dearest family and friends and to all those who have suffered, struggled and survived throughout the horrific 2020/2021 Covid 19 pandemic.

THE SILENCE OF SNOW

CHAPTER 1

Premonition
(A Friday evening in London)

A SHARP crack followed by breaking glass; then a loud reverberating crash had Ellie jumping out of her chair in fright and heading for the window. Silence, but for only a moment: although long enough for a cold shiver to find its way down the back of her neck. 'Someone walking over your grave.' Ellie remembered the dreadful intuitive feeling she'd experienced just before she'd heard of her brother's horrific accident. That was a twin thing she reassured herself, but this was something quite different.

She gingerly opened the window and looked out. Down below, just for an instant, two pairs of guilty yellow green eyes held her gaze. Ellie breathed out in relief as a pair of suburban foxes made off, over a low wall, after creating chaos amongst the building's usually well-ordered dustbins.

All in all it had been a long day: difficult clients, an extremely grumpy boss and a thoroughly unsatisfactory lunch meeting, with food that didn't suit her. Ellie went to the bathroom mirror, circling her taught shoulders to relieve the tension. She was looking forward to an evening with Jake planning their imminent holiday together. Her stark image in the glass showed a pale face with staring dark navy blue eyes, heavily ringed with tiredness.

'God,' murmured Ellie to herself, 'what on earth is the matter with me? After all it was only a couple of bold feral foxes after an easy dinner.'

Strangely she'd been suffering disturbed dreams recently, which left her tired and nervous during the day and less able to cope with ordinary office upsets.

It was time to get a grip on herself or she'd be late. Going to her bedroom cupboard, Ellie drew out her usual safe choice: a smart black trouser suit with a simple cream silk shirt. Always the same, yet the garment suited her slim figure, especially as she often had to go straight from the office to an evening event. Some high heels, a bit of jewellery and a different printed scarf wrapped around her neck, would ring the changes. At least tonight she'd managed to get home for a shower. She dressed and then went across to study her appearance in the long mirror. A calm and cool reflection now looked falsely back at her, belying the previous few moments of anxiety. Her dark hair cut in its modern short bob looked good; Jake said it suited her. Minimal makeup enhanced her flawless skin while the diamond studs in her ears induced a little necessary sparkle.

The front doorbell buzzed furiously. The taxi driver obviously didn't intend to hang around out of his cab for too long in the cool night air, thought Ellie. She could hear the taxi clearly now in the street below, with the sound of its familiar comforting engine reliably ticking over. She decided not to bother with an overcoat as she'd hardly be outside for more than a couple of minutes. A quick spritz of Jake's favourite scent and she was ready.

Locking the flat door behind her, Ellie felt her old self again. She really must not be so easily spooked in the future just because she'd had a bad day. It was ridiculous. The cold air hit her as she walked outside dispelling her sombre thoughts and tiredness of spirit. Warmth at the prospect of seeing Jake again filled her with joy. They had the whole weekend ahead to themselves, with no annoying plans, parental or otherwise.

❋

"Are you alright if I drop you off at the corner Miss? There's a lot going on around here tonight and with the one-way system an' all, I shan't be able to turn around that easily; there's so much traffic."

"Yes of course, no problem," answered Ellie quickly getting out her money. "I can see the place I'm going to from here; it's all lit up. Thank you very much."

She handed over the fare and, with a spring in her step, set off up the street trying to avoid all the hordes of onlookers milling around enjoying a night out in Soho.

The Night Jar Brasserie was smart and alluring, slightly exotic even, with strange looking plants and sophisticated furnishings. As usual Ellie was there before Jake; he was always late. She headed for a free comfy-looking stool at the end of the long bar. She asked for a glass of pale pink pinot grigio and, once it had arrived, sat back quietly sipping the reviving cool liquid while she waited. Ellie felt happy and steady again, she and Jake had been together for eighteen months now and she wondered if their relationship would last. They were definitely known to be an item; he was good fun yet not quite as romantic as she would have liked. Maybe that was her fault; perhaps she was holding back a little. She was well aware that he considered her to be, in his words, a rather quiet and very private person.

Suddenly Ellie's thoughts were interrupted as the neighbouring stool, which had become free, was quickly claimed.

"Good evening! I'm so sorry to disturb your peace but it seems this is the only empty chair in the entire room. I suppose Friday night is the problem!" He laughed good naturedly. Ellie appraised the polite newcomer taking in his clean-shaven face, clothes and hearing a well-educated accent.

"Don't worry," she answered, "I'm just waiting for somebody before we have dinner." The man's grey eyes twinkled.

"Actually I think I know who you are waiting for Ellie. It is Ellie isn't it?"

Ellie sat up both surprised and alert for a moment, then she looked once more at the agreeable face in front of her.

"How on earth do you know my name? We've never met," she exclaimed. The man chuckled.

"Don't be alarmed," he reassured. "It's simple really. I'm a work-mate of Jake's and he once showed me a picture of you in his wallet."

Ellie let out a sigh, instantly understanding "Oh goodness! Has he still got that funny old picture of me by the sea?"

"Yes he does. It's a good likeness but doesn't do you credit in the flesh," he laughed and continued easily. "Anyway, I'm Nicholas. Nick for short." He held out a welcoming hand before adding, "Would you like a top up while we wait for our other halves?"

Ellie glanced at her watch, returned the handshake and answered happily, "Yes, please – why not? Jake's always half an hour late and I'm always early!"

Ellie had texted her twin, Giles, from the taxi. They kept in close touch and often seemed to know when something was wrong with the other. She felt like checking up on him because of that odd premonition she'd just had, after her fright from the fox burglars outside her flat. While her new acquaintance, Nicholas, was ordering their fresh drinks she took out her mobile for a quick check to see if Giles had answered. He had and he'd replied. *'Yes, I'm fine, how are you? You sound a bit strange. What's up?'* Good, Ellie smiled to herself; she'd reply after dinner to tell him how this new place rated. The stranger placed her new glass of wine in front of her.

"Here we are then: my treat for picking up my old mate's girlfriend!"

"Thank you very much," Ellie answered taking a large swig to hide her embarrassment. Funny though that Jake had never before mentioned this good-looking friend of his – Nicholas – or Nick.

* * *

CHAPTER 2

Tension
(Saturday afternoon)

THE man who seemed to be in charge had a shambolic appearance: canary-yellow-coloured hair and a weak clammy handshake. This was Jake's first impression of the individual standing before him. The untidy slightly alien looking person also suffered a noticeable twitch to his cold steel grey eyes, which were half hidden in unhealthy dark deep-set sockets. Closer scrutiny revealed a large body, relapsed into slack fat, only partially concealed by creased ill-fitting clothes, completing his unpleasant overall image. Jake absorbed every detail in a matter of seconds. This lot must certainly be low down the pecking order. Real low life: Jake stepped well back.

He knew that there was bound to be somebody far more professional to whom they would be answering. Yet Jake's alert intelligent eyes gave none of his thoughts away. But his superiors must be well briefed on the situation? After all it was they who had arranged this meeting with the motley crew's controller. These men wouldn't have been capable of setting up anything without guidance, they'd only be acting to orders from some heavyweight higher up the hierarchy. The very thought of this man, standing in front of him, even having a phone conversation with Jake's people back at headquarters, was almost funny – if it hadn't been for the present precarious predicament.

No doubt there was much more to the story. Jake had most likely only been told what was necessary at this present time, probably for his own good and for that of Ellie. He was briefed that these people were from one of the Eastern European countries, Russia most likely, yet he wasn't to let on that he understood and could speak the language himself.

Jake then glanced towards the minions assembled, tense and alert, either side of their gross boss. Each had their hands ready for quick removal of their weaponry, barely hidden inside their rumpled open jackets. No question that these thugs projected their intimidating strength, but Jake was sure that any cruel ideas would emanate from the man with the yellow hair. That would surely be his forte. He had that easily identifiable look of ugly aggression; one which laced with vodka indicated how much he would likely enjoy the violence he dealt.

As the group tried to stare him down Jake wondered how he would be seen through their eyes? Cool, experienced and unflappable, he hoped beyond all else. If only he could achieve what was expected without having to call upon his combat training. With this mob he'd prefer to keep his hard-earned confrontational and physical strengths in reserve, at least until the numbers were more even. Jake had a sophisticated phone with its special capabilities well camouflaged. He had only to press a button to summon backup. It looked just like the perfectly ordinary run of the mill mobile that thousands used, but it was a brilliant espionage device. Jake carried no weaponry of his own, as had been specifically stipulated when this meeting was arranged.

As instructed, he had to set up a further rendezvous, but in a particular place and at a certain time. Only then, he had been told, could the operation become viable. Jake had a small part in the op, it seemed, but that was understandable considering he wasn't long qualified for this covert type of field work.

Jake undid the middle button of his jacket and took a more casual stance then, making plain what he was about, offered the boss-man a cigarette. The man grunted his thanks and in turn produced a grubby looking lighter out of an even dirtier trouser pocket. The lighter was in the shape of a topless woman. The man must live in seedy bars. Even from a distance, he stank of cigarettes and unwashed clothes. Jake wondered where these criminals were based in the UK and where they'd come from originally; definitely somewhere in Eastern Europe. They obviously had easy access in and out of the country. So, someone up the pecking order must have plenty of clout.

He noticed that the minders had all moved in closer, smirking, raising their hands a little to advertise their strength with their hardware. The manoeuvre could have been almost laughable except that the weaponry was likely loaded. Here in a suburban dead-end rundown street they were well off the beaten track, with nobody around to see or hear. He must be careful: back up, if summoned, was some minutes away.

"Well" said Jake, deciding it was best to get on with it and speak slow and clear. "So you want some cash and we need the little lady returned – all in one piece," he added for good measure. "So how about tomorrow at midday in the old grave yard, beside the church around the corner from here?"

He inclined his head indicating its proximity. They wouldn't try anything on there, not on a Sunday, when there were people around after the weekly service.

The big man gave a grunt, sniffed and wiped his nose on his arm, then turned to the surrounding group, thick orange eyebrows raised in question. He shuffled from one foot to the other relieving the tension a little. He wasn't used to giving orders thought Jake and lacked confidence; seeming uneasy with the task he'd been given.

Jack waited for an answer. Why was it, he thought, that mobsters such as these always wore their dark shiny trousers too long? The men all glanced shiftily at each other before nodding in unison yet still without talking. The henchman probably didn't speak much English. 'Good,' thought Jake; the yellow-haired git really wasn't too sure of himself and needed the support of the unlikely looking gang. Who on earth, in their right mind, would hire people like these to work for them? He'd give a lot to know who was behind this whole kidnapping idea, as the man who'd taken Ellie was, he'd been informed, of another calibre altogether.

"Alright," answered the big dishevelled man of few words, swivelling around on heavy heeled shoes.

It was over for the moment.

"Tomorrow then," agreed Jake raising his hand in a mock salute and matching his assailant's lack of words, turning smartly and walking unhurriedly towards the warehouse exit.

The air smelt sweet and clean after the stifling musty atmosphere in the derelict empty building. Jake hit the button on the car key which released the door lock with a satisfying clunk. Seemingly still in no hurry, just in case a concealed pair of eyes was watching, he opened the door, got in and then sped off with a sigh of relief. He was glad the meeting was over without frayed and short tempers exploding. The canary or *'kanaari'* as, in his second language, Jake now privately nicknamed the wretched man, was without a doubt the worst possible example of the human race. He dreaded to think about what might have gone on with Ellie. He ran his free left hand fingers through his hair to relieve the tension. A characteristic gesture for the young man when in a bad situation.

The thought of Ellie cooped up God knows where for a second night, was almost too much to bear. His stomach was in a knot. The very idea of any one of those men touching her he couldn't and mustn't even contemplate. But he hadn't shown how much he cared, although they surely must know of his relationship with Ellie. Yet this had to be simply seen to be a business arrangement or he'd have less bargaining power.

If only Julian Birchall and Guy Hargreaves were around, his mentors and friends. But they were both out of the country involved in another mission. He must concentrate on every element of training they'd taught him at the Hereford base. He'd enjoyed the tough physical side and the idea of some backup fieldwork. Hopefully, before long, they'd all be together again on a normal footing and he'd continue with his work with the MOD, in his office at Northolt; he loved it there being involved in all the classified global comings and goings. Driving on back into the city, he made sure he wasn't being followed then pulled in to the kerb, put his own personal feelings to the back of his mind and made the expected call back to Headquarters.

✻

Ellie stared up towards the only light in the room. A mere slit of brightness high up in the ancient wall told her it was afternoon and her watch agreed – just after four pm. She couldn't really remember how she came to be in this place or for how long she'd been here. She must have been knocked out with some lethal concoction in the bar where she'd arranged to meet Jake on his way back home last night. They'd never been there before. Someone in her office had said that the cocktails were special. I wonder if they knew just how 'special', thought Ellie grimly. Jake must have been kept late at the office. She had arrived early and had spoken to somebody soon after arriving, or perhaps he'd spoken first. She recalled a youngish man sitting down beside her, both polite and well spoken, in a city suit. Good looking. How could she have been so easily taken in? But he'd introduced himself saying that he was a friend of Jake's, he'd seen her picture from Jake's wallet and so had recognised her. From this confession Ellie had immediately decided that the man named Nicholas, or Nick as he had soon suggested, was alright. It must have been him: she'd quickly felt dizzy and he'd helped her outside. That was the last thing she remembered. The bloody bastard!

Ellie wished she had some more water; the bottle beside her was now empty. She heaved herself up unsteadily into a standing position, thinking about the predicament in which she found herself. She was cold, not surprising considering it was well into Autumn. She felt queasy still and frightened, but as yet not strong enough to take any action should it become possible. She looked disgustedly over at the bucket they'd left for her and turned away, wrapping the horse blanket around her more firmly. That was her one comfort, she loved horses and the familiar smell instantly reminded her of happier memories as a child, although she wished she also had her warm overcoat.

She still had on her smart work suit. In spite of feeling dirty and dishevelled, even her shoes had somehow managed to remain firmly on her feet. Her short dark hair was still firmly held back, on one side, with the tortoiseshell clip – one Jake had given her on holiday just last year, which she had so carefully chosen last night; all of which now seemed a lifetime ago. Ellie looked at her hands. They shook, yet the nails were unbroken and the pink nail polish remained untarnished. So as far as she could tell she hadn't been in any way physically abused. She had no serious bruising or soreness anywhere. She just couldn't remember quite what had happened. Rohipnol – it must have been that particular drug that he had used to befuddle her brain and make her incapable of putting up any sort of a fight. But why was she taken? What was her worth? What did they want and who were they?

Ellie knew that Jake had another life, all muddled up with friends they'd made on holiday in the Lake District. Julian, Guy, Oliver and the doctor, Marc. They'd all got on well and Ellie had particularly liked Rose, Olly's other half. She had gleaned lots of intriguing information from Rose about what the men got up to when they went off together. All highly secret stuff it seemed. The Secret Service she thought most likely, in which case she just had to fix on the likelihood of Jake being aware of what had happened to her and hope he was already on the case. She had to keep faith that eventually he'd come for her. Her limbs felt numb, anything for a hot bath and home thought Ellie dejectedly, tears starting their silent journey down across her cheeks. She moved over to the door knowing it would be firmly locked. She sensed that she was in the middle of nowhere so there was no point in shouting. Best to walk a bit then sit down again, regain her strength and wait – it was all she could do.

✳   ✳   ✳

CHAPTER 3

Marking Time
(London)

ENDURING a sleepless night, Sunday eventually dawned and midday finally arrived. It had seemed an interminably long wait. Jake had spent much of the inactive hours of the night castigating himself for not having arrived early, for once in his life, at the bar where Ellie had been awaiting him. But the time had not been wasted, he had at least rested and by the time he'd dressed and eaten a simple breakfast his head was clear. The group who had taken Ellie had declared their demands: the meeting had been arranged, *'alea iacta est is'* – so the die was cast.

For this particular mission, which involved Jake's private life, the hardest part had been keeping himself in work mode; putting his own feelings on hold. Guy and Julian had been in similar circumstances and had explained how they'd managed to keep control of their own emotions. Now Jake tried practising their advice. His outward cool exterior remained, although his insides were churning: but he was in control.

It had been difficult, early last evening, when Ellie's parents rang to speak to her, as they always did on a Saturday evening. He'd had to lie through his teeth, saying she'd gone off to see some girlfriend who was in trouble and that it was all very hush hush and secret. Well, at least that last part was true.

In this most enigmatic world, which he'd joined, Jake had already been on several small quick ops but he had never before dealt with something which touched him personally. His bosses were adamant that he was the one the abductors had particularly named to negotiate the deal, which meant that they were certainly aware that Ellie was his girlfriend. If considered necessary they'd use that knowledge, thought Jake even more worried for her safety.

But he was glad to have a hand in achieving her release, as he couldn't have sat idly by and waited this one out; not with Ellie in danger. In the cold light of day he knew he was up to the job, his superiors had faith in him so he'd give of his best and stick to what he'd been trained to do. The meeting in the cemetery would he hoped, if he handled things well, manoeuvre matters along toward a successful end to the mission.

※

Jake walked between and around the headstones making for the centre of the churchyard. As expected, there were a few people around and the undesirables were already arrived, over in a far corner, leaning on either side of tall tombstones and trampling all over the well-kept graves, smoking; both oblivious and thoughtless as to where they were standing. No sign of Ellie: he hadn't presumed she'd be here, but where was she for God's sake? No money and nobody would move, his people back at HQ had assured him; not until she was seen to be safe. He'd left his tracking device in the car, just in case they insisted on searching him.

Call it ESP but Jake reckoned Ellie was in the vicinity and not far away; the airport also was right in the area. He approached the group with apparent confidence and a fake smile. He wasn't in the least bit intimidated, just determined to act as he'd been told. The 'kanaari' man was turned to watch his approach, flicking his ice-cold eyes down to the case Jake carried. No greeting of any sort; just an unwelcoming glare.

"The money?" the man demanded pointing rudely to Jake's briefcase as soon as he came near.

"On the computer of course," replied Jake airily, "but only when we have the girl."

"I asked for cash and transport," the man spat back.

"No can do," Jake answered coolly, putting the case down carefully beside him. "The money only goes in when we have the girl and you're on your way."

The canary definitely had Russian origins, Jake thought, taking in every smallest detail as his assailant reddened, at first looking uncertain, then thoroughly annoyed. Jake just lifted his hands in mock exasperation.

"It's your call!"

On schedule Jake's driver appeared through the nearest gate of the cemetery holding up some car keys for them to see. In the moment of quiet confusion they could all hear an engine running.

"Your call!" Jake said again, this time adding a mildly impatient sigh and indicating that he was ready to go.

"The plane? Is Ok to go? My pilot, crew?" asked the man of little speech.

"It's there, with your crew ready and waiting, but we need the girl, now – and she'd better be unharmed. Where is she?"

"Nearby, you'll have her as soon as we have the money – on board. She's still in one piece, as you English say." The man sniggered having actually managed a reasonable length sentence for once. The jerk had made up his mind. He had obviously realised there was no alternative and so turned to one of his men.

"Go and get the *suka*," he shouted, "but you," he pointed belligerently again at Jake, "you and the suitcase come with us. *Ty doizhen sledovat.*" Good, reasoned Jake, it's working. So far so good. He let the tension fuel his adrenalin.

"Right let's go!" Jake marched off towards the exit to his driver, another well trained colleague, with the ill-assorted group of crooks in close pursuit.

The boss man went up to Jake's driver, gave him the once over, then grunted "*Sledovat!* You follow!" and climbed into a minibus with blacked out windows parked across the road.

If he could just get them all onto the plane and retrieve Ellie unscathed, only then could he hand over the reins and relax. This is what he'd been told to do. God alone knew what would happen next and as for his lovely Ellie? Just keep her safe until I get there, prayed Jake silently, as they followed the minibus.

They skirted the airport perimeter in tandem and drove through a secluded entrance to where small private aircraft were parked. Their plane was out on the tarmac with its engines already fired. Headquarters at their best, thought Jake glancing at his watch, happy in the knowledge that he was being closely monitored. On schedule – almost to the minute. The rush of adrenalin steadied and his confidence rose realising that backup must be in place and was as efficient as ever.

❋

With a deep breath Jake ducked his head and entered the expensive Bombardier jet first, with one of the Russian minions close behind, wheezing loudly as he climbed the boarding steps. The crew were waiting to receive them. A cool look of authority bathed the pilot's face as in that first instant, when he and Guy saw each other, Jake managed artfully to force recognition off his face while he inwardly heaved a sigh of relief.

Guy, Jake's friend and colleague, stood in his immaculate pilot's uniform looking every bit the commercial employee he was expected to be. The three other crew stood smart and welcoming beside him; Jake nodded to the men, the air hostess was extremely attractive; Jake felt immediately drawn to her eyes which seemed to convey an unusual depth of understanding.

The yellow-haired thug came in next and stopped dead in front of Guy. His large face creased into a puzzled frown.

"Where's our pilot?" He turned to look around then noticed his own pilot sitting beside another crew member towards the back of the plane; both men were in rumpled uniforms, heads down, looking very sorry for themselves, appearing fearful and undoubtedly expecting trouble.

The big man let out a furious oath and pushing rudely past both Jake and Guy, strode off down the aisle shouting mostly in disjointed Russian.

"What the shit's going on here? *tchyo za ga lima?* What's happened?"

The steward hurried up behind him just as the angry thug raised a fist to the quivering Russian pilot, who'd struggled still cowering, to his feet. The steward quickly intervened.

"*On u-shihp-sa,* a car crash, last night, after too long in a bar. Your pilot is concussed with stitches in his head, Sir. He can't fly, he is sleeping all the time."

The pilot sank to his seat again, thankful for the intervention. The canary boss didn't attempt to lower his voice.

"Shit! *derr mo!*" he swore again. "Who is that then?"

He pointed discourteously back towards the front of the plane as both Guy and the co-pilot now emerged from the cockpit. Jake and the stewardess were standing to one side in the kitchenette area patiently awaiting the outcome of the confrontation. It was almost as if this particular crew had seen it all before, thought Jake intuitively, wondering just how they might know these people as they seemed to be handling the situation unusually well.

Guy walked forward handing over his credentials, politely enquiring if there was a problem?

Jake listened attentively admiring Guy's cool explanation as to how he came unexpectedly to the job. He said that he was asked to do many last minute flights when people were let down or the pilot taken ill. He was used to it and as long as he was paid well, he never asked any questions about his passengers or what they might be carrying. His credentials were meticulous and had been given the Ok by the gentleman who'd hired the crew.

Guy obviously had tongue in cheek when he used the word 'gentleman' in front of this uncouth lout; Jake had to keep a grin off his face. Guy was being exceptionally diplomatic he noted as his friend and colleague continued to state his qualifications. Guy said that he was cleared to pilot anything that flew, except for fighter jets and the larger aircraft carrying missiles. He'd get himself home. The return journey would be covered by his pay.

Jake felt the tension as the big man considered what Guy had said. They were all waved away as the canary man took out his mobile to ring his superior for confirmation. Jake, listened as best he could. Although mostly speaking slang, the yellow *kanaari* and his henchmen were definitely of the Russian race.

But where was Ellie?

✳

It was Sunday afternoon and Ellie's legs felt swollen and numb. Fright she thought; it could do that to you. She'd had nothing to eat since yesterday, at lunch time, when she'd been given a stale cheese sandwich and water.

She was exhausted, her throat was dry: Ellie was both hungry and cold. She'd been blindfolded, virtually dragged out of her prison and shoved into an old jeep; then driven at speed through bumpy, twisting lanes until they arrived at some small airport, which she didn't recognise when the blindfold was removed. She was given her shoulder bag and told in gruff badly spoken English to tidy herself up. As she did so Ellie could see a private aircraft way out on the runway. Presumably it was their goal.

The jeep rushed through the entrance then slowed to hover a little distance from the plane. There was a minibus with darkened windows already parked alongside. Whoever was in that plane could now see them, Ellie realised, wondering what on earth was going to happen next. She looked around surreptitiously. There didn't seem to be many people about; just a couple of ground staff waiting to see the plane off. The tower over on the right would control the plane's movements but were they aware of her own situation Ellie mused?

For God's sake, was she to be taken out of the country now by these vile thugs? If so, there was nothing she could do. Her hands were shaking, she felt sick and she needed the bathroom. Was there nobody to help her?

A man appeared at the door of the aircraft and waved them forward. Her driver grunted and the one beside her started to stroke her thigh.

"It's goodbye little one, huh? *YA khochu trakhnut tebya,*" he whispered close to her ear. "I would have liked some more time with you." He pressed his leg hard up against hers and lecherously ran his fingers across Ellie's cheek. His breath stank, his fingers were dirty, nicotine stained and gnarled, it was all Ellie could do not to retch; she edged as far away as she could, up against the car door protesting as best she could. Although in another language she'd understood perfectly well what he'd intimated.

The driver muttered something rude and unintelligible over his shoulder to the man beside her, then he drove to the bottom of the steps and stopped, hissing instructions over his shoulder.

"Go! *Otva li* get out! Now!"

Once more Ellie was dragged out of the jeep and made to haltingly ascend the steep steps. There was no point in struggling, she was weak and there was nobody to rescue her. She just took as much time as she dared, hoping that perhaps cars with flashing lights would appear to surround the plane and prevent it from taking off. The very idea of being taken out of the country against her will by these monsters was terrifying.

But... miracle of all miracles, Jake stood facing her as she entered. He was frowning.

"Oh!" was all that Ellie was capable of uttering. A large ugly man with yellow blonde hair appeared, shoving past Jake and grabbed her roughly by the shoulder.

"You know this man, *da?*"

She shrugged off the rough hand, stood up straight and looked searchingly at the man whose bed she shared – Jake's right hand was just in her line of vision and she sensed rather than saw it move slightly from side to side. Without hesitation she turned to stare back at the horrendous yellow-haired bully.

"We have met before," was all she said.

"Thought so," he sneered. Then the man shouted towards the cockpit "*Poydem!* let's go."

"Hang on a minute!" Jake moved to intercede, holding up his free hand, while the other clutched his briefcase. "Either you let the girl go or no deal! None whatsoever!"

"*Zasranec!*" The Russian swore, turned his back and started pacing the narrow gangway huffing and puffing with impatience. The crew, the lovely dark girl and the steward, the two appeared closely connected, waited up by the cockpit seemingly unfussed but a little confused at the altercation. The co-pilot sat uninvolved in his seat concentrating on his flight details. Jake knew that Guy, also in the cockpit, was in earshot and this realisation boosted his spirits.

"Either my man comes to get her or no deal. I repeat no deal. You'll leave with nothing at all. Nobody will move or release the money until they have the girl safely released and unharmed." Jake stood his ground firmly, lifting the case with the computer to make his point.

The big man turned back furiously and glared.

"Shut up *ty idiot*! I can't think with that noise." He swiped hard at the face of the sniffing wheezing individual standing nearest.

Jake saw Ellie cringe at the violence. But she stood bravely near the open door with a gang member holding her roughly by the shoulder. Jake knew that Guy would have heard every last word.

There was silence now and the atmosphere inside the plane was hot and intense. The English pilot then came forward once more: Jake alone heard Ellie's stifled intake of breath as she recognised their friend. Guy once more betrayed no sign of recognition and glanced at his watch.

"Excuse me, Sir." He addressed the boss man. "I'm afraid we need to leave on schedule; the bad weather is imminent and if we delay any further, our airspace slots en route will be lost."

The thug absorbed this information which seemed to stir him into action.

"Alright, call your man for the *suka*." He pointed to Jake, who just managed to hide his disgust at Ellie being referred to again as a bitch, as he took out his mobile.

"And the rest of you *otva li*. Out – Now! And take those idiots with you." Waving his hands around wildly, the yellow-haired monster indicated the two wounded members in the back who gingerly got to their feet and shambled along the aisle towards the door.

The man holding Ellie released his hold ready to join the others, who all couldn't get out quickly enough, once the order had been given.

"Not you two! *ostavaysya zdes*!" The Russian bawled, pointing to Ellie's jailor and another man who was half out of the doorway. Both men turned back with a look of unhappy resignation on their faces.

As the jeep and the minibus sped away another smaller vehicle, with blacked out windows, arrived to collect Ellie. Jake checked out of the window then, seeing his own transport safely arrived, indicated for her to leave.

Ellie, who had slumped down onto the nearest seat, gathered herself together and rose quickly to her feet. She held her head high and said a formal courteous 'thank you' to her lover, the man who had come to her rescue. With one last contemptuous glance at the man in charge, she ducked her head to exit, blinked against the strong sunlight and started in slow dignified steps to walk down to the waiting car and freedom. Jake thought he'd never been so proud.

* * *

CHAPTER 4

Relief

(A country police station North of London)

MARC sat waiting, uneasy, yet well prepared for the bad state in which he might find his patient. He had been informed that he or she was safely on their way, but that was all. He didn't know the circumstances or what to expect and he had once more been made to reconfirm the Official Secrets Act.

Marc and Emma had been on her delayed birthday break, in an especially good pub in the country to the North of London, when he had received the phone call. He was to go to a police station, some ten miles away and to await instructions. Emma wasn't at all pleased. It was such a treat to be on their own without having to worry about their two little children for once – he could understand how she felt. But when he had originally joined the territorial army, part time, he had known that he'd like to put his medical skills to use in an 'out of the ordinary' way. So, with advice from friends, he had taken specialized medical training. Since when he had been mobilised on many occasions, in a very discreet and secret world. At these times he had someone to cover for him when it affected his part time GP work at his local surgery.

Marc looked up as the sound of an engine coming to a halt outside disturbed the silence. The station was quieter on a Sunday, early in the evening in the colder months. Most folk would be tucked up safe at home preparing for the next working day. He moved across to the window. Two people were helping a woman out of the car. She was wrapped in a blanket but able to walk, he saw immediately. Good, she wasn't a stretcher case. He checked he had everything ready and continued to wait. The door opened and his patient was brought in. A young woman looked out from underneath a warm hood.

My God it was Ellie, Guy and Julian's friend – Jake's girlfriend! He walked forward to greet her holding out both hands.

"Ellie, come in, it's alright now, you're safe." Ellie stared at Marc in confused astonishment, her eyes filled and she promptly burst into tears. He quickly ushered her into an empty interview room, then nodded to the plain clothes police escorting her; one went out and the other, a woman, discreetly left a recording machine behind a curtain before leaving the room. Marc had heard the click as she'd flicked the on switch. He took Ellie by the arm and helped her across to a chair.

"Marc, why are you here? What are you doing, what's happening? I don't understand any of it and Jake... Jake... he's in some big trouble and Guy he was there too but dressed as a pilot. Who were those terrible people and why... why did they want me... me of all people, what could they possibly want?" She slumped down onto the uncomfortable armchair in the corner, pulling the blanket closely around her. She was shaking, Marc noticed, as he perched himself on a stool beside her. He took her small cold hands in his.

"It's alright Ellie. I had no idea that it would be you walking through the door just now. But one thing I do know: If Guy is in any way involved in what is going on, then Jake has the best backup support he could possibly need. So you must try not to worry. Now I want to check that you're not hurting anywhere. Did those men abuse you in any way?" he asked gently.

"No! Thank God!" Ellie, calmer now, replied with feeling. "Although I'm not sure how much longer I would have lasted intact: yuck they were disgusting. I'm just so cold, I can't seem to stop shaking. I'm dirty and tired and so hungry."

After a meticulous check, Marc could thankfully confirm that she was indeed untouched, except for some superficial bruising on one of her shoulders. He let out a sigh of relief.

"Ok we'll get you a cup of tea and some biscuits then you'll be coming back with me to where Emma and I are staying."

"Oh no," Ellie sniffed. "I suppose I've ruined your weekend haven't I? I'm so sorry I'm just so worried about Jake with those dreadful violent people. I think they were talking Russian some of the time and I don't think that they were intending to let Jake go either. They wanted money in exchange for me. That much I worked out, but he wouldn't even think of transferring it until I was safe. Both he and Guy were so cool and in control. I hope I didn't let them down. I'm sure they were going to make Jake go with them. Oh God! I hope he's alright: Guy too. But I don't understand any of it and what on earth could they possibly want with me?"

"Well I have a feeling that you were just a small part of a much bigger picture. No way did you let anybody down Ellie. You've been extremely brave. You must try not to worry; Jake and Guy have both been trained. They are professionals in a very elite secret world. They know what they're doing. Now let's get you that tea and then back to the hotel, I think a hot bath and a meal is called for. The man in plain clothes is a Home Office man. He may just need to ask a few questions and explain a few things before we can leave. Its standard practice in these rather delicate cases. I had to sign a form for confidentiality as well, so don't worry, I shall be with you all the time."

"I'm so relieved to see you," muttered Ellie, sinking down further into the old chair in an exhausted heap as Marc went to the door to order tea and biscuits. When he turned back, she was completely engulfed in the blanket, almost as if all the horror had reduced her in size. He could tranquillize the immediate physical affects but hoped he'd also be able to pour balm on any mental damage.

※

Back at the hotel Emma, feeling relatively fed up, went down to the bar to order a drink. She'd rung home to check on the two girls but, speaking to her mother, had declined to let on that their plans had been thoroughly disrupted. She'd do that in the morning. From past experience Emma knew better than refer in any way to Marc's additional work. It always worried her mother who had guessed it was something apart from his normal doctors job.

As she walked into the cosy fire-lit sitting room of the hotel, Emma noticed a person seated quietly on her own by the window looking just a little out of place. Why on earth didn't the woman sit by the fire, thought Emma, heading straight for the comforting warmth. Odd, but perhaps she too was waiting for someone. This person in no way appeared to be enjoying a leisurely evening with that glass of orange either, she mused. On duty, with no doubt at all and most likely a plain clothes policewoman of some sort or other. Emma ordered a glass of Sauvignon from the bartender. At the same time she also asked if she could re-book their dinner for an hour later. Emma then went to sit beside the fire where, through the open door, she could see into the hall and reception area.

Some half an hour later Marc appeared with a woman huddled in a blanket. Emma stayed put, sensing that he'd wish her to remain incognito for the moment. Marc noticed her, smiled and discreetly shook his head indicating, as she had thought, for her to stay where she was. Emma had assessed the situation correctly: the woman by the window immediately got to her feet and went over. There was a low discussion before she took the blanketed lady upstairs. Marc waved and walked through to the bar, ordering a drink from the barman en route as he came to sit beside Emma, kissed her cheek and sat down with a tired yet relieved sigh.

"God almighty, what have you got involved in now?" she asked with an amused smile.

"Well," grinned Marc "you aren't going to believe this but that," he replied pointing toward the stairs to the upper floor, "was someone we both know and, if she is up to it, she's going to be having dinner with us. I'm afraid it's *de rigueur* as that poor girl has been through one hell of an ordeal, which of course I can't tell you too much about." He finished, rather smugly thought Emma.

"Hey ho!" sighed Emma. "Here we go again! I sincerely hope that once again none of the others are muddled up in whatever it is. There's a party organised for next week, which I can already see being cancelled."

Mark turned quickly away from his wife's alert and beautiful eyes, to take his drink from the barman, who had happily arrived at just the right moment.

✳

The telephone rang shrilly beside the bed. Emma, lying with her feet up jumped with the unexpected disturbance. She'd been miles away in thought wondering just what was going on while Marc was taking a quick shower before dinner. She felt a little ill at ease yet picked up the annoying instrument thinking it must be the hotel reception. It wasn't anything to do with the hotel, it was their friend Rose, ringing from London. Emma had told no one where they were going to be this weekend. How did Rose have the hotel number?

"Hello Rose, how are you and how on earth did you know where we were?"

"I don't know where you are exactly, but I had a message from Marc to ring him on this number and I've only just picked it up. Are you alright you two?"

"Yes, but there's something going on of which as yet I'm not a part. Why has he asked you to call I wonder?" Emma was mystified.

"Well," answered Rose, "the message said would I kindly have the spare-room made up, so I assume that one of you, or both for some reason, want to come and stay? This is absolutely fine of course, better than fine actually as Olly is away on some TA tramp anyway, so I'm by myself with nothing much to do as the office is closed for redecoration. At the moment I'm dealing with everything from home."

Emma looked up as her husband came out of the shower, a questioning look on his face as he saw her on the phone.

"Hang on Rose, perhaps we are about to be enlightened. He's just come out of the bathroom. I'll hand you over. Lots of love then, bye." Marc leaned over her to retrieve the phone but Emma held on to it, with her hand over the mouth piece.

"What is going on here exactly?"

"I'll tell you all that I can in a minute." He kissed her quickly and grabbed the phone as he walked out onto the small private balcony, firmly shutting the French window behind him.

Emma went to brush her hair. She looked long and hard in the mirror. Her dark hair glistened with good health except on her face the worry lines were more pronounced after the beginnings of this latest intrigue. Her eyes were bright, but alert and perhaps just looking a little scared. It's because of the children, she thought, that she felt more fearful about physical safety these days. She stood up. Her figure had almost returned to its pre-motherhood state. Poppy was four and a half now and little Lilly Anne just over a year old. The worst of the baby stage seemed to be past, although Emma already dreaded the time ahead when as teenagers they would no longer be safe under her own roof every night of the week. But that was still a long way off, thank goodness. No mother loved her children more. Or her husband, come to that, Emma decided. She must be strong and support Marc in whatever he was about, take everything in her stride. They'd been through much together in the past.

Marc came back in, his dark red hair damp and shining in the light. The towelling dressing gown had kept him warm outside and as usual he was full of good humour and concern for her wellbeing above all else. She loved the unusual colour of his brown eyes, one with the dark fleck. Those eyes were fixed on her now.

"I'm so sorry about all this my darling, spoiling our long weekend away, but you see this friend of ours is in deep trouble and needs our help and that of Rose as well. I will of course tell you all that I can now…" Emma interrupted.

"Come here and get warm for goodness sake, it's cold out there you'll catch your death, after your shower, then a fat lot of good you'd be to anybody. Apart from which we have half an hour before dinner." She held out her arms with an invitation he certainly couldn't resist.

❉   ❉   ❉

CHAPTER 5

Team Effort
(On the plane)

JAKE sat, near the front of the plane, quietly considering his situation while absorbing everything around him as he'd been trained. Guy was behaving as would any normal airline pilot. Jake could just see his friend, now in shirt sleeves, concentrating and carefully watching his controls. He was making the odd adjustment as he chatted through his head-phones on the VHF frequency to the air traffic control tower about en route weather conditions. Was Alexei the co-pilot one of theirs or ours Jake wondered. The young man was of foreign extraction as was Katya, the very pretty smart stewardess, busy preparing coffee and pastries. They certainly looked as if they knew each other well and worked together as a regular team.

The boss-man or evil '*Kanaari*', as Jake had privately named the monster, sat towards the back of the aircraft with his equally coarse untidy henchman. The last remaining minion, who had brought Ellie to them, sat on the nearby aisle seat opposite Jake, glancing at him warily from time to time. What was the idiot expecting? That he'd open the door and jump out still clasping the briefcase? The stewardess, he noted, kept as far away from the boss man as possible, except for getting up periodically to offer more coffee. They'd crossed the channel, flown out North of Paris and now were probably over Germany. Jake imagined they were heading out of Europe and the EU to somewhere discreet, outside of British jurisdiction. They would want no interference with the bank transfer. What were they up to? What was it all about?

He got up, indicating to the imbecile opposite that he needed the lavatory, at the front of the aircraft, just outside the cockpit. The man leapt to his feet and made to take the briefcase. Jake merely shook his head and took it with him, momentarily blocking the man's view between himself and the pilots. The door into the cockpit was open and Guy turned around in his seat and winked. The yellow *kanaari* had risen to his feet to see what the mild commotion was about. Jake heard Guy give an instruction to his co-pilot.

"Alexei, we're on auto at present, please go inform the boss of our flight details – here are the notes." Jake fiddled with the door then waited for the co-pilot to politely squeeze past before entering the small washroom.

With the noise of the aircraft engines and the bulk of their bodies filling the space nobody could have seen Guy turn his head to say quickly to Jake, "We're heading for St Petersburg. Don't worry. All is under control, we have friends meeting us."

"What about the co-pilot and the steward and stewardess, ours or theirs?"

"Independent crew I think, working together as a team, I imagine."

Jake felt a knot of excitement invade his stomach and a surge of adrenalin boost his confidence as he shut the door firmly behind him. Now that Ellie was safe he realised just how much he actually loved this job. Pushing back his unruly brown hair from his forehead he studied his mirror image. Dark circles of tiredness framed his alert green eyes and worry lines creased his brow. Jake splashed cold water over his face, letting it run over his wrists till they were ice cool. Drying his hands he found he was looking forward to the task in hand, whatever it turned out to be. He felt on top of the situation, now he knew he had the best back up that he could wish for. He went back to his place, put the briefcase on the empty seat beside him and asked the stewardess for some water. Looking at his watch he reckoned they had just over another hour and a half to go – with his hand firmly gripping the case he could risk a short snooze to prepare for the unknown next phase of the operation.

*

Emma and Marc went down to the hotel restaurant to wait for their guest but she was already at their reserved table, in a discreet corner of the room, eating nuts with a large glass of red wine in her hand.

On seeing them arrive Ellie, smiling through her tears, immediately got up and came into Emma's open arms.

"Oh my God Ellie! It's you! Are you alright? I can't believe you're muddled up in this latest horror!"

"Neither can I. It's all like the worst nightmare. I'm alright now that I'm here with you two, thanks… just a bit tearful and shaky, also worried about Jake. Sorry!" Marc pulled out a chair.

"Come then Ellie, sit down let's get you fed, you must be starving."

"Yes I am but I've been stuffing bread and I had all those biscuits at the police station and after that glorious bath I think I'll survive. How lucky it was for me that you two were here, so near to it all."

Ellie, in Emma's slightly too large jeans and jersey which Emma had given to the lady policeman for her, looked exhausted despite her upbeat conversation. Emma, understood so well how she must be feeling as she'd suffered in a similar situation herself a few years back.

Ellie appeared all huddled up into herself clasping her knees. Her newly shortened hair had somehow lost its shine and her huge dark blue eyes seemed bigger than ever but looked dull and lustreless. Her skin was paper white. Although they hadn't known each other long, Emma's heart went out to their young friend after her horrible ordeal.

"I've brought down another wrap thing for you to snuggle into. You'll feel cold I'm sure after the effects of the bath wear off."

Emma placed the warm coral coloured shawl around Ellie's thin shoulders and kissed her again, before sitting down close beside her and opposite Marc. She had chosen a table especially near to the blazing fire.

"We thought that perhaps you might like to sleep in our room tonight with me," Emma continued, "Marc is happy to swap for a night."

"I'd like that very much indeed, if you're sure you don't mind: and Marc, please do tell that policewoman that she can go. She's very kind but not exactly a cosy person to have around."

Marc laughed.

"I know what you mean; there are actually two of them, the other a man. They'll be around but as you are with us now, they can stay out of the way. Now let's concentrate on ordering dinner, then I want you to feel that you can talk about it all or not, as you wish. Remember I am both friend and doctor for the time being."

He looked across the restaurant, through the double doors, towards the reception hall. There was nobody else about, most people had eaten and left the dining room for coffee in the sitting areas or in the bar on the other side of the hotel. The policewoman would be there also. They would be here albeit discreetly all night, just to check that nobody unexpected or uninvited came in.

*

Later after a nourishing dinner with plenty of red wine Emma took Ellie up to their large room, produced a spare pair of pyjamas and tucked her up in their big bed. She was totally worn out. Emma kissed her goodnight and left the bathroom light on, so that she'd know where she was, if she woke up in the night. The poor girl was asleep before Emma left to go downstairs to join Marc for a nightcap.

Marc watched Emma as she approached with a determined look on her face. He smiled in admiration. She had taken all the intrigue in her stride. Now he was about to be grilled, it was already hitting him in vibes, as she crossed the room towards him. Emma sat in the chair opposite, put her elbows on the table, picked up the drink he'd ordered for her and fixed him with an authoritative stare.

"Ok, now you'd better fill me in with the whole story as I'm not about to ask Ellie to divulge any more of her horrific experience, but if we are to look after her I need to be aware of what's going on; at least about some of it." Marc sighed, his wife was a strong character, but she was right she did need to understand how things stood.

"Alright, I'll tell you as much as I know of the situation which poor Ellie has been living through, but as yet I'm not aware of the bigger picture myself. Neither are Headquarters who are, as we speak, working on every possible scenario. I'm afraid Guy is also out there with Jake."

"Oh no! Not Guy as well, he's always involved in some intrigue or other. What about Julian? I suppose he's in it up to his neck too?"

"I don't know, really I don't, however I'm sure that things will become clear once these wretched people make up their minds what they want from us, other than the money." Emma looked worried and took a sip of her drink.

"So do you think that both Julian and Guy are in real danger once more? Also Jake, he's only been in the force for a short time, surely he's not really experienced enough to deal with this sort of thing?"

"I have no idea; I'll just tell you what I can, but we mustn't speculate. Although the so called 'Cold War' is no more, in certain respects we now have more trouble than before in finding out exactly what the Russians are up to."

"Oh! Good Heavens!" Emma interrupted, "Not the bloody Russians!"

❋   ❋   ❋

CHAPTER 6

The Eye Of The Storm
(In flight)

AS they flew on across Europe Guy considered the predicament. He knew perfectly well that this particular group would not let Jake out of their clutches until they had landed in Mother Russia and the money was safely transferred. But he felt sure there was far more to the story than the cash, although it was an obscene amount they were demanding.

Somewhere out there someone was manipulating a much bigger agenda. This motley crew were just being paid to fetch and carry and do somebody else's dirty work.

Guy had already been told to change course slightly for a smaller airport South of St Petersburg. Unfortunate, as at the main Clearwater International airport he had backup arranged. It would be difficult to get word to them of the altered destination without his co-pilot becoming suspicious. He wasn't sure yet which way the man's loyalty lay.

If these Slavic people had control of a private airfield then the operation would become far more complicated. They obviously knew how to cover their tracks and Guy had a gut feeling that he might even be told to refuel and continue on yet another flight. There was indication that another Baltic country was involved. Intelligence back in the UK had managed to infiltrate and decode a message from a Russian government source, which had been confirmed by a British covert agent in Moscow. Jake's name was mentioned as was that of his girlfriend, Ellie. The very vulnerable Estonia immediately came to mind.

As a senior officer, Guy had seen Jake's credentials when they had been so meticulously checked before the young man joined the Reserve Force attached to the SAS. Jake was born in the UK, well-educated and well connected yet, although you'd never have known, he was actually only half English. Few knew that he had a wealthy Estonian grandmother, of Swedish descent, who still lived in some style in the countryside of Estonia. The Baltic nobility had been powerful and influential people in past times. They settled in the manor houses and palaces that had dominated the rural countryside until Estonia finally became Independent in 1991.

Jake spoke Swedish as well as Russian and he had a good understanding of most of the Baltic languages. This command of different dialects had made him a valued member of Guy's elite group, when he had been officially recruited a year previously.

The people on board were speaking in a gutteral Russian dialect, so it was obvious to Guy that Jake would understand what was being said. But these people were only the couriers and Guy suspected that whoever was behind this nasty situation had taken the trouble to investigate Jake's lineage. Jake could just be the prize.

Time would tell where they would all end up. For the moment the thugs had the upper hand, but Headquarters were still able to track their progress. Guy felt quite certain that there was much more behind the whole affair, which would soon become evident; as it was unlikely to have been a mere kidnapping of Ellie for money. Everyone knew Mother Russia's eyes were always on the countries by which she was bordered.

※

The weather was deteriorating as forecast making the plane shake and skew in the rising wind.

Jake had exceptionally fine-tuned ears, so he could hear a little of the conversation between the man in charge and his shifty sidekick, a few seats behind him. They were loud, rough spoken, uncouth people which made it more difficult to understand their slang, especially against the whine of the aircraft: but as the plane flew on across Europe in Guy's firm hands, the truth began to dawn on Jake. He stared out of the cabin window at an unsettled night sky and his heart sank. One of the men was speaking of Estonia.

He himself was the catch, Ellie had merely been the bait and both he and his superiors had fallen for it – hook line and sinker. But then again perhaps those back at GCHQ had dropped him in it on purpose. Jake supposed he was most likely the best qualified for this particular mission. But what could these people possibly want from him? A cold chill crept down his back undermining his confidence and fuelling extreme unease. His grandmother, of whom he was very fond, was still an exceptionally wealthy woman. She lived in a lovely manor house on a large estate just on the Estonian side of the Russian border. She was often in the public eye and he, Jake, was her only grandchild. If his thinking was correct whoever was behind this operation would be an extremely dangerous and exceptionally powerful individual. He would be capable of manoeuvring political events and attempting to bribe key figure's in the Estonian government and for that they'd need a lot of money. Thank God his own parents and sister were away on a holiday on the other side of the world and completely unaware of his present predicament.

Jake wished he could transfer these thoughts across to Guy, but there was no way he would be allowed to the lavatory again so he'd just have to sit tight, listen to as much as he could hear and wait to see where they landed. At least

Ellie was safe. He half turned his head to concentrate again as the two behind were conversing once more.

Unfastening his seatbelt Guy told the co-pilot to take over and set off towards the back of the plane to talk to the boss. As he went past Jake he reached up seemingly to adjust a cabin locker door, rattling it, creating a diversion. Jake stood up and quickly took his opportunity.

"Let me help!" Then more quietly he whispered, unheard above the engine drone, "it's Estonia and it's me they're after – Ellie was just the bait."

"I know. Nothing to be done right now though. But our destination must remain as planned; St Petersburg airport, as the weather really is worsening." Guy answered appearing to struggle still further with the locker catch as the two men towards the back of the plane had now risen from their seats and were hurrying down the aisle towards them.

"That's it! Thanks." Guy clicked the latch into place and turned to speak to his employer.

"We're in for some turbulence so would you please sit down and fasten your seat belts. I'm having trouble getting St. Petersburg on the radio at the moment," he lied, "we may have to divert and circle for a while till I get our landing instructions. They're obviously very busy getting everybody safely down."

That'll prolong the agony and shake them up a bit he decided.

"We are expected at the small airport!" snapped the angry man in charge.

"Yes I'm sure, but St. Petersburg is the best option in rough weather. I've been given my coordinates. Other flights also have had to alter course so we must await the info and follow instructions." The man was about to argue but the plane shuddered and lurched sideways, as if ordered, unbalancing the Russians.

"Do what you must then but get on with it," the ugly man answered glaring and red in the face; with fright Guy surmised, pleased.

"I'm sorry Sir," he answered politely, "but unfortunately I'm not in control of the weather, which is closing in. In this storm we need a runway with the required facilities and preferably one with which I am familiar, otherwise, in this particular plane, it is simply not safe enough to land." The plane switched again and both men were literally thrown back into their seats, looking thoroughly shaken.

"Now I must return to the cockpit to fly this aeroplane. Please do as I ask and put your seat belts on for your own comfort and turn off your mobile phones," he added with a slight grin directed at Jake as he turned back his way. Jake's minder was also beginning to look ever more anxious and already had his head between his knees. Guy hoped for Jake's sake the man wasn't about to be sick, so he indicated the bags in a side pocket near at hand.

Jake had sat quietly listening, admiring Guys tactics. A surge of adrenalin boosted the younger man's confidence again as he realised just how professional Guy was as he neatly out manoeuvred these uncouth, violent people. They would land at Clearwater International after all, where help would be at hand. He nudged his quivering companion and handed over a couple of the paper bags hoping they wouldn't be required.

❋　❋　❋

CHAPTER 7

The Estonian Connection
(Turbulent airspace)

GUY readjusted his headset and while he still had a few more minutes on automatic spoke again to his co-pilot.

"We have already warned Clearwater international that we have a Code 7500 threat when we entered Russian airspace. Now we need to warn the tower that we have a Code Red landing. Tell the crew to prepare. It'll be manual and rough with the crosswinds. There's very low cloud. We may lose radio contact, but I'll leave the automatic on as long as I dare, until we have a visual and can see the landing lights, then I'll take manual control. We might have to go round again but we'll most likely be the last in today so that shouldn't be a problem."

Alexei nodded his understanding and did as he was told. It was snowing hard and for the moment there was a complete white out. A pilot's nightmare in a small plane: with such a low cloud ceiling they were going to be landing almost entirely blind. Guy needed full concentration on getting them all down safely.

By his side, Alexei so far had proved extremely professional and Guy had decided with relief that the man had no ongoing or regular link whatsoever to these thugs. It was obvious also that he, along with the steward and pretty stewardess, were an independent team recruited for clients by a private aircraft company.

Alexei gave their altitude height and ETA then asked for every bad weather facility available to be made ready. Guy switched over to listen to the short clipped response in exceptionally good English. For St. Petersburg, he supposed, these conditions were normal; they were told that everything was prepared for their arrival. There was one other aircraft coming in behind them which posed no problem: just stay on course and clear the runway as fast as possible. Guy gave an indistinguishable sigh. No problem my foot. Despite the appalling weather, just how much did those in the tower at this International airport know about the tense situation on board? He hoped that by now they were well informed and aware of his aircraft's precarious plight.

Realising that the cabin crew stood behind him, braced just inside the open doorway awaiting further orders, he raised his voice.

"Make sure that all the passengers and yourselves are properly strapped in and prepare as for a basic crash-landing. It will be pretty bumpy. Alexei give out the two-minute warning and Katya, please shut the cabin door now." That'll put the fear of God into the bastards Guy thought with satisfaction. He didn't have to deceive his Russian passengers any further. Absolute concentration was now needed for they were not only to land in a blizzard but also with crosswinds, which were going to make keeping control of the aircraft extremely tricky.

Katya took a deep breath, counted to ten and set about her task. She was used to rough weather flying but these violent people were another thing altogether. She caught Jake's eye again as she moved carefully around the cabin, keeping her balance, while making sure everybody was strapped in. He smiled, cool as a cucumber; she remembered learning that funny English saying as a child, when on occasion she had solemnly and slowly counted to ten. Both

Jake and the pilot obviously had special training. Thankfully, Andrei had taken over responsibility for looking after the horrendous boss man.

"To all passengers – this is the two-minute warning prepare for a rough landing – Brace! Brace! Brace! Heads down!"

The Bombardier jet shuddered and shook in the turbulent wind as it made its approach, slewing violently sideways as it hit the snow-covered tarmac, bouncing its way down the lit runway while Guy struggled to bring it quickly to rest, balancing the aircraft against the strong North Easterly wind, trying to keep it straight until they achieved the first available turn off the main landing strip.

"Look for the way off!" he shouted to his co- pilot. The tower were giving instruction on the head sets but it was difficult to see through the swirling snow and Guy knew that he mustn't miss it, for a large aeroplane was coming in close on his tail. In these appalling conditions he was glad not to be landing the bigger plane himself.

"It's there!" Alexei pointed. "There! It's coming up now! Turn! Turn!"

A flashing light with an arrow had suddenly loomed through the murk, so Guy moved the Bombardier Global as swiftly as he dared, skidding it safely off the main runway, leaving it clear for the huge Boeing 737 thundering in behind them. God alone knows what would have happened had they missed the turn off. Both men let out a sigh of relief.

"Job well done!" murmured Guy grinning at Alexei, "You must have cat's eyes!"

Out of harm's way they taxied slowly back towards the private parking spaces as directed by the control tower. Guy issued further orders: he told Alexei to call for the stewardess. Looking thoroughly relieved both the young woman and the steward appeared instantly in the doorway of the cabin.

"Well done crew!" he grinned at them. "Give everybody back there a double shot of vodka, quick now Katya as they'll be stressed and completely disorientated. I suggest leaving the bottle with the big boss. He looks like he could do with it!"

He winked at the air hostess who responded with a bright smile and the two of them turned to do as he'd suggested. They both appeared completely unfazed, almost as if they were used to dealing with such unusual and fraught circumstances over and above the call of duty.

"It's blowing hard out there and it will take us a while to organize the welcome party and transfer vehicle. I need time to re-think our next step." He turned to his co-pilot who merely nodded.

"These people cannot be trusted in anyway whatsoever," Alexei mouthed quietly. That was all Guy needed to hear.

Even on the ground, as the plane taxied to the allotted parking slot, far off from the terminal buildings, it was being severely buffeted by the stronger gusts. Everybody needed time to recover from the exhausting flight. Guy hoped that the instructions to the crew would serve his purpose in helping their adversaries relax and become a little less of a threat while he tried to anticipate their next move. They weren't preparing to disembark, they didn't seem to be in a hurry to get off and for some reason Guy didn't think it was anything to do with the weather.

When Guy brought the plane to a standstill, he finished the necessary arrival tasks then unbuckled, regained his jacket and both he and his co-pilot stood to see what was going on at the back of the plane. The atmosphere was both tense and volatile again. He could hear arguing now that the engine noise had died. Jake, calm as ever, was sitting with the same henchman at the front of the aircraft, looking as if he was trying hard to repress a grin. Jake's minder, as intended, already appeared very much the worse for wear. The wretched man was waving a large tumbler of vodka around in one hand and brandishing a gun in the other. Jake, aware that the safety catch was on, with some difficulty was trying to persuade the thug to put his gun down. The remarkably pretty and calm stewardess was standing by to assist.

A good sign, Guy decided, as she could prove helpful later. Jake had obviously built on a friendly relationship during the flight, so both she, the steward and also Alexei were certain allies. He noticed how they kept their distance from the boss and were barely able to hide a look of disdain as they served the other two gang members. This crew were well turned out, efficient and appeared perfectly comfortable even under extreme pressure.

At the back of the aircraft the boss man, standing, was arguing forcefully again on his mobile; an empty glass on the seat tray beside him. Guy noticed the big man's hands were shaking. This was most probably from the frightening experience they'd just had and, judging by the explosive conversation he was now having, trying to explain why their plans had been so thoroughly disrupted by the weather. The third thug sat white faced and limp across the aisle, leaning away from his superior and surreptitiously glugging back the vodka as fast as he could. Two out of three would soon be well under the influence, Guy concluded with satisfaction.

Putting on his most professional and disarming smile, for the sake of the stewardess, while avoiding the flailing arm, Guy calmly placed a firm hand on the shoulder of Jake's twitchy companion.

"I'm sorry about the rough landing, but the weather is out of my control I'm afraid. Please give me that gun as it might just go off by mistake and I don't think your boss would like that. Why don't you give it to me as no one's going anywhere – just for the moment."

The man was in such a state, yet Guy could see that he understood. He looked as if he might have handed it over except the wretched head man, who'd been watching, already on his feet and still talking on the mobile, appeared speedily at Guy's side. He shouted rudely into the phone then, pushing Guy and the crew out of the way, shoved his hand out to the gibbering henchman.

"I'll have the gun *mu'dak*. Give it to me you idiot and stop the drinking!"

The glass was knocked clean out of the wretched minion's hand, spewing alcohol everywhere as it flew to the floor. The spilt patches of vodka mingled with the stale sweaty aroma of the frightened man; only intensified the heavy stench of fear within the confined space of the aircraft. The boss grabbed the gun then glared at Guy.

"You – only the pilot! *Ne meshay*, No interfere! We wait here now for further instruction. We need fuel. See to it."

The ugly individual turned away to continue his mobile argument at the back of the plane. 'Fucking Hell', thought Guy, aware that he must calm things down as best he could, otherwise somebody would get hurt. He quietly returned to the cockpit intending to try to alert the tower, but Alexei had already seized the opportunity of the distraction whilst voices had been raised. The tower had confirmed that for the time being and throughout this storm the airport was now closed to all other traffic. Alexei had managed to reaffirm their mayday state. The answer had been immediate; they were prepared and expecting further instruction. So help was at hand, they were ready and waiting, but staying back until the Russians' next move became clear.

One of the Russian minders appeared outside the cockpit door, leaning in slightly to make it obvious that he'd been sent to keep an eye on the pilot. Too late thought Guy with a barely disguised chuckle.

Guy was sure that their abductors had planned to fly on to their original destination once the Bombardier had refuelled, hence the ongoing argument on the phone. They'd been stymied by the weather conditions. If they waited out the storm and didn't disembark here at St. Petersburg, that would put paid to the 'helpful' welcome Guy had in place within the International arrival's building. But for the next few hours they would all remain trapped where they were by the storm.

The person to whom the boss was talking was most likely in charge of their cronies at the final destination. No way was this man fronting the whole operation; this yellow-haired lout was showing no respect to whomsoever he was speaking to. An interesting scenario: it was obvious now that this lot were at the very bottom of the pecking order. After supposedly speaking once more to the control tower about practical arrangements, Guy returned to the main cabin to regain the yellow man's attention.

"Sir! Excuse me?"

Everybody stopped what they were doing and the big man turned quickly around, furious to be confronted once more. Guy spoke loudly for everyone to hear.

"I'm sorry Sir, but we'll be going nowhere anytime soon, not in these conditions. They won't give us permission for take-off; as you can see the runway is completely covered again and at the moment they can't refuel us either. Apart from which I am not prepared to risk your lives, mine or even this aircraft. If you look out of the window, the visibility is now nil. The weather has completely closed in," adding as if it were a mere afterthought, "would you like me to organize some hot food in a private VIP lounge in which we can ride out the blizzard?"

As things stood, Guy realised that this would be the only chance of making good use of his backup. His colleagues, with Julian at the helm, would know they had landed and most probably could see the stationary plane lit up out on the smaller jet parking area. They'd have the necessary info that the Bombardier was grounded for the moment. The other big plane had come lumbering noisily in behind them, to park some distance away nearer the arrivals hall, where a bus was already in place to take off the passengers. There wouldn't be any other smaller local planes caught out on such a night so they were isolated in their private slot.

Jake realised he was holding his breath again, yet watching closely to observe any sign from Guy for a coordinated move against the Russians. In spite of the minions now seeming more relaxed, thanks to the vodka, the two of them would still be outnumbered. So it was out of the question to take action without weaponry, unless Guy had something hidden and to hand. On the ground, their support team was obviously waiting to see what the Russians would do before trying to negotiate a stand down.

Guy had nerves of steel: he could feel the adrenalin rush as he waited for the big man's response to his suggestion. He was itching for action. Jake had kept his cool throughout and would be a capable team mate to have beside him. He wondered if Alexei the co-pilot would be able to give any sort of physical backup. He'd got on well with him during the flight and thought that, as they were obviously all close friends, the steward and the stewardess Katya could also be relied upon. They definitely were not permanent employees of these horrendous people and so he dare not risk the lives of the crew. If only – if only he could manoeuvre them all safely into the airport, then he knew that the tables would turn and this particular mission could be quickly wound up. This bunch of mobsters would be no match for Guy's crack team awaiting them incognito in the arrivals building.

The atmosphere in the plane was laden with expectancy while everybody waited for the big boss' decision. He was obviously considering Guy's offer; this they could all see, he was vacillating at the thought of a hot meal, his face still red from the excess of vodka and with fury at the person on the end of his mobile.

The *kanaari* or yellow man, as Jake now silently thought of the man, strode back to where he'd been sitting, grabbed the bottle once more, poured himself a double shot and gulped it down in one. Then with his mind made up returned to fix Guy with a steely stare.

"Nobody gets off this plane. You stay and refuel when is possible and get something hot sent out to us. *Ty slyshish*, You hear?"

The Russian shook his fist rudely in Guy's face. Jake thought the big man was going to throw a punch as he was so agitated, but Guy calmly stood his ground and held the crook's furious glare, while trying to defuse the situation. Guy was weighing up the risks of action, keeping himself in tight control. Jake could see his colleague's curled fingers, with one hand held tight to his side, showing white knuckles. Guy must have been longing to smash the man's nose in one efficient forceful swipe, thought Jake. He waited to see if they were to make a move or not, holding his breath again. Guy had removed his jacket earlier and Jake could see the toned muscles in his colleague's upper arm flexing slightly underneath his shirt.

"Do it!" The monster spat, daring Guy to refuse.

Guy's face was set with a contrived blank expression and with a resigned sigh he merely nodded politely and returned to the cockpit. What else could he do with a half cocked PSS pistol aimed at his head.

There was a significant and deathly hush amongst all on board the aircraft. For all their different reasons nobody wished another rough flight and everybody could have done with a hot meal with time to stretch their legs out of the enclosed area and stale air of the small aircraft.

*

Jake had been listening to the loud mobile conversation. It was as he had thought; their destination was Talinn, Estonia and his heart sank. He hadn't been back there to visit his grandmother for five years. The last time he'd been in the country she had been full of disgust at Russia's tactics manoeuvring, she felt sure, to annex her beloved Estonia once more. Irina used her wealth helping them remain independent at all costs because, as everyone knew, Russia still had designs on all her neighbouring Baltic countries.

At this moment Jake felt his own vulnerability. Amazing in this job how your spirits lifted and dropped according to the outcome of action. He knew he had to keep on top of any mood swing. He hadn't been in the least bit frightened by the dangerous flight as he had every confidence in the pilot, his colleague. He still had absolute faith in Guy and as his adrenalin flowed in the tense unsettled atmosphere, his brain immediately went into action working out new possibilities to somehow turn events around to their advantage. Everything was more hazardous when guns were being waved around within a confined space.

If they weren't to be allowed off the aircraft and when the weather cleared they flew on to Talinn, or somewhere else, Guy's team here on the ground would be less than useless. There would be just the two of them to rethink their plight, to somehow communicate and prepare for arrival at their next, as yet undisclosed, destination.

Unless the ground force managed quickly to discover any new flight schedule and there was another team in the Baltic area already on standby, in these weather conditions, there'd be no support to meet them in Talinn. Yet, one thing that Jake had already learnt was that HQ thought ahead and always had a contingency plan. He just hoped that somehow Guy had managed to get a message through and that back at home they already had prior knowledge of the Estonian connection.

❄ ❄ ❄

CHAPTER 8

The Thrill Of Fear
(St. Petersburg airport, Sunday evening)

A HEAVY-WEATHER snow cat eventually appeared out of the murk, from the airport buildings, carrying heated containers of a goulash meat stew. The yellow-haired boss man had stipulated forcefully that there were to be no police and no military, which had backed off out of sight from the plane, dousing their lights as they withdrew: just the one man to drive the machine bringing the food.

On gaining access to the aeroplane the poor man, met by the Russians toting their guns, couldn't wait to deliver the meal and retreat. The steward and air hostess handed it around served in china bowls from the aircraft's well-equipped kitchenette. With audible sighs and varying degrees of gratitude, both those in control and those under their supervision tucked in; heartily aware of the need for sustenance whatever their roles. Hot nourishing food soon began to sober up the Russians, who had over-indulged in alcohol whilst recovering from their traumatic flight and emergency landing. But by the same token the welcome food refuelled the energy levels of both Guy and Jake.

Guy was obviously taking stock of their predicament while Jake pensively watched the retreating lights of the snow cat as it returned through the escalating storm, to the safety of the airport buildings. Once the delivery man reported back to the team dealing with the emergency, the army would be well briefed on the drama unfolding inside the plane.

The whistling wind was gathering force outside, buffeting the aircraft with ever strengthening gusts. It was a filthy evening, there was no way the plane could fly again until this blizzard abated and it looked as if the severe snowstorm would continue on through the encroaching night. With an ongoing flight out of the question, just what exactly would these people do next? There didn't seem to be any option except to stay put: no negotiating was feasible while the Russian boss absolutely refused to speak to anybody, except whoever it was on the other end of his own wretched mobile. He was taking out his phone yet again, so Jake would be able to eavesdrop and try to get a gist of another ensuing volatile conversation.

Guy also knew that there was nothing more he could do for the moment. He was quite sure that he and Jake together could overpower the three Russians; but in such a confined space he would be worried for the lives of the crew in particular of Katya who, although intelligent, appeared too brave for her own good. He noticed now that the yellow man was keeping her nearer and slightly apart from the other crew members, as if he intended to use her in some way should he have a problem.

Guy was sure that his arranged 'welcome' team, waiting incognito both outside and within the arrivals hall, would by now also have been updated. He wondered exactly how much support the airport authorities had already called in themselves. They would have received info direct from the UK when the flight took off and also his report of a Code 7500 hijack alert when they entered Russian airspace. Presumably a special force army group would have been activated and put in position before the storm hit. Now in these extreme conditions and without air assistance any other top guns would have a job getting to the airport.

For the moment all that he could do was gather his wits and try to keep the situation calm inside the aircraft.

The yellow man was still glued to his mobile indulging in yet another slightly more agreeable conversation. Guy could see Jake discreetly leaning a little into the aisle, trying to hear what was being said. He hated this unexpected lull in the action. His muscles were tense, his fingers tingling, itching to make a move and yet he must not show it. He knew that Julian, waiting with his team, would be feeling the same and that they'd have everything ready should they manage to disembark.

Guy felt that somehow he had to instigate action. The very idea of spending the entire night holed up with these frustrated and fractious muppets with their loaded guns was not a good idea. He heard one of them give out a large obscene belch. Right! Almost as one with his young colleague, he saw Jake also move to stand up announcing a wish to visit the washroom. The idiot sitting next to him, now with a full stomach, was easily mollified. He merely nodded and sat back in his seat. Jake, carrying his briefcase, walked down the aircraft towards his pilot.

"Any ideas? I think he's now planning to get off here," he mouthed.

"Right. Ok I'll give it a couple of minutes then see if I can move things along."

The noise of the storm muffled their words and the bulk of their bodies hid their faces from view. The air hostess, standing across the aisle from Guy, seeing Jake's intention also moved toward the washroom. She opened the door and produced a fresh air spray which she used liberally within the small space while Jake waited.

"There you are, Sir," she said as she held the door open for him. She leaned in close to whisper, "We're not with these dreadful people, you must know that – if there's

61

anything we can do to help?" Jake turned quickly, instantly drawn into the depths of those tantalising eyes once more.

"No, nothing, the guns are loaded. Just stay cool as you are." He smiled, noticing her discreet name pinned on the jacket she'd just put on again. As he shut the door he said "thank, Katya," for all to hear. The name rang a nostalgic bell. He used to know a child with those mesmeric dark eyes, a happy plump little girl he'd nicknamed 'Kit'. But that was long ago when he too was a mere child. He thought that her real name had been Katrina or perhaps Katherine; the girl had been expert at climbing trees and keeping up with him getting into trouble. They had once, for a short time, been a team.

"Your welcome!" Katya had smiled back energetically. She really was a stunning looking girl with those unique eyes.

As soon as Jake had regained his seat, Guy approached the Russian boss. The man was standing staring morosely out of the window.

"Sir," Guy spoke loudly enough to be heard against the raging gale outside. "I'm afraid I can't hear what the control tower is reporting on the weather. The storm is producing too much static. Perhaps I should try to get across there to receive information in person?"

The surly man just looked ever more annoyed, yet somewhat resigned.

"*Nyet!*" he replied brusquely. "You do as I say." With sour breath he thrust his face up close to Guy who flinched back managing to keep his hands to himself – but only just.

"Change clothes with young Englishman. Now!" Guy remained outwardly calm yet inside he experienced a fearsome surge of adrenalin, as understanding of the big man's intentions flooded his brain.

"I beg your pardon Sir, but that is not possible. I'm a professional pilot and am unable to remove my uniform whilst working. I'd lose my job!"

"Do it! *Sdelay eto srazu!*" came the retort, "or you lose life as well as job!"

Guy knew that he was outmanoeuvred. There was nothing he could do. It was Jake they were after and they had every chance of getting him away undercover as a member of the uniformed crew. Jake also was left in no doubt as to what they were about once he was made to don Guy's uniform. The co-pilot, Alexei tried to intervene but Guy, indicating the guns, merely put a hand on his arm.

"I'm afraid, Alexei, that we have no choice but to do as we are asked. My responsibility is for the wellbeing of my crew, which includes you and all the passengers; whoever they are unfortunately," he added drily.

Only Guy's eyes showed tension as he caught Jake's glance. The big man then made the horrified Alexei also take off his outer clothing, somehow managing to squeeze himself into the smaller man's uniform. He squashed the cap on his head and donned his own overcoat. Then, looking at his watch, he turned to shout orders to his two remaining henchmen, who slumped down into their seats, looking thoroughly relieved. Meanwhile Guy made sure Jake had his leather flying jacket on top of the uniform and thrust a warm woollen hat and scarf in the pockets. They both now knew somehow that Jake was to be furtively taken off the plane. The others were to follow, although they most likely would be using one of the usual entrances into arrivals, to deflect attention.

"No overcoat, I'm afraid, only the leather flight jacket!" Jake gave a positive nod to his colleague and friend.

"Don't worry, I'll survive, I hope," he added bravely." I'll keep in touch. It's done," He whispered tapping the briefcase. Guy realised with some comfort that Jake had obviously managed to set his second mobile with its secret tracking device. His own phone had been removed on boarding the plane. Katya stepped forward.

"I think that you should at least wrap that scarf around your neck, Sir." she said taking it out of the pocket then hurriedly whispered. "Their coming now. I'm so sorry Jake. I wish we could do something."

She really did have the most beautiful eyes and she was worried for him, but how did she know his name? Jake had little time to speculate further.

All Guy could do was to return to the cockpit to press the alert button on his own concealed phone, with the hope that Julian would come up with some extra-sensory inspiration. They often managed to waylay each other's thoughts. On a mission they were so perfectly in tune; an extraordinary gift which had served them well during troublesome predicaments in the past.

✳

At the back of the airport buildings the British team were all keyed up and waiting for action. Julian heard the soft buzz on his mobile. He knew instantly that Guy was trying to tell him something. He puzzled as to what that might be.

The weather had completely closed in. Even in their thermal gear it was bitterly cold. The plane was grounded and going nowhere. It would by now be thoroughly iced up as well. But what was going on inside the aircraft? He'd discovered that food had been delivered and so it looked as if the Russians intended to sit tight, but now that Guy had used the alert button Julian knew that some kind of move was imminent.

Earlier Julian had noticed that there were three large Russian army vehicles pulled up outside the building. One lot of soldiers had gone inside and another lot had split up to presumably cover all exits from the outside. He called his own team up on the two-way radio.

"Movement is imminent. I want everybody ready, cover me while I talk to the officer in that lead army vehicle. I'm not sure how friendly they'll be or if they'll appreciate our interference."

Julian made sure his weaponry was held in a relaxed manner and frustratingly kicking the snow from his feet walked across towards the first parked vehicle. There was something menacing about the dark camouflaged lorry, half covered in snow waiting in the murk with its engine running. The so-called Cold War was supposedly over, but the Russians were communists and must have strong feelings of enmity towards anyone intruding or interfering within their own country. He clapped his hands together, to keep the circulation going and stamped his feet, then took off his gloves and turned away from the swirling snow; cupping his hands to light a cigarette. The cold was extreme and it hurt to inhale, he took two drags then dropped the cigarette, re-covering the lower part of his face again with his wool army balaclava against the biting gusting wind.

At this moment he wished that he had a better command of the Russian language. He approached the lorry and heard the driver's side window slide down with a slight crunch as it hit the snow piled up on the window's lower edge. An unfriendly darkened face peered out of the gloom to stare out at the intruder. Julian unable to see past the driver to the inside sensed there was a whole team concealed in the back. He could smell the hot, damp humanity within. In the distance he could hear the faint throbbing sound of snowmobiles, the most sensible way to get around in heavy snow such as this.

As Julian was about to introduce himself and try out a simple Russian greeting, the main doors of the arrivals burst open and out came a bunch of, as yet, un-identifiable people muffled up in a strange mix of ill-fitting uniforms and unsuitable clothing. They were quickly surrounded by soldiers from the second lorry. Julian's own shadow force appeared from around the sides of the building to stand to one side; looking to Julian, awaiting instructions. At the same time another half dozen soldiers jumped out of the back of the truck, nearest Julian, with guns raised. The driver opened the door and indicating calm to Julian, ordered his men to stand down. All guns were lowered in one well-coordinated move.

The group of ill-assorted people split, two were quickly taken over to the leading military vehicle by a couple of soldiers and shoved, none to gently, into the back. The officer gave a curt salute to Julian, shouted another order to his men; they all piled back into the three vehicles and with a squeal of brakes and a shower of snow took off and disappeared into the night. Julian turned to approach the rest of the dishevelled group. A sly moon glimmered for a moment above the building fully lighting the scene in front of him.

"For God's sake Guy what the hell are you wearing and where the fuck is Jake?"

* * *

CHAPTER 9

Cold Dark Forests
(Russia)

HEIGHTENED by the bumpy ride across the snow-laden landscape and with the blizzard blinding his eyes, Jake felt the adrenalin coursing through his veins; albeit with a frustrated rush. Since leaving the aircraft there had been no opportunity to extricate himself from the present untenable impasse. They had never even entered the airport buildings. So there had been no chance of escaping the clutches of his abductors.

Back on the aeroplane Guy had also been powerless as he dared not risk the lives of the crew. But Jake knew that HQ would want more information on where these villains were headed and what they were planning. He was the one team member who understood their language and could help fathom out their intentions.

The three snowmobiles had appeared from out of the harsh and dense freezing air at the far side of the aeroplane. There had been a slight scuffle between the yellow man and Guy as Jake, in Guy's pilot's uniform, was taken off the aircraft. The other two Russians looked relieved to see them depart. Jake caught Guy's encouraging glance as he left the plane. As he faced the blast of freezing air and set off down the slippery steps, he hoped that his colleague might have managed to get off a message during the disturbance as they'd left. They needed backup and fast: God alone knew where he was to be taken.

Jake had managed to activate the GPS emergency tracking device on his second modified mobile, still concealed in a hidden compartment attached to his briefcase. Nobody had bothered to search him further once his own phone had been removed and he was found to be carrying no weaponry. The mobile activation would alert Guy and pin-point Jake's whereabouts at least for a while, until the phone was found by someone other than himself. With the wrong person using an incorrect entry code the instrument would self-destruct, becoming useless.

Jake had noticed an airport vehicle in the distance appearing out of the gloom from the arrivals building; it's lights sweeping the area as it had approached the plane. With much gesticulating, whilst being hastily shown the simple brake and accelerator system on one of the snow-mobiles, Jake had been ordered merely to get on and to 'follow'. They had taken off speedily, out of sight, from the far side of the plane. He wondered what would have happened had he refused to leave. Mounted on the middle machine, with the heavily togged Russian soldiers, each with an SV-98 Sniper rifle slung over their shoulder, both in front and behind him, he'd had no choice.

With the yellow *kaanari* shouting orders, riding double immediately behind him, Jake realised there was nothing he could do for the moment but accept his plight. He had managed to wedge the briefcase, containing the all-important computer and mobile tracker, firmly between his knees: the man who'd brought and handed over the snowmobile had helped secure it with a strong strap. Nobody had tried to take it from him and nobody could open it without his help. These were the two factors which gave some comfort.

The Russians needed him in one piece, both to open the briefcase and transfer their money. Also Jake felt sure that his own commanders needed him to uncover more detail of the unfolding agenda, which was already indicating a very much bigger conspiracy.

A fourth man on another machine met them at the airport perimeter. He escorted them through the surrounding broken security fence, along a partially camouflaged tunnel under a major road and onto a deserted minor route. This they followed for several kilometres before turning up a narrow track into a deep forest. The tops of the trees were shrouded in heavy snow creating a cavernous ceiling for those passing by below.

There were no cars in sight, no lights amidst the dark trees, no sign of human habitation at all. But for their muted engine noise there was an eerie silence, not even the cry of a bird to be heard. A world's activities placed on hold by an ever-thickening blanket of unrelenting snow.

Jake had little idea where they were, except that his wits told him they were headed East of the airport and towards the Estonian border, some two hundred kilometres away. He thought fleetingly of his grandmother. Her lovely old Estonian country house was nestled in a forest clearing not far from the Russian border, at Narva. He wondered if she was in residence or away on her frequent travels. She owned large tracts of forest all around her organic farm, which was subsidised by the government.

Irina was an intrepid character full of energy and with a mind very much of her own. She'd have a fit if she knew of her grandson's present ordeal. Irina had seen much in her long life. She would certainly expect the very best from Jake, he reflected: but how the hell was he going to get himself out of this particular hole? As yet he had no fixed idea.

Snow had found its way down the back of his neck; the wet scarf was now frozen solid and he felt an unsettling stab of unease. He'd been left to his own devices on a dangerous mission and had been captured by the enemy. It had never been intended for him to leave the UK in the first place, but now it all began to slot into place. He was uncannily near to the home of a much loved family member, almost as if it had been organised: perhaps it had.

The wind, as they continued to speed along, was bitterly cold; while the sky had lost definition as it was blurred and as one with the ground; thoroughly disorientating. The way ahead was only just visible so their tyre tracks would be immediately covered over, leaving no tell-tale evidence of their flight. The men, in front and behind him, were well kitted out. The *Kanarri* had thrown on a thick coat over his stolen ill-fitting uniform and he also had warm gloves and a fur hat, virtually obscuring his ugly features.

Jake hadn't been able to see his escorts' faces when he'd been told to get on the snow-mobile, back at the airport. They had face coverings and were clad in full winter military gear. Jake was glad of Guy's flying jacket and that he had decent gloves and a thick woollen hat, although it was now frozen hard as a board. He thought for a moment of Katya, the girl with the mesmeric eyes, as she'd tied the scarf around his neck. She'd shown such concern knowing that his clothes were totally unsuitable for these outlandish conditions.

The snow was piling up on the handlebars and creating drifts against the front of his legs. It even found its way into his leather boots, so his feet were fast becoming numb inside his sodden socks. When he moved his head and with the shaking of the machine under him, the folds of stiff scarf released shards of ice which slid down to settle between the seat back and his stiffly frozen leather jacket.

Jake knew that only pure adrenalin, pumping around his body, kept him warm enough to survive such temperatures.

With the yellow-haired man now immediately in front of him and another of the Russian escorts behind him shouting orders to keep up, whenever the gap widened, they struggled on for several more kilometres. Eventually Jake could see a misty light ahead promising a way out at last from the grim trees.

What next he wondered, feeling the need for physical movement before his hands, inside their frozen leather gloves, actually stuck to the handlebars and his feet turned to solid blocks of ice within his thin boots. He'd be unable to keep the briefcase wedged in front of him much longer as his legs were becoming numb with cold. He swiped another pile of snow from his lap. The yellow man in front had become a solid phantom-like figure: no outline could now be seen of a living person, as the relentless falling snow clung to the obscured icy form.

A few minutes later Jake realised that the dim light was coming from a vehicle parked in the gap where the track, he thought, must join a road of some sort. He would be glad at least to be out of the extreme threatening blackness of the dark forest.

Needless to say the Lada 4x4 was black with darkened windows. Jake, still clutching the briefcase, was manhandled inside to where another brutish Russian was already seated. There was much vitriolic swearing as the yellow *kaanari* pushed in after Jake, morosely greeting the others; who quickly jumped out to retrieve the vacated snowmobiles. They were not a happy bunch, this lot, the adverse weather had obviously thrown all their plans. The driver didn't even bother to get out.

At least Jake appreciated the sudden rise in temperature. He was squashed between the yellow man and the heavy lout on the other side. The former then shouted at the driver so that soon they were bouncing their way along an ever-widening track. Jake glanced back to see the grouped snowmobiles already beginning to disperse, re-entering the dark forest in two different directions with their lights momentarily piecing the all-pervading eerie gloom.

The rough track finally met a proper highway where a snow plough had done a good job part clearing one lane. A difficult task, considering the driving snow. It was still coming down hard and fast with no sign of letting up. The *kanaari* man on his left suddenly slapped Jake's knee and pointed to the briefcase smirking.

"All good, yes?"

"We'll see," answered Jake shortly, trying to avoid inhaling the stale vodka fumes.

"Your girlfriend, she's Ok now; yes?"

"I bloody well hope so," Jake muttered looking ahead. The big man nodded with a snigger, wiping his nose on the sleeve of his arm.

"She's nice, very nice! *Seks,*" he grunted. Jake wanted to punch his flabby jowls.

At least the wretched man was in a much better mood, now that they were warmer, which meant that Jake might have a chance to build some sort of a relationship whilst he planned his way out of this mess. The piles of snow that they'd brought with them into the car were now thawing into damp pools, covering the cigarette stubs on the dirty floor. Jake could feel the damp beginning to seep through the thin soles of his boots.

These people really were scraped from the very bottom of the barrel. The smell of hot humanity was stifling and there was no air. He hoped the beef stroganoff would stay put although he'd been taught how to stave off vomiting. Jake wasn't overly confident anymore, with no backup team within reach. These Russians weren't as chaotic as they looked – at least the man at the top must have his head firmly on his shoulders to have rescheduled their plans so quickly. Perhaps he'd get to meet him at the end of this journey and even be able to glean some of the crucial intelligence which was so desperately needed back at home.

He wasn't being beaten up which was one thing for which to be thankful. His companions were now talking between themselves and his mobile tracking device would be uninterrupted. Thank God for that. These hired guns must be the very lowest of the criminal hierarchy and they would have no idea that Jake both spoke and understood most Russian dialects. They were unlikely to have acquired any facts of his past and of his childhood visits to this part of Estonia. They would have been told next to nothing, just given the orders for carrying out Ellie's abduction, his seizure and transportation with the money to wherever they were bound.

A cool head was essential, but the most important thing of all was that he must remain positive and patient as his immediate destination and the Russian intent became clearer. Until then there was nothing to be done except rest, as best he could, listen to any conversation and try to glean as much information as possible.

❅ ❅ ❅

CHAPTER 10

A Change Of Plan
(The Estonian border)

GUY and Julian took the small bedraggled group from the aircraft back into the airport complex. There were few people around as all flights had been cancelled earlier in the day. Some of the passengers, off the diverted Aeroflot 737, were still in the building trying to organize accommodation and re-booking themselves for the first available ongoing internal flights. Cleaners with mops and buckets were clearing away the debris of dirty melted snow puddles, brought in by the constant flow of people during the day.

The men were found a table, in a quiet discreet area, away from listening ears and the stark lighting of the food service counter. Julian's team were directed to a different part of the room to get hot drinks and to rest, while they could. Guy ordered coffee tea and biscuits to be brought to their own table. Everybody removed their dripping outer clothing and still adjusting to their changed circumstances sat down both exhausted and relieved. Katya appeared back from the washrooms looking remarkably fresh, considering what she had endured since they'd left the UK. She took her seat between her two fellow crew members with a sigh of relief.

The atmosphere within the characterless room, although loaded, was now at least without fear.

Guy sat down beside his friend and colleague, Julian. They talked quietly together for a few minutes letting the others settle. Both men felt thoroughly frustrated with the way they had, for the moment, been thwarted by the Russians. He was worried for Jake who must by now be well out of his depth and far away. It had never been intended for Jake to fly out of London. His part of the job should have ended with Ellie's release. It was the first time Jake had been used for something so crucial out in the field since joining. But Guy still had full confidence in the young man and as yet the hidden GPS tracker was working well. He wasn't out of touch. It was only if the big uncouth boss with his minions lost their tempers and resorted to violence... then Jake was in the shit for he was outnumbered and had no chance of escape without help.

The situation was in the Russians' control at present, so hopefully they would be feeling at ease and satisfied with the way things were going. They seemed to be headed North West for the suburbs of St Petersburg. In the deteriorating weather they surely must be stopping soon. What the hell were the intentions of these people? Guy needed to know what they were up against and he needed to know fast. Information from the UK was taking a long time in coming.

Hot drinks arrived and everybody took their mugs with relish. Julian turned towards Guy clearing his throat, he had so many questions, but was stopped by Guy's hand on his arm.

"Just a minute my friend, all in good time." He glanced around the table. "First I want to thank Alexei, my co-pilot, Katya and our steward Andrei for a difficult and thoroughly professional job, so very well done, under extremely dangerous circumstances."

He looked towards the three of them where they sat closely huddled together with their hands clasped around their warm mugs. Andrei asked if he could light a cigarette.

"Yes, of course," answered Guy. "There's no-one much around, or anywhere near us to complain; go ahead, you've earned it." He looked up to check for smoke alarms then pushed a small bin, left for rubbish, towards Andrei. "Now I need to ask you some questions, I think you all speak good English?" They all nodded in unison. "Am I right in thinking that you work as a private freelance team and not exclusively for those unpleasant Russians who took our friend Jake with them?" The co-pilot uttered a disgusted oath at the very thought of any respect for such people.

"No! No! They are terrible people," Katya, the obvious spokeswoman, cut in.

"Yes we work together, but we dread flying anywhere with such filth, but they pay and we need the money for our families back home."

"You're Romanian?" asked Guy reasonably certain of the accent and demeanour.

"Yes." replied Andrei smiling. "Katya is my long-lost sister. Alexei is Estonian and a good friend. We all found each other at college."

"How did you come by this particular job?"

"We were booked by phone, as usual, by a small Russian company based outside St Petersburg not far from the airport. They never supply us with the client's name or business. Only the flight details." Katya politely interrupted. She spoke excellent English.

"We never know what sort of people we will be looking after until we board the plane, but they are supposed to have been vetted when they pay for the airport facilities. On this last flight all of us wished we could have helped you, but it became impossible with that volatile monster, the guns... and the storm. Poor Jake, I hope he's alright. He was so calm – such courage."

Katya lowered her eyes and took a deep shuddering breath. Guy admired this brave girl who minded so much about his colleague. They were a superb team of people; their behaviour under duress had been faultless, which deserved reassurance.

"You were all most professional and held your cool admirably at the worst moments. Now we would like to get the details of the company which hires you. It might help in finding out where our friend has been taken." Katya looked crestfallen.

"I am so sorry but we have nothing with which you might trace these people as they always call us and never leave a number or an address. Originally we went to the airport with our credentials. These were checked and handed over to the department looking after the private plane sector. Our qualifications were verified again; then we were added to their books. But this lot found us through someone unknown to any of us. I'm so very sorry," she finished disconsolately.

"It can't be helped," Guy replied. "Katya, where did you learn such perfect English?"

"Thank you. I learnt at first from a friend, a boy when I was a mere child. Then in school it became easy." She coloured and looked down at her hands clasped around her mug, on the table.

"Well I must say you speak very well indeed. Now we can give you a gadget for your phone which will record their incoming numbers for us, should these people call again."

Julian looked towards the co-pilot. "Alexei have you flown this particular Russian group before?"

"Yes, the yellow-haired boss, but once only and not with Katya or Andrei. I was called in to fly with their own pilot as the co. was sick. He was as aggressive as today and

78

the other crew were even worse with disgusting manners. In future I shall tell the company that we will never fly with these people again."

"The trouble is," Katya intervened once more, "they pay us so much it's sometimes hard to refuse."

"Katya and I have a friend's small child in our care and we have the little girl's ageing grandfather who we try to look after as well," Andrei explained, putting his arm around his sister as he spoke.

"Ok, don't worry we do understand," Julian smiled at the good-looking pair. They were decent people. Katya was exceptionally alluring. He suspected that she pulled in most of their work! She smiled back looking relieved.

"I'm so worried about your poor friend, he's such a nice man, what can we do to help him?" Katya asked genuinely concerned. Guy took over again.

"Do you understand Russian?" he enquired.

"Yes, I don't really speak the language but I understood a fair amount of the conversation the big ugly man had on his mobile, whenever I was within hearing distance."

"Good! That's where we can start then. First I'd like to hear more about that other flight Alexei. Please tell me everything that you can remember, no matter how unimportant it may have seemed at the time." Guy replied adding, "Julian – listen well please."

❋

Jake, in the confined uncomfortable space of the 4x4, was also listening carefully to the conversation between the men in the car. They were obviously wary now of how much he could understand, because quite often the driver was told to shut up by the boss. After four hours, the last on worsening roads with little sign of snow-plough activity, Jake, from memory, thought he'd recognized a small town through which they'd just struggled. They were nearing the Estonian border he felt sure, which gave a measure of comfort at first followed by a rush of extreme un-ease. They weren't very far from his grandmother's estate.

God forbid that she was in anyway mixed up in this fast escalating mission or its far reaching consequences. He could feel his brow breaking out in a cold sweat, in the dank claustrophobic atmosphere of the car. It was hard to imagine his indomitable, fiercely independent grandmother as vulnerable; but still it was an unnerving possibility that she might in some way be involved: she wasn't exactly young anymore for all her boundless energy, courage and determination. In spite of many friends and a long-standing lover she was on her own much of the time having lost his grandfather many years before.

Just as these thoughts were swamping Jake's head, the obnoxious *Kanaari* heaved himself around to slap Jake hard on his back, creating a rush of fury which he had to dampen. With the inevitable warning smirk the wretched Russian growled, "Now we best friends, *da,* yes? You say nothing, just answer questions and give passport and green card."

Jake had to really control himself from smacking the rough ugly man right back in the face. He took a deep breath to steady himself and wondered if there would be any chance of a bid for freedom.

But it wasn't merely about escaping anymore. He now realised that he had to see this thing through. His grandmother being so near was just too much of a coincidence. Her life might well be in danger and so he had to know that she was unharmed. Finding himself in an unexpected ongoing mission he needed to help. He'd been well trained and Jake wanted to prove his worth and show the team of what he was really capable.

They arrived at the border, were waved through the first stop exiting Russia and stopped at the entry into Estonia. The Estonian guard strode forward to apprehend the vehicle. The man hardly bothered with the Russian passports, just flipped through their details which were obviously in order and possibly familiar as well. When Jake took his own documents from his briefcase and handed over his passport and green card, he rather hoped that they'd find something not to their liking, enabling them to hold him there. The guard peered in through the open window while the yellow *kanaari* pretended to be having an amicable joke with Jake. Meanwhile Jake stared out at the man trying to transfer the feelings of his intense and fearful predicament, if they could just sense a situation it might be reported.

"You English?" the man asked scanning his passport with interest.

"Yes, mostly but my grandmother's partly Estonian."

"Really? Where does she live."

"Quite near here actually." Jake replied looking straight back.

"On holiday?"

"Not really." He answered deliberately.

The big man interrupted with a loud chuckle.

"Yes, Yes! On holiday, with just little business." The guard ignored the Russian and looked again at Jake.

"You Ok? You see your grandmother? You don't look happy for holiday."

Again the yellow man butted in, leaning close.

"*On plokho sebya chuvstvuyet.* No! he's not good, had bad rough flight from UK in private plane, too small. Our

81

friend not like that." He laughed pointing to his stomach. "But he recover at good hotel with us." He slapped Jake on the back again, making him jump and Jake's irritation grow almost beyond limits. He leant as far away as possible from the putrid smell of stale breath and dirty teeth.

"One minute!" The Estonian guard held his hand up to call over one of his colleagues, to whom he then turned, to have a quiet few words. Both men, together with a sniffer dog, then approached the 4x4. Jake felt a surge of hope as the man opened the car door. "Please out now, all of you. We look at car." He ordered.

The immaculately well-trained dog took its time walking around the car then around each of them, sniffing. It then walked back to its handler and sat down obviously satisfied. The guards then searched inside the Lada, underneath and in the boot, with a hand-held Xray scanner. Jake remembered seeing the Russians strap something to the underside before they'd set off from the forest. They obviously had a safe place to hide their weaponry with a method for blocking the detector: nothing was found.

The first guard continued to slide suspicious glances at Jake, who aware that he was being presented with a further chance to convey his situation, stared back hard at the man whenever he had the opportunity, otherwise keeping silent. The big man, standing near, kept up a jocular exchange with the second Estonian, whilst they searched, covering for Jake's silence.

When Jake's briefcase was checked there was nothing untoward to see, besides his computer, only normal contents. The hidden compartment with his ultra-thin mobile, with its special protective sleeve concealing the all-important tracker device, was not found. It was well hidden in a flat pocket on the bottom behind the leather case's double layer of stitching. In the dark and under only sparse covering against the swirling snow, the guards weren't for hanging around outside longer than necessary.

Jake had only one more chance. As they all re-entered the vehicle and the engine was fired, he managed to mouth four words to the guard who had first approached the car as they arrived. In perfect Estonian he whispered, shaking his head, "No! No! Not happy at all!"

The man appeared taken aback. But the yellow man was there right beside him in a flash, before he could say anything else. He indicated for Jake to get in with a false smile fixed on his heavy features. The guard held the door for them still looking uncertain. As Jake got in he turned once more to the border guard and said 'thank you', in English.

As they sped off Jake turned to look out of the back window. The two men stood close together watching them leave and deep in conversation once more. Jake felt a lift in his spirits and a return of that energizing sense of purpose. At least this particular crossing might well be reported as interesting; not quite the same as usual with the obvious uncomfortable relationship between the rough Russian occupants and the unhappy, young Englishman of a very different calibre.

Also Guy would be tracking their progress and with any luck he would, with info from the UK, have hit on the likely connection to Jake's grandmother by now. Jake didn't feel quite so alone anymore.

The Russians had been disagreeing again, once they'd moved off from the frontier. They weren't happy with how things had gone at the border, their changed plans, or with their own arrangements for the night ahead. That much Jake could glean from the bad tempered mutterings.

Suddenly their ugly boss turned to Jake and slapped him across the face again, giving him a fright. The man was still almost spitting with rage and Jake knew that he was the reason.

"You stupid, what you do that for? What you say just then, hey, hey?" He punched Jake again hard on the upper arm, where it really hurt.

Jake just managed not to retaliate and stay calm. Shaking his head morosely he muttered, "I only thanked the man politely... as you do," he added with feeling.

The Russian uttered a rude disapproving grunt.

"Not good, looking sad, not spirit for holiday. Now... we cover your eyes," the big man said with obvious pleasure. He produced a large, damp, none-too-clean, cotton scarf out of his overcoat pocket and proceeded to tie it roughly and tight around Jake's head.

Jake let out a sigh. "Is this really necessary?"

"*Da!* Yes – is!" the big man answered crossly, slapping Jake across his ear again.

"Much more of that and you won't bloody well get your money!" warned Jake trying to keep his temper whilst rubbing his ear. "Remember that!"

The yellow-haired man merely snorted, muttered some Russian obscenity and wiped his nose on his sleeve yet again, before readjusting the foul smelling rag more tightly around Jake's head. Jake sat back, his hearing ever more alert without his sight. Now he could feel every bump beneath him and every turn of the 4x4. Why the blindfold? Was there a specific reason? Jake felt ever more worried for his grandmother.

After another twenty minutes or so, he knew for certain that her home was much too close for comfort, as he'd recognised the judder of the level crossing tracks with the hard right and left double bend just before it. Then a further half a mile and the 4x4 turned left into the back entrance that led to Irina's hunting lodge. Things were beginning to become ever clearer.

*　*　*

CHAPTER 11

Irina
(St. Petersburg airport: The Hunting Lodge, late Sunday)

THE Bombardier aeroplane belonged to a South American businessman, owner of a suspect company already under surveillance by the FBI. The man travelled constantly, had homes all over the world, a mega-sized superyacht and a transatlantic aircraft in addition to the Bombardier. He also had a diverse selection of friends who were entertained frequently wherever he went. Several Russian oligarchs were on his party list including a high-ranking army general and a senior politician. He had an ex-model wife, two sons and a daughter, all educated entirely at the best private prep and public schools in England. One son was already engaged in 'business' with his father, whatever that enterprise might be. The publicised companies were considered to be the fronts for very much more.

Julian and Guy sat together in the bar of one of the international airport hotels. The crew from the flight had gone to their homes in the suburbs and the rest of the elite force were holed up in accommodation at another hotel within the same airport complex. The exquisite and efficient Katya had organised all this for them before going off duty. Both men felt her to be in some way mysterious; an exceptionally brave girl probably with many other hidden talents on top of her exceptional command of the English language.

They had been instructed to stay in touch with the airport officials tasked with organising private aircraft, also with the control tower for the rescheduling and refuelling of the plane when flights were resumed. The tower was on notice to keep an eye for lights indicating any disturbance in the vicinity of the stationary Bombardier. Guy had been told that a small special force Russian army group remained elsewhere within the airport. Clearwater International would remain closed until morning at the earliest so, during the enforced pause in the action, everybody involved could appreciate some rest.

Guy sat fingering a glass of beer beside Julian as they watched Jake's mobile tracker on the computer. He had fired a load of questions off to Headquarters back in the UK and was impatient for the answers. They now knew that Jake had passed through the border into Estonia. As soon as he could see for certain where they were headed, Guy had put through an order to have the young Englishman stopped and held there. Unfortunately, the Estonians had been too slow, they had concentrated first on an illegal crossing to one side of the main crossing: at Narva the day-guards had just gone off duty and the night-watch had taken over and received the message too late. Guy suspected that HQ had decided not to intervene further until they discovered the vehicle's destination. Poor Jake had really been dropped in at the deep end!

The report from the frontier soon came in, confirming that the man they were looking for had indeed entered Estonia in the company of some Russians. The young Englishman had seemed to be a little uncomfortable, one of the guards had noted, but otherwise appeared to be in good health. All their paper-work was in order; their vehicle had been searched and so there had been no reason to delay them further on such a night. They were warned not to try to venture too far, but they'd been reassured that the

Englishman had a relation he was to visit in the vicinity. Julian was thoughtful.

"This definitely looks as if it has something to do with Jake and his grandmother then, doesn't it? Her place must be the destination?"

"Yes, I reckon so," Guy responded. "She's certainly just there and I believe she has a lot of land right on the border. We'll get a helicopter up to Narva as soon as it can fly and probably establish a base there. We'll see where the tracker stops for the night; by then I should have all the info I've requested, with Irina's exact location. This could well be a glimpse of the bigger picture we've been waiting for. Jake's grandmother is quite involved politically. She's known to consort with all the Estonian hierarchy. She's a good old-fashioned patriot. The Estonians are well aware of Russian ambition and continuous aggression along their borders. If she lives not far from Narva where Jake crossed, they could certainly be heading there. Time will tell, this is definitely something much larger than we first thought."

Guy's mobile flashed urgently beside him, he looked at his friend and colleague.

"Right, here we go, let's hope this call gives us the information and also a green light. I don't appreciate this forced inactivity as I'm sure you don't either." He put the flashing instrument to his ear. As he did so they both felt the adrenalin rush as at last they prepared for action.

✻

Irina sat without moving in her favourite chair by the fireplace in her forest home. The hunting lodge was deep in the woods and several kilometres away from the main

89

residence. She should have been at a concert in Talinn with her long-standing lover and friend Gustav.

The Russians had waylaid her at the end of her main drive; they had been ready and waiting. She had thought it was somebody wanting to warn her of the impending storm and had made it easy for them by stopping and lowering the window to speak.

But it wouldn't be long before Gustav realised that something must have happened, as she was never late and had planned to be at their hotel in the early afternoon, before the snowstorm hit. Now here she was uncomfortably bound to her own chair, in her own house, being carefully scrutinised and guarded by three reasonably polite yet formidable Russian soldiers. Now another stranger had just arrived; an immaculately dressed and well-educated young Englishman. Who on earth was he and what the hell did they want from her? Not money, no: but they knew that she had the ear of several influential people in her government. It was information and much else that they were after, but they weren't going to get it from her, no way.

The newly arrived young man quickly undid the straps binding Irina to her chair. Apologising profusely, in well-educated English, he offered her some water. He then asked if she would like the fire to be lit. He spoke excellent Russian also, it seemed, as he appeared quite comfortable with giving orders to her Russian guard.

Irina surmised that this person was both suave and polite in character. As he spoke to her it became obvious that, wherever he'd been born, he'd spent plenty of time in England. His manners also were faultless, under any other circumstances, he was charming. She'd like to hear his name and she needed to assess his upbringing and his nature. So far he didn't seem to be in any way a violent man.

How best should she respond? With dignity, forthrightness and just a little understanding she felt. He can't be much older than my own grandson Jake, Irina decided, as the young man talked confidently in English about what he wanted of her.

It seemed that the Russians wished to take over her house for a while to be used as headquarters for some clandestine shenanigans. She already had a good idea what this was all about. Something she'd been expecting for years; but what an earth did this attractive young man have to do with such catastrophic devilry?

"Absolutely not!" Irina responded indignantly. "I'm afraid that Russian people have no standing whatsoever here in Estonia and whatever you are up to, of course, you have no permission from me to use my house as a base. Whatever made you think that you could and what an earth is a well-spoken man like you doing with such rough people as those anyway?" She waved her hands imperiously indicating the Russian guards on the other side of the door.

"Irina," if I may call you by your first name?"

She merely nodded at his deference; a log shifted catching his attention and he turned to pick up a fire iron to deal with it. Irina let out a sigh of mild annoyance and reached for her glass of water. She needed to try to build some form of relationship with this mild-mannered man. To do so with the soldiers would be well-nigh impossible she felt. She was glad that she was in her tidy clothes, as she called them. Because of the intended visit to the concert, she'd had the hairdresser visit the day before and her nails had been re-polished in preparation for the evening event. She felt better able to cope with this unusual young man knowing she looked her best. She replaced her glass, patted her hair in place and looked towards her adversary now sitting on the arm of the chair opposite.

"Well, young man, what do you have to say for yourself?" she asked with a raised eyebrow. "I need an explanation about this extraordinary predicament in which I find myself?"

He smiled at her just too charmingly, thought Irina, then nodding, cleared his throat.

"But of course, Comtesse," he replied, easily reverting to the French equivalent of her title. "You move freely between Estonia and Russia, do you not?" Again she simply inclined her head.

"The thing is that we need your help and your hunting lodge, as it turns out, is in the perfect location."

Irina was beginning to get the drift of what he was saying, albeit in a roundabout way.

"Who exactly is 'we'?" she asked. "Also, if you are asking for my help, why was I trussed up like a chicken? It's not as if I can go anywhere, with these gun-toting Russian soldiers breathing down my neck and the blizzard outside! Do you have a name?" she added.

The man smiled condescendingly.

"Yes it's Nicholas or Nico," he replied with a smile. "Irina, I can see that we have put you in an awkward position and I have apologised already for the indignity of being tied to your chair before I arrived. Misplaced judgement I'm afraid and the overly zealous soldiers responsible shall be reprimanded." He indicated the army gathering outside in the hall. "But surely I do not need to remind you who really is in charge here? We would like to have your permission to use your house as our base, given gladly, but if not then I am very much afraid that we shall just have to take it over anyway."

He laughed, almost charmingly as he turned away for a moment to gaze into the fire.

Irina remained silent, a frown on her face. She was thinking hard, how could she delay things? She asked for some more water. Nico called in one of the Russian guards, held out the glass and gave the order. This man was definitely used to giving orders, she thought. Nico or perhaps Nicolai? She had a feeling this man wasn't as English as he seemed. The accent was just too perfect, but the Russian was exactly right. Irina could see her late husband's comforting old grandfather clock reliably ticking away in the far corner. It somehow gave her renewed confidence.

She thought that by now, her oldest friend and lover Gustav would be taking some sort of action. He would remember the musical evening planned here at the hunting lodge with the Romanians on Friday night. He always looked forward to the event and stayed the night with her afterwards. Nicholas, or more likely Nicolai bent to attend to the fire again as a log had rolled out onto the hearth. She opened her mouth to speak, but at that moment everybody could hear the deep muffled sound of a vehicle, of some sort, navigating a way through the snow and arriving outside. The Roma card she'd have to keep up her sleeve for the moment.

Men's voices and the slamming of doors ensued, as a draught of cold air blew through the old building. The young man politely excused himself to deal with the new arrivals. Irina drew in her breath and let it out slowly. Footsteps on the flagstones, she relaxed her knuckles on the chair arms, moved her arms around a bit and rotated her feet a few times, to keep her circulation going as much as she was able. She wasn't used to sitting still for so long and her neck and back ached. It didn't suit her for she was a busy person and she was accustomed to giving the orders, not taking them.

The tension was palpable as she heard raised voices and angry footsteps approaching. Irina, smoothed her hair, took another deep breath, stood up and turning her head towards the door prepared herself for the next shocking experience.

*　*　*

CHAPTER 12

Enemy Within
(The early hours)

WALKING into one of his family homes under duress, filled Jake with an anger fuelled confidence. How dare these people ride roughshod over other people's lives to further their own evil ambitions. He felt desperately worried and overly protective for his grandmother but his mentor back at HQ had reminded him not to let personal feelings cloud his judgement. Yet at this moment his fury was hard to control.

He forcefully shook off the rough hands guiding him inside and turned around quickly to rebuke his abductors entering his grandmother's house behind him.

"This is my family's home, now take your hands off me and..." pointing to their snow laden boots, "deal with your feet before you come in."

The yellow-haired monster appeared bewildered by Jake's commanding voice and sudden change in temperament. He took a step back, nearly knocking over the other car passengers on the icy top step behind him, while the three Russian soldiers in the hall, with little sign of aggression, stepped up to make a formal stand in front of the newcomers; fairly senior army officers Jake surmised, but with no evident weaponry and no tendency towards immediate violence.

With some relief that the situation appeared calm for the moment, Jake felt less aggrieved and anxious with the lessening of tension. He looked them all up and down then spoke with a determined glare.

"Now take me to the man in charge!" With that the door into the sitting room, on the other side of the hall opened and a good-looking well-dressed man, of a similar age to himself, advanced towards Jake with an arm out-stretched in greeting.

"Good evening Jake. How do you do?" Perfect public-school English Jake noted, somewhat astonished, yet keeping his hand firmly in his pocket.

"How do I do? Not at all well thank you – as you can see for yourself!" Jake waved a hand at the motley Russian crew behind him with disdain; they were now looking rather uncertain of themselves. He indicated his own cold wet and dishevelled state. "Might I ask who the hell are you, bringing these unwelcome people into my grandmother's house?"

"Do please come in," the young man answered smoothly, "and I'll explain everything."

"First I must see my grandmother to make sure that she is unharmed," Jake answered in an authoritative tone, "and please get rid of this obnoxious lot behind me, they are not welcome in this house." The man stood politely to one side as Jake marched past.

"Yes, don't worry I shall dismiss them and your grandmother is fine, I do assure you..."

With relief, Jake could hear Irina calling him from the sitting room; she'd heard his voice. Her own was strong as ever, in spite of her age, the late hour and the circumstances.

"Jake darling, I'm in here by the fire. I'm alright, come in, come in for Heaven's sake!"

Jake flung the door open and in three long strides was at her side and bending down to her.

"Grina – what on earth is going on here, who are these people, what the hell are they doing here?" Jake, already had a perfectly good idea what this was all about, but he couldn't let on as he didn't wish to compromise his role as part of the special forces.

Irina hugged her grandson to her, whispering quickly, "Bloody Russians! I always knew they'd come." Then loudly: "Darling you are freezing cold and wet, you'll catch your death, now go up and change at once. There are some of your grandfather's shooting clothes still in the cupboard in the blue room upstairs. Nico let him go up," she demanded pointing to the door. The young man, who had followed Jake into the room, merely nodded courteously.

"But of course." He beckoned to one of the army officers issuing a command in Russian. The man immediately stepped forward to make sure that Jake was unarmed.

Jake put his briefcase down firmly beside his grandmother while the soldier frisked him. The man then made him open his briefcase, but there was nothing to see and Jake in relief quietly let out his breath.

"Ok! I won't be a minute Grina." He gave her a quick kiss. "I'm so glad you're alright, now sit back down; I was really worried when I realised these people were bringing me here."

"I'm glad you did come here," answered Irina with feeling, "but don't you worry darling, it takes more than a few Russian men flexing their muscles to worry an old Estonian lady like me. Unfortunately I've seen it all before. Now off with you, go and get dry. Then when you come down Nico here or should I say Nicolai... will tell you all – I hope?"

She inclined her head towards the young man who looked just a little startled as he realised his cover had been blown. He had thought that he spoke English like an upper-crust Englishman. Jake picked up his briefcase and the officer followed him out.

Irina let out a long sigh. She didn't feel half so vulnerable now that Jake had turned up.

✳

Jake came bounding down the stairs in double quick time. As promised, Nicolai had already dismissed the motley crew who had brought him here and Jake was more than glad to see the back of them; particularly the violent yellow *kanaari*, who had never ceased to try both his patience and his temper. Now the household was comprised of just himself, his grandmother, Nicolai and the three army officers sitting around a table in the far corner of the hall noisily playing cards.

Back in the sitting room the young man rose to greet him. He'd put another log on the fire and there was a mug of tea and some heavy looking cake for Jake. He pulled up a chair and picking up the tea, looked from his grandmother to Nicolai.

"Now Grina would you like to tell me exactly what is going on here, and you perhaps…" looking towards the polite young man, "could kindly ask your men to show some respect and keep their voices down. Then perhaps you can tell me what you are up to which necessitated the kidnapping of a young woman, back in the UK, demands for a large amount of money and my being forcibly brought into Russia, in the company of an uncouth violent mob?" There was dead silence.

"Perhaps you could also shut the door, for some privacy. It's very draughty in her for my grandmother and it makes the fire smoke."

Irina had to stifle a girlish giggle. Nicolai gave a barely disguised sigh and with a slight bow to Irina, dropped his gaze and strode to the open doorway to issue more instructions to the soldiers in the hall. Irina turned to her grandson.

"Jake tell me everything darling. You can call me Irina now, if you wish, you're no longer a child after all!" Jake smiled at her fondly.

"No Grina, I'd never change your name, you've always been Grina for me and Grina you'll stay!" Irina nodded, secretly pleased.

Nicolai returned to stand quietly at the far side of the fire place, hands in pockets, surveying them both as Jake told his story.

Irina listened with mounting horror as she learned of the rough flight and dramatic ride through the bitterly cold dark forests, which her beloved grandson had just experienced. After hearing it all she regarded Nicolai with cold violet coloured eyes.

"So! All this doesn't seem to sit very well on your shoulders young man. You don't look and behave as a violent man, you are quite charming really, surely you must come from a good family? How on earth did you ever get involved with such people? My grandson and I both wish to be enlightened. I have already worked out that, although you have obviously been well educated in England, you aren't English at all are you? – You are one hundred per cent Russian."

She held up an imperious hand and Jake just managed to contain a chuckle. Nicolai was also looking somewhat astonished.

"How did I know? Because Your English is just too perfect and your Russian includes just a wee bit of school boy slang! I myself speak the Russian language, Estonian, English and of course French. Never mind. Tell me – am I to believe that you are responsible for this state of affairs. Are you yourself in the business of abducting elderly women or do you answer to someone else altogether who we have yet to meet?" Neither Nicolai or Jake could resist a slight barely controlled chuckle: the lady was indomitable.

"Irina, I am the one who should be dictating this conversation and I am only holding back out of politeness and good manners, some of which as you, quite rightly guessed, I learnt in England. Tomorrow I have to leave you for a couple of days. You and your grandson will be held here in your own house, free to move within, but under the, shall I say… care, of the men outside in the hall. I am sorry that they might not be as gentlemanly as you might wish, but this is merely the night watch, who will be replaced with a fresh unit tomorrow. I will try to make sure that next time the men are more to your liking." He glanced at Jake with a meaningful smile and added, "But they also will, of course, be well armed."

"And what might I ask do you want of my grandson?" demanded Irina, not to be put down in anyway.

"He has funds for us which he will transfer into a Swiss bank account," he countered quickly before changing the subject. "He will, as well, be responsible for your own good health and safety. More than this you have no need to know or worry about at present. Now I think that perhaps we should have some rest. Irina you are free to go upstairs to your room, also your grandson. Tomorrow before I leave we will see if the internet connection has been restored, after the storm, for the funds to be transferred, then all communication here will be cut once more. The men in the hall will rest where they are and I shall be perfectly comfortable in here."

He stood up. Irina remained where she was. Now she would play her card.

"There's just one thing Nicolai." The young man sat down again, with an amused raised eyebrow, noting his real name being used and wondering what was coming next. "Now that I know your proper name I shall show you the respect of using it." She nodded, as if agreeing with her own decision before continuing.

"In a few days' time I have the Romany people invited here, to the lodge, to entertain us with their gypsy music and dancing. They are gifted people and come to work on the estate every year. The night before they leave to go home, they come for their money and – to show their appreciation, they perform for us. A long-standing elderly friend of mine, who lives nearby, always attends, also two of my nearest neighbouring families. On Wednesday my staff are expecting to begin the preparations, which means that they will need to make the lodge ready and to start bringing equipment and food here from the main house. Now if I cancel this event news that something is amiss will spread like wildfire. What would you have me do?"

Jake, remembering his old friend Gunari and those happy days from his boyhood, had to hand it to his grandmother as her inspired revelation had the desired effect.

Nicolai's calm reserve began to unravel a little. He seemed just very slightly agitated. This planned occasion was something the Russians couldn't have foreseen. If it was allowed to go ahead, it could possibly instigate a turning point in this whole unsavoury business. It could well present a way into the house for Jake's colleagues.

Jake's heart was thumping, he had to appear unperturbed by his grandmothers request. He waited to hear what Nicolai would decide, hardly daring to breath. He turned to stare into the fire giving the impression that he really didn't care one way or the other.

"I need to think about this overnight. When is the actual party? How many of these Romany people do you expect?" Irina also was keeping her cool.

"It's on Friday and they usually bring about five dancers and maybe five playing their instruments. Of course, perhaps I could cancel the other two families with some feasible excuse, but telling the Romanies, who so badly need their pay..." she trailed off with a sigh "...is more difficult."

"I see. I will let you know tomorrow before I leave." He stood again. "Now I am sure that we are all tired so we should get some rest." He went over to the door and held it open. Irina and Jake walked through, the men in the hall immediately arrived at their side. Jake held up a hand.

"No! I will escort my grandmother to her room myself thank you." He turned to nod to Nicolai and set off up the stairs after Irina, still carrying his briefcase.

"I am afraid that there is to be no communication outside this house so I must look after your suitcase over-night, just in case the lines become available again." Jake handed it over happy to know that his special facility mobile was safely concealed upstairs and that there was no way his computer could be infiltrated.

"When you are settled, I'm afraid we shall need to lock your doors, so when you are ready please kindly leave the keys on the outside." The young man called after them. "Thank you for your calm good judgement and hospitality. I wish you both a good night."

"Hardly likely to be going anywhere in this weather," muttered Irina without turning around.

Jake couldn't help but smile at the audacity of his extraordinarily brave and inspirational grandmother.

* * *

CHAPTER 13

Irina And Jake
(Monday)

IRINA and Jake were both awake early. Jake had managed to climb out of his window and to swing himself up and over the wrought iron balustrade onto Irina's little balcony. He'd done this on a couple of occasions as a young teenager when he'd come in late from visiting the Romany encampment. He used to love mucking around, in the forest, with people of his own age. He was glad to know that they were still there and reassured to feel certain that Gunari would by now be well aware of what was happening.

The last time he'd climbed in to the hunting lodge, it had been summer, but now in unsuitable clothes, getting over the thin intricate old barrier in winter proved to be a much more difficult task. The snow was deep on the balcony and the frail iron guardrail was completely iced over and very slippery. When she realised that her grandson was outside the window Irina helped him in, thoroughly enjoying this clandestine adventure.

"Darling are you a member of a special forces team or something, 'cos you seem very fit and on top of this situation? Good Heaven's the muscles in your arms are firm. Come in, come in" she whispered, "before you catch your death in this cold! You are not even wearing proper winter clothes."

"Yes well the thing is…" Jake lifted his feet one at a time to gingerly knock the snow off his boots onto the narrow balcony, "quite obviously I wasn't even expecting to leave England! Also Grina, you aren't supposed to know that I have any hidden talents at all! Whatever happens those downstairs must never know. I've concealed my magical mobile beneath the floorboards in my old room, where I used to stash my sweets; luckily I took it out of the case when I first came up to change. It had its very own hiding place in the inner lining of my briefcase."

Irina's eyes twinkled with excitement. "Well isn't that a thing! But my darling boy I always knew where you hid your sweets you know – just never let on!" She chuckled; then in a low voice she enlightened Jake further about the coming evening with the gypsies. She also explained her absolute certainty that Gustav, in Talinn, would be moving matters along by now.

Earlier Jake had tried to get a text message off to Guy wondering, given the appalling weather, if or not it would be received. He gave details of their exact location, numbers of Russians in the household and of the impending Romany musical evening, planned for Friday night. His mobile had appeared to stand up well to the harsh conditions; it had triple the usual strength and charge time of any normal phone and many more facilities. The message had disappeared off into the ether but whether or not it was to arrive safely with his colleagues he couldn't tell. He could only wait to see if he received a reply.

Gunari and his Romany friends had created an obvious way for Jake's colleagues to infiltrate the hunting lodge. Irina was sure that the Russians were about to walk into Estonia using her estate as the entry point. Hopefully Gustav would have already alerted the Ministry of Defence, as only last week during a dinner together, they had been discussing this very possibility. Even the Romany leader had remarked on Russian activity on the other side of the border, when last Irina had visited him in the forest.

Jake also was confident that Guy would be in touch with Gunari once he had received his earlier text. Knowing both men and aware of the implications surrounding his own and Irina's incarceration, Jake knew that no stone would have been left unturned. It was imperative that the musical evening went ahead at the end of the week.

＊

The kitchen at the hunting lodge was always well equipped and stocked during the shooting season, so Irina made them both boiled eggs and toast with bread from the freezer and coffee with long life milk. They felt better for each other's company even though they always had a Russian soldier lurking within earshot. Irina had made it quite clear to Nicolai that she was not going to feed the soldiers and had given them a kettle, a carton of milk and some sugar in the little study off the hall beside the front door. As planned, Irina asked the young man whether she would be allowed to have one of her staff bring up some fresh food from the main house when the drive had been sufficiently cleared.

"Yes, I see no harm in that, but whoever you choose will then have to stay here to look after your needs and help in general. You will also inform the main house that you have decided to stay here to oversee preparations for your musical evening."

"Ah, that is good, so my evening with the Roma may go ahead, as usual?"

"Good," smiled Jake with a fake sigh, quickly hiding his relief. "Grina, it will be a little like when I was a child."

"But I think it would be best if you cancelled the other guests. Perhaps just let the elderly gentleman come to keep you company."

"Oh my goodness! Gustav will be so pleased. He's never yet missed one of my soirées with the gypsies. I'll just mention to the others that I have a touch of flu so it's best they keep clear, shall I?"

Nicolai thought how helpful Irina had become; that must be after the arrival of her grandson, who seemed quite a nice quiet sort of man. He didn't expect any more trouble from Jake now that he had seen that his grandmother was not to be harmed.

"I will help you with these telephone calls. Please make sure that you order everything you need to be brought. Once we have transferred the money Jake, if I may call you by your first name?" Jake nodded, "the telephones and any other communication will no longer be available to you. As far as the rest of the world are concerned, for the next few days the lines are being repaired. I shall be away until the end of the week, but I shall be here for your party Irina. I wouldn't dream of missing it."

"Excellent!" replied Irina, well pleased. You might even enjoy the evening's entertainment, we always do. Now I suppose you aren't going to tell us anything more about your imminent plans?"

"Yes, what exactly are you doing here?" asked Jake apparently completely bewildered. "Will you all be leaving once this money is seen to have gone through the various channels?"

"No I am afraid that we need to be here a little longer than that."

At the last question Nicolai looked wary but smug. He wasn't about to give them any further information. He was quite oblivious to the reality that both Jake and his grandmother were well aware of what was happening.

"Now I will go to see if we can install some form of communication."

The telephone calls were made with the help of a Russian army communications engineer, with the required technical facilities, who had been ordered to the Lodge. As far as the recipients were concerned, it was just a temporary line set up and used by the ordinary Estonian emergency services.

Nicolai stood beside Irina telling her what to say and she left a message for Gustav signing off using her full name Katarina… their secretive code in times of trouble. This gave her an immense feeling of satisfaction. The money was then transferred with apparent success through a series of bank accounts, eventually ending up in Switzerland.

The weather cleared. After introducing Irina and Jake to a newly arrived more presentable looking army officer named Colonel Bobrinsky, Nicolai took his leave promising to return on Friday in good time for the party.

The senior officer Bobrinsky, once Nicolai had left, looked both bad tempered and unhappy to be there; but at least he was a smarter looking individual. He ordered his other two men into the hall where they also sat looking ill at ease and glum. Although, the Contessa decided, that their appearance was a slight improvement from the last lot.

"What on earth are we going to do with ourselves under such depressing-looking supervision?" asked Irina. Jake walked her over to the fireplace pretending to reorganise the fire for the coming evening.

"We keep calm and at least try to build some sort of relationship with Bobrinsky," Jake replied adding even more quietly, "and remember Grina… what I have upstairs." He put his hand to his face and touched his ear.

"Yes, but is it charged?" she countered helping sweep the scattered, dead embers off the hearth back into the fireplace.

"Not needed," Jake answered, looking more confident by the minute.

*

By Monday morning, having picked up Irina's message, supposedly about her Friday soirée, Gustav was convinced that something was seriously wrong. They knew each other very well; they were on the same wavelength and on the answer machine, Irina had used her full name. She was always precise with her plans which they'd discussed when they spoke the day before. He had warned her of the impending storm and she had assured him that she would be at the hotel in Talinn in time for a late lunch prior to the concert.

On the message machine she had left no explanation whatsoever for her failure to turn up. Quite obviously she was not alone and had been told what to say.

Gustav, in his seventies, was a fit, old fashioned and distinguished looking aristocrat. A courageous senior cavalry officer in his prime and a former minister in the government, he not only had guts but was blessed with an astute intellect and an alert brain; neither of which had diminished with age. He still managed to keep a foot in the door of the Estonian government. He kept his position mainly because of his connections and past experience in dealing with the Russians, who continued to create a constant problem along their borders.

Irina had the reputation of being extremely outspoken on matters regarding the 'Great Bear' and she had good reason to be wary, with her estate being located right on the Russian border. She was convinced that one day they'd come across in force and that she would be directly on their route.

Gustav also knew that as far as the Russians were concerned, Irina lived right in the centre of a strategically weak area where an aggressor might well consider breaching the border.

As lunchtime on Sunday had passed with no news from Irina, Gustav called up the mainline of the old manor house, only to find that the lines were down. Irina's mobile was usually on the blink, having run out of juice. They were completely out of touch which still could possibly be due to weather damage. Early on Monday he had called up his own office, to give instructions that he'd be out for the afternoon and to make an urgent appointment with the War Minister. Luckily the man was also an old friend to whom he'd gain immediate access.

Now Gustav approached the Government buildings; despite the falling snow he hesitated a moment, as usual, just to look up at the blue, black and white Estonian flag. It flew free at the top of the building. Blue for the sky, black for the earth and white for the spirit of freedom.

'Hum' he thought, with a genuine sense of unease, 'are we about to be severely tested? And is my dearest Irina correct in her thinking? Is she perhaps in serious danger? Were the bloody Russians making yet another move to annex Estonia?'

Gustav shook his head, smoothed down his thick, silver hair and ran determinedly up the steps. The man he was about to see had already received information from the British about the involvement of Irina's grandson in an enigmatic and expensive transfer of funds and of strange aircraft movements during this last dangerous storm.

Gustav hadn't seen Jake since he'd become a man, yet he'd been very fond of the boy with, he remembered, his unique and adventurous spirit. He sensed and hoped that if he was under extreme pressure in these testing circumstances, he would be holding himself together well. He felt sure that he would. He couldn't help but wonder if perhaps he was already here in Estonia, hopefully even taking care of his grandmother.

* * *

CHAPTER 14

Reassurance
(The English country pub)

"WELL then, what shall we do today? Do we stay here in the pub until further notice?" Emma looked over her coffee cup across the breakfast table at her husband. Ellie hadn't appeared yet so they had a moment to themselves to make a plan. Marc was tucking into toast and marmalade with a vengeance and she could sense that he was not happy with being out of the picture and away from all the action. He finished his mouthful, took a sip of coffee, put his cup down and fixed her with his extraordinary and unusual coloured eyes.

"To be absolutely honest – I'm not quite sure whether or not we can move until I've spoken to my liaison in London. He's due to call in; it's early yet, so until then I suggest we continue to enjoy our breakfast and wait for Ellie to come down." He started on another piece of toast.

Emma hated this situation and although she was certain he didn't mean to be, Marc did appear smug. She well understood all the confidentiality, but it was thoroughly irritating! There was something about being kept in the dark by her husband that really got to her, especially when they had been through much together, in the past: then she had almost been treated as an equal.

It is all very well, she thought sniffily to herself – this clandestine stuff. Marc only worked for the elusive people occasionally, but when matters interfered with their private life she felt that she should be told exactly how things stood. Otherwise how on earth was she supposed to react in a helpful manner. To make it worse, this time the whole saga seemed to be revolving around a very vulnerable young friend of theirs.

Marc knew that because he was so low down in the hierarchy, he was unlikely to be enlightened as to what was really happening elsewhere. His priority was focused on the care and safety of Ellie: he looked up and realised that he was in for another interrogation. He cleared his throat ready to deal with a barrage of, no doubt, astute and understandable questioning. Emma was intelligent and didn't miss much, but just as she was about to start they both spied Ellie approaching, still looking pale yet obviously better for the secure night's rest. Marc stood to greet her.

"Good morning." Ellie smiled and kissed them both. "What a lovely peaceful night: thank you Marc for letting me share with Emma last night. I'm so sorry to have kicked you out of your room. I never even heard Emma get up this morning."

"It was my pleasure and neither of us wanted you to be alone after what you'd just been through."

"How are you feeling this morning?" Emma asked gently, pulling out the chair next to her. Ellie slumped down with a sigh.

"Ok I suppose. I'm just so worried about Jake… and Guy of course. I can't stop thinking about it all and imagining what might be going on and wondering where they have got to. I have all these awful images in my head…" she trailed off, her eyes filling with tears.

"To be honest, I kept waking in the night and… and feeling so helpless not knowing and not being able to do anything. I've been trying to think if there's something, anything that I can remember which might help. Especially about that man, the one who abducted me. I do recall thinking that he was too good to be true. Does that sound strange? I don't know, just a funny feeling that he was too perfect in some way... his looks, attitude, his accent even; overly posh. I can't quite put my finger on it. He was so very charming and well mannered. What an idiot I was to be taken in so easily."

"You're not an idiot Ellie, no way: don't push things," advised Marc kindly, covering her hand with his. "Interestingly enough what you have just said could be helpful and I shall pass it on. If anything else comes to mind, however small and insignificant that you might think it is, just tell me. But for now you must try to recover from all the drama, which is well and truly over I do assure you. Jake is in exceptionally good company with Guy and I suspect that Julian's around somewhere in the background, as they nearly always work together. So you must try not to worry too much – I do realise how difficult it is but you know what they're like – they're probably wrapping things up now as we speak and having a pint somewhere."

Emma glanced at her husband with a raised eyebrow, passing over a very distinct look of 'I very much doubt it' for him alone. Being in the army, elite or otherwise or even the TA was one thing, but the Secret Services was quite another. Thank God that, when required, Marc merely helped out the Reserves with his doctor's hat on.

"Well I suggest we spend a peaceful morning here and wait for instructions," said Emma. "What do you think Marc?"

"Yes, they'll be in touch when they can so until then let's have some more coffee and Ellie you must eat." He signalled for the waiter. "What would you like?"

"I'm not really very hungry, but I suppose I should have something." She looked at the menu, "Perhaps some scrambled eggs, with toast and tea for me, please." Emma's heart went out to her young friend, there really was nothing worse than not knowing what the hell was going on. Her whole world had been turned upside down, the men had all vanished and everything seemed wrapped in secrecy. Marc ordered, then checked his watch.

"Hopefully I might have some news in an hour or so. Meanwhile we'll just have to sit tight."

Ellie looked miserable. "What shall I do all by myself, at home, in the flat? I suppose I can't go to work either, for the moment. What on earth shall I tell them? Actually I think I'd be too frightened to go out at all: what if that man found me again?"

Emma took her hand. "Ellie you won't be on your own, you're going to stay somewhere safe… We can tell her now, can't we Marc? I mean it is all organised."

"Yes of course. Ellie – we will look after you until this is all over. You'll be staying with Rose. Olly is away with the TA and Rose is working from home, at present, while her office is being redecorated. Your work people will be told that you aren't well: that you're down with flu needing a few days' rest in bed. Anything you need will be brought to you, so you mustn't worry."

Ellie managed a wan smile. "Goodness you're quick at arranging things. I'd love to hole up with Rose, if that's really alright; but I do need to contact my parents who are used to me calling them up at the weekends. As I couldn't ring them this last one they'll be wondering if something has happened. Little do they know what has been going on, thank God, as Mum would have a fit. As for Giles, with my special twin insight I'm sure that my brother already senses something's wrong. He's bound to have been trying to get hold of me and wondering why I'm not at home. I think I should ring him also – just to set his mind at rest as we are so very close. Perhaps I can just say that I'm staying with friends as Jake has to work away from home for a few days. He does sometimes do that."

"You'll be able to speak to them as normal Ellie, don't worry, they needn't know anything different other than you have a mild go of flu and will have to stay away from the office for a week or so. I'll give you a new mobile for the time being." Marc reassured. "Do you know what happened to yours?"

"Yes I lost it, possibly dropped it in that bar, where it all started and I became ill. But I don't think that awful man got it, at least I hope not. He must have been too busy getting me out of the building, without raising suspicion, to look for it. The last thing I remember was that I'd see what the food was like and tell Giles about it later, then placing the mobile on the shallow shelf under the bar while I was waiting for Jake."

Ellie put both hands up to her face. "Oh Heavens! Giles! I know he'll be really anxious that something has happened to me, we're always texting each other and I never got to answer his text on Friday night. I suppose the man was busy spiking my drink while I was checking my messages. My biggest mistake. It might still be there if it hasn't been pinched. It was an upmarket bar, not in the least sleazy with a decent type of barman. I'm sure if they found it they would have kept it safe."

"Don't worry about it. If the mobile is still there we'll retrieve it, but just for the moment you'll have to tell your family that you've lost it, so will borrow one just to keep in touch until you get your own replaced. That's the best plan. The new one which I'm to give you is no ordinary mobile as it can't be traced. I will plumb in the numbers of both your parents and brother, otherwise it will be solely for you to keep in touch with us – either calls or texts at any time of the day or night, I will always answer. I suggest you text your brother immediately so that he's not worrying, then you can ring your parents too. I will also see to it that Jake can contact you as soon as he is able on the new phone. You will have an emergency button for immediate assistance as well. So Ellie, I do assure you, you will never be alone." Ellie sank back in her chair looking relieved.

"As I'm sure you now realise there really is an ongoing, secret mission in progress at present. That's why, just for the time being, Jake can't get in touch. It will only be for a short time and I promise to update you whenever I can." At this last mention of Jake, Ellie looked a lot happier.

"Thank you," she said. "I had no idea just how good you obviously all are at this undercover intelligence business." They sat silent for a moment pondering their own thoughts.

The sudden intrusive noise of Marc's phone made them all jump and he moved quickly off out of earshot. Emma could feel his tension. She and Ellie watched his face as, holding the instrument tight to his ear, he listened. Despite feeling a nauseous wave of fear wash over her, Ellie concentrated on stirring her tea determined to hold herself together. Everything seemed to have been taken in hand which was a relief. She felt safe herself now, but she was terrified for Jake, having seen for herself those dreadful people with whom he and Guy had flown off. She sat quietly praying for some good news for Marc to bring back to the table. The conversation looked like being a long one.

Little had Ellie imagined, when Jake told her of his secondary job, that it could ever touch their private life and in such a violent manner. She had thought that his Intelligence workplace was at some highly technical SIS headquarters just outside London where he, most likely, spent his time helping decode and infiltrate terrorist organizations. He had very advanced I/T skills and had previously worked for the Home Office and the MOD which had also been fairly hush hush. Now she felt thoroughly shaken with the realization that he was actually out in the field, dealing with the dangerous and frightening physical aspects of the job.

Breakfast arrived for Ellie and as the waitress unloaded the tray and poured the coffee Ellie studied Emma's face. She seemed so calm and compliant with what Marc was doing. Emma caught Ellie staring at her and wondered what she was thinking. She smiled encouragingly.

"Hopefully we'll have a bit more information about what's going on in a minute," she said hoping to dispel any negative thoughts. Marc had moved further away and out of sight as the hotel staff began discreetly clearing away some of the earlier breakfast tables. Emma felt a cold sliver of fear slide down the back of her neck and shivered. She quickly began to rearrange her hair to cover for this weird and ominous sensation.

"Yes, that would be good," Ellie answered quickly, "but Emma how on earth do the women who are married to these men cope, when they go out on dangerous operations all the time? I just can't imagine how they can live with it on a day to day basis. I don't think I could."

"Yes you could Ellie, because you are brave and loyal; you've just proved that. After a time the wives and other halves just get used to it. I don't even like Marc's smaller part in it at all, but I go along with it because his one calling is helping people who need medical assistance. Yet there do seem to be a growing number of cases, away from the public eye so to speak, like now." She smiled.

"Yes, but you have children, don't you get frantic with worry? I know everybody says that once you've had children you become a lot more concerned about your own physical safety because of the responsibility." Ellie, Emma noticed, seemed to be enjoying her scrambled eggs.

"That's just an inbuilt parental thing. My job in life is to help keep everybody in the family healthy, happy and safe and under duress I'd fight tooth and nail to do that. When you are feeling stronger Ellie, I'll tell you about something that happened to me one winter, not long ago, in the Swiss Alps before the children were born. It's some story and involved Rose, Olly and all the others, which is one of the reasons we are all so close. I think you have also met Alicia and Adriana?" Ellie nodded. "Well they both go to work and try not to think about what Guy and Julian are up to when they are sent away. Sometimes if the mission is a long one then the girls move in together, so they at least have each other for company. Both of them are amazingly staunch, although we keep a close eye on Adriana now that she has two babies on board. They know they are welcome to be with us anytime and they often come over. Marc's a very calming influence on us all, even more so when he has a little harem to look after!"

"I can see that," Ellie answered swallowing a mouthful of toast and smiling. "I now have had first-hand experience of both Guy and Jake's professionalism. Olly's in the TA isn't he? Does Rose mind about that?"

"Yes, Olly loves anything to do with the army as he says his ordinary job is thoroughly boring in comparison. He's a great character is Olly and game for anything! Anyway now Adriana's well past her six months, she and Julian are throwing a party, so the men had better all get back home or there will be big trouble."

Emma laughed, trying to lighten the atmosphere; but Marc had been gone a long time.

✻

Rose was looking forward to having Ellie to stay. She hated being alone for more than a night or two and Olly had gone on some Territorial expedition, or so she thought. He'd been gone for three days already. He'd sent his usual sign that all was well by text; the usual picture of a rose and two xx's. So she had no real reason to believe that he wasn't out on the moors somewhere on a routine training exercise, running around with a huge backpack getting ridiculously fit. It was just that she was always suspicious, from past experience, when both Julian and Guy were also out of touch at the same time.

Since Marc had called her, enlightening her about poor Ellie's situation, her brain had gone into overtime trying to remember exactly where Olly had said he was going on this last TA adventure. The trouble was she obviously hadn't been listening, if indeed he had told her at all. Rose knew perfectly well that the expertise of some of the most experienced in the team were sometimes used for further assignments; recruited by the crack SAS Intelligence officers, to whom both Julian and Guy reported. She was also well aware that on a tricky mission the Service liked to assemble the same back-up team, with those who had already worked together, whenever possible.

Rose experienced the tell-tale slightly queasy anxious feeling in her stomach. She was probably right in her thinking. Why couldn't she be married to someone with an ordinary job? Olly was a good estate agent. He could sell oil to the Arabs. He had risen to become a partner in a very upmarket firm in the West End. But, in the past, he had always been fascinated with intrigue of any sort. After meeting Julian and Guy, they had all become close friends. Olly had eventually persuaded them that perhaps on certain occasions he could be useful to them in their other work, if he trained to become part of the Reserve Force. Over a long period of time, mostly and boringly at weekends, he had set about becoming ultra-fit. He loved all his adventures and hard field exercises with the TA. So, Rose supposed, he was the perfect target for recruitment into further entanglement with the secretive world.

Rose walked down the passage to check everything was ready for Ellie in the spare-room. She'd put some flowers on the table beside the bed and added some light reading and a bottle of water on the shelf underneath. She fluffed up the pillows, patted away the wrinkles on the duvet and straightened the towels on the rail in the bathroom. Then she caught a glimpse of herself in the mirror. Her dark curly hair looked dishevelled and her face was paler than usual accentuating her freckles. A bit grim looking and anxious, she thought, so that impression had to go before Ellie arrived. The poor girl needed a calm cosy nest in which to recover, whilst waiting for the return of Jake from God alone knows where.

✻   ✻   ✻

CHAPTER 15

Friends Indeed
(Rose's flat, London)

AT eleven thirty am precisely, the loud door buzzer shattered the silence: they were exactly on schedule. Rose looked around one last time, just to make sure that she had everything ready to welcome Ellie into a cosy, tranquil atmosphere. She flicked on the switch of the kettle, then moved quickly across to lift the entrance handset, to hear Marc's familiar dulcet and reassuring tones.

"Come in! Come on up! You know the way. Lift to third floor. I'm here ready and waiting."

Rose pressed the enter button and opened her apartment door into the passage. She wondered if her suspicions were correct and that Olly might also be muddled up in this latest drama.

Perhaps Marc would know by now of his whereabouts. She hadn't heard from Oliver for three days, although that was often the case. He loved all the hush hush and slightly secretive duties of the TA Reserve Force.

Muted voices rose up inside the building and the street sounds diminished. The slam of the heavy front door reverberated up the stairs and then Rose heard the whine of the ancient mechanism as the lift struggled into action. A few moments later the lift gate clanked open into the corridor and Emma's smiling face appeared, followed by Ellie, with Marc bringing up the rear. Rose, now entirely restored to her usual ebullient self, ushered them all in, closed the door, said hello to her friends and immediately enveloped Ellie in a gentle welcoming hug.

"Dear Ellie, I know it's for a horrible reason, but it's just lovely to have you here." Ellie held on tight responding with relieved warmth.

"You are so good to have me, I'm afraid I'm a complete mess." Marc stepped in quickly.

"She's not in a mess at all Rose, Ellie has been exceptionally brave during a really frightening experience. She kept her head throughout, so both Jake and Guy must be very proud indeed!"

"How do you know I kept my head?" Ellie turned towards Marc. "You weren't even there." She looked hesitant.

"No, but the man waiting for you with the car at the bottom of the aeroplane steps saw the way you left Ellie; 'slowly and with great dignity' were his actual words." Marc was smiling gently, trying to soften the effects of trauma.

"When this whole saga is wrapped up, we'll all have one hell of a celebration," Emma added positively giving Ellie an affectionate hug.

"Well I'm definitely up for that," Rose agreed. "Now I suggest I show Ellie to her room then we'll have a cup of coffee while discussing a plan of action. Come on Ellie let's get you settled in." In spite of Olly being out of the picture for the moment, Rose was in her usual optimistic and bossy frame of mind, thought Emma, although she must also be apprehensive as to Olly's whereabouts.

Rose picked up Ellie's bag and they disappeared down the passage while Marc and Emma moved towards the open plan kitchen. Emma took out four mugs from their usual place above the steaming kettle and started to spoon in the coffee.

"Definitely the right decision to bring Ellie here to Rose," Emma said softly to her husband.

"Yes she'll be fine and hopefully I'll soon be able to get word to Jake that she's okay; although we'll have to keep an eye on her as she mustn't wander off out on her own. I might get a bit more information tonight when I call in to update them that Ellie's settled in here. They'll want to put some surveillance in place outside, just in case."

"It all sounds to be a pretty harrowing situation particularly as the wretched Russians seem to be involved and relations with them…," hearing the others coming back down the passage Emma stopped quickly raising her voice and calling, "Ellie do you have sugar? I know Rose's addiction to sweeteners but there is sugar here as well."

"Yes, one please. Oh dear! I still really do feel exhausted even though, thanks to Marc's sleeping pill last night, I actually dozed quite well." She sat down heavily at one end of the sofa.

"Hardly surprising," Marc answered, "why don't you take your coffee with you and go to put your feet up for a bit. There's no hurry about anything now and you must sleep whenever you feel like it. Listen to your body. You've had a shocking experience Ellie and it takes time to recover from something like that. So please just take it easy." She got up looking relieved.

"Ok I think I might take your advice and disappear to my lovely room for a bit, if nobody minds." She put her hands together, obviously still feeling wobbly. "Thank you everybody, thank you for everything."

The three friends sat for a while considering their predicament, as they discussed a plan for the days to come. Rose seemed completely unfussed: she said she was up to date with her work as she relied on her computer and her mobile anyway. She always woke early with Olly away and

125

worked until breakfast, so Ellie could have a lie in and be peaceful. Then perhaps they could all meet in the park for a walk each day and as for the rest… just take it from there, depending on developments.

Rose also admitted then that she'd heard nothing from Olly for the last few days. When he left he'd just texted her with the usual single red rose and a couple of xx's, which normally meant he was about to go out of touch. Marc had talked to Adriana before he and Emma had left the pub with Ellie. Apparently Julian also appeared to be 'away' at present. It was likely that he and Guy were aware of each other's movements, if not together. Marc suspected that his entire team of friends were probably involved in the current mission, which had begun with Ellie's abduction.

Ellie was fast asleep when Emma and Marc left, agreeing to call Rose in the evening and promising to return the following afternoon for a walk.

"We'll go home now and I'll take you out to dinner tonight at our local Brasserie, so at least you won't have to cook, or wash up!" Marc put his arm around his wife as they left the building. "I'm so sorry my darling that all this happened, cutting our weekend short."

"Never mind it can't be helped. I feel so worried for Ellie as Jake's not really used to taking part in these specialist field operations, is he?" She sighed, not expecting an answer. "I just hope to God that both Julian and Guy are well in control and that they haven't put Jake in the firing line. He's lacking in experience."

"If they aren't on top of the situation now, they soon will be. As to what happened on the plane I understood from Ellie that Guy already appeared to have the upper hand. Jake wouldn't have been called in unless he was considered fully trained, prepared and able to cope. Headquarters are meticulous about the people they use and the teams they put together. They assume responsibility for everyone they send out."

"Alright, now let's go home and continue our little holiday," answered Emma. "There's obviously nothing more to be done for the moment and Mum has the children until tomorrow night. Let's make the most of it."

As they walked back to the car hand in hand, Marc hoped that he had managed to reassure his wife. Underneath the calm exterior he actually felt extremely nervous about the whole ongoing mission, in which he himself was now also involved. He hadn't told Emma, but he was pretty certain that they'd been followed, for a while, as they'd left the pub earlier for London. But having been brought up with a brother who had gone on to become a rally driver, he reckoned he was quite capable of losing a tail in the intricate one-way system in the Great Metropolis that was his home. So when they encountered traffic on entering the city, he had stopped a couple of times, dived down a little known short cut and backtracked to regain the route to Rose and Olly's flat, coming into it from another direction altogether.

However, the building was very well protected. Unbeknown to any of the girls when they had left just now, a specially trained team for around the clock surveillance had already been put in place.

✳   ✳   ✳

CHAPTER 16

Olly In Pursuit
(Heathrow to Geneva)

OLIVER always seemed to be given surveillance jobs. He thought it was probably to do with his colleagues and friends Guy and Julian. After various adventures together and with his extensive TA training behind him, they must have put his name forward, recommending him to the various powers that be. Once he had passed all the physical and mental tests and exams, Oliver was informed that he was now considered to be a good enough candidate to be put to use by the Special Reserve Force, for surveillance purposes. He had been chosen, ahead of many other candidates, for being best able to blend, follow people discreetly and also to put people at ease and chat them up. He was exceptionally good, he was told, at extracting sometimes vital information very quickly. He loved this latter task; he chuckled to himself thinking that this had probably been the main reason for his successful recruitment.

Oliver's present job had entailed Saturday evening being spent in an upmarket bar from where Jake's girlfriend, the unfortunate Ellie, had been abducted. The barman, Leo, had been extremely helpful as he clearly remembered Ellie, her companion and the incident on the Friday night. He had found her mobile and he had given a very good description of the well-spoken, perfectly mannered and smartly dressed Englishman escorting her. Leo had summed up by saying that he thought afterwards that the young man had been 'just a little bit too perfect, perhaps'.

The description given by the barman, immediately confirming Ellie's detailed statement, had formed the basis of an excellent identikit picture of the man Olly was supposed to be watching and tailing. Consequently, the enthusiastic barman was alerted and briefed in case the abductor returned to the bar; as he did once more, on Sunday at midday. Apparently the man had apologised politely for his hasty departure with Ellie the previous Friday evening. He went on to tell Leo that his friend Ellie had been absolutely fine the following morning and then he asked if by any chance Leo had found her mobile.

At this point, the well briefed barman had gone over to the chest beneath the window, to check for him. He'd stood, facing out towards the street apparently to open the window further, but in reality to alert Olly who was in position outside, before bending to supposedly search through things left behind by his customers. Thoroughly enjoying his new role, Leo had returned to the bar where the man had been patiently waiting.

Leo sighed theatrically. "I'm so sorry, I have a small umbrella, a tie, a scarf and a pair of ladies gloves in the chest. I also put three credit cards in the safe but I have no mobiles; that's all that's been left behind since Friday night. I'm afraid someone may have taken your friend's phone." Warming to his performance Leo continued, "May I offer you something to drink or a coffee whilst you're here?"

"No thank you, but I appreciate you looking. It's not safe to leave anything around anywhere these days is it? No matter, I must go, thank you again, by the way you have a great place here," the young man said in his impeccable English, then, smiling, said goodbye and turned to step out into the street.

Leo, standing in the doorway, decided that there was no doubt the man was just too good to be true; the type that he'd never trust. What you see isn't always what you get with his sort, he thought. He noted that the man glanced to either side of him before hailing a taxi. Definitely suspicious.

As the taxi moved off, the barman also saw a private car from the opposite side of the street move out into the road after it. The driver let a small delivery van in first behind the taxi, then positioned himself to follow. Leo could see the man named Oliver, bent over the wheel in hot pursuit. He sighed to himself with satisfaction thinking himself lucky. He wouldn't change his job for the world, no way, as you never quite knew what was going to happen next.

Leo had liked the young girl, Ellie. He remembered her well when she first came in alone. They'd chatted together whilst she'd been waiting for her boyfriend, who'd never turned up. He'd like to have broken a heavy bottle over that man's head if only he'd known, at the time, what he was really about and that he wasn't the man she'd been waiting for at all. He was glad to have helped them in their search for her. He just hoped that they'd find her well and unharmed. Poor girl, what an evil bastard.

He wished he'd seen what exactly had happened, on Friday night, after that smooth talking man had joined her, but he'd been far too busy to concentrate on any one person. When they went out, he had thought that Ellie had merely had one too many. If she ever returned to the bar he'd offer her and her real boyfriend a free drink and dinner in the restaurant. Leo hoped he'd have that opportunity and that he'd be told how this particular incognito tailing escapade turned out. Leo was a kind gentle soul at heart, but the idea of one of his customers being treated in such an appalling way made his blood boil.

*

Staying well behind, Olly followed the taxi all the way to the airport. Once at Heathrow, he dumped the car, as arranged, at the curb edge behind the queue, handing the key to his colleague hovering nearby on the pavement. He then walked through the automatic opening doors into the airport building after the young man. There a woman, part of the surveillance team, with a light blue scarf around her neck was lurking just inside the main entrance. She stepped to his side smiling. Together, arm in arm, they followed their quarry as far as his departure desk. The man joined the small business class queue for an Eastern European destination. Their task achieved Olly and the girl walked on by.

It transpired that the man was booked on a flight into Tallin, Estonia. The departure board showed that all flights after his were delayed until the following day due to expected bad weather conditions.

GCHQ were beginning to piece together the bigger picture. Olly was put on standby until further notice and sent back to his billet at the main TA Army Reserve base at Marlow. Meanwhile he wasn't allowed to make contact with anybody: he knew that Rose had Ellie with her and that their flat was under protective surveillance. He had been told that Marc was keeping an eye on the girls and was also in touch with their base. He had been informed that Guy and Jake were both heading for Russia. More than that he wasn't told. Where was Julian he wondered?

The most difficult part of his job, as one of the more irregular army reservists, was that he was unable to contact Rose when he was out and about. Whilst at the base, on a specially designed mobile, he could at least send her his usual reassuring text of a rose and two xx's. Then she knew that he was safe. But Rose was the most sensible of women, she never had a freak out, was always level-headed, fun and loving, apart from which she was insatiable in bed. He loved her completely and utterly. But now Olly couldn't wait for his next orders. Once involved in this particular mission he wanted to see it through to the end.

*

After twenty-eight hours of twiddling his thumbs in frustration, On Monday evening Olly received his orders. The man they were after was now on a flight from Tallin Estonia to Geneva. Oliver was to fly to Switzerland from Northolt without delay. By the time he had grabbed his small travel bag there was already a car with a driver in army uniform ready waiting outside.

*

Zak, an old friend from his past, was waiting outside the Geneva Terminal building, parked in the short-term park area immediately outside arrivals. Taxis were coming and going collecting people as they came out through the doors all dressed in their warmest clothes. Oliver was easily recognizable in his army greatcoat and scarf with his usual tidy jeans and well-worn desert boots. He was in good time and at least half an hour in advance of the scheduled landing time for the Talinn flight.

The two men had time to catch up and discuss plans as they sat watching and quietly talking in Zak's jeep. They had permission to park immediately outside so as not to miss their target. In matters of criminal movement touching their country, the Swiss authorities were always efficient, discreet and most helpful.

The early evening flights were beginning to bring in the business men; keen to get home or off to a late meeting, competing for the taxis and private limousines hovering outside. The darkening night sky promised snow, so if they were correct in their thinking as to their man's destination, they had a further journey yet to accomplish. Zak hoped that the motorway would remain open.

Olly noticed a limo with darkened windows hanging back a little away from the main queue. Sure enough a few minutes later their quarry, looking immaculate, appeared through the automatic doors. He raised a hand to acknowledge the driver as he stepped outside and climbed quickly into the waiting vehicle. Zak pulled out of the parking area following a small private bus and joined the line of exiting cars achieving second place behind the limo. Unexpectedly their quarry then turned away from the motorway heading instead into the city of Geneva.

"He's not going where we thought he would," remarked Zak putting his foot down to make sure he didn't get caught at the lights.

"No," Olly looked at his watch, "but I bet I know where he's headed first!"

"A bank?" suggested Zak.

"A bank," replied Oliver, "and, no doubt, a private one which has remained open especially."

Some twenty minutes later watching from further along the street, they were proven correct. The man disappeared inside a smart building with a discreet brass nameplate to the left of a pair of heavily carved doors. Olly took the opportunity to report back to Headquarters. The man was only gone for a mere ten minutes before emerging once more escorted by an immaculately dressed older man. They shook hands, the young man checked his watch, stepped quickly once more into the waiting limo, which then retraced it's journey through the Geneva rush hour to the airport.

"Shite!" exclaimed Olly. "He's going to fly again."

"Don't worry, this time you stay with the car and I'll see where he's headed," said Zak opening the door.

Olly watched Zak disappear through the departure doors after their objective. He looked no different, just the same stocky fit and reliable person with a shock of dark hair and those twinkling brown eyes. He was a great character to work with: he thought ahead and could arrange things in an instant. He returned after a few minutes and with a wide grin got back into the car.

"As your boss thought. He is going up to Gstaad, but in a private jet."

"Bloody hell and we're here!" answered Olly.

"No problem, my brother's up there, ready and waiting. We were warned this morning. We'll have his final stopping place for tonight in no time."

"There must be somebody this guy is going to meet up there and this person could be the one at the top of this game plan or at least the financial connection. Gstaad is one of the true hot spots for the very wealthy in the skiing season," Olly concluded.

"Yes, I'm well aware of that," muttered Zak as he negotiated his way back into the traffic heading out onto the motorway, away from the city towards Lausanne. "This is what London are obviously thinking and this year it seems we are being invaded by the Russians."

"Interesting," agreed Olly. "Actually that's very interesting, particularly as I have been informed that both Jake and Guy were headed for Eastern Europe."

The traffic was bad as they caught the tail-end of rush hour getting past Lausanne, where the lanes narrowed through the wine area, but then they had a reasonable run up into the twisting mountain roads. As they left the motorway the constant stream of slower local evening traffic kept the smaller roads clear of snow.

Zak drove straight into Gstaad station where they found his brother smoking, leisurely perched on a covered bench. Putting out his cigarette he ambled over, kicked the snow off his feet and got into the back seat.

"Hello Pieter, it's good to see you again, how are you?"

Olly and he shook hands.

"*Hallo* Oliver, yes very well *Danke*. It's good to have you here once more."

Olly was genuinely thrilled to be back. He loved these spectacular mountains.

"Let's head off to that quiet little Brasserie in the next village, I'm starving. I could eat one of your delightful Swiss cows I'm so hungry. You can fill us in on the way down, Pieter."

Zak negotiated his way around the milling traffic, waiting to pick up the many people off the incoming trains arriving from both directions. Soon with Zak's deft manoeuvring, they were back in the main street and heading away towards the Brasserie in Schönreid.

"Now Pieter what have you got for us?" Oliver was enthusiastic and conscientious about his work.

"Ok! For a start, our man is at the new Castle Haute Hotel, up the mountain, where his dad and family are holed up. They're not English, no way…" Pieter paused having their full attention, "they are as cold as the cold war itself. Our man is Nicholai Peronovich and his father is one of the wealthiest oligarchs on the planet."

Silence ensued.

"Good God," muttered Oliver, "the man apparently has no accent at all. The barman in London said he was well educated and spoke perfect upper-class English. I asked him. The guy must have been educated in the UK then?"

"More than likely," agreed Zak parking outside the restaurant, getting out of the four by four and walking determinedly towards the building.

"Come on. They're going nowhere at this time of night without us knowing. I've put the concierge onto it: they're settling down to dinner. It's going to snow some more, so let's eat."

"Right, good, well done Pieter. You two go in. I've just got one more quick call to make to my boss."

After Olly finished his report he stood for a few minutes, remembering being here with Rose. It was a beautiful night and new flakes of snow were beginning to settle. It had come early. How she would love it. He thought about the time he'd seen her ski in the dark. The piste had been lit on either side and she was like a little shooting star, in her black suit with a light fixed to her forehead, as she shot past even the very best skiers.

He wished she was here with him now, but then this was something in which he didn't want her further involved. Olly was well aware that this mission wasn't about to finish: it was just beginning. The Russians obviously controlled the overall operation which was becoming ever more worrisome as their influence became more evident.

He felt an ice-cold snowflake slither down the back of his neck, shook himself, turned his collar up and walked into the restaurant's welcome warmth.

❈ ❈ ❈

CHAPTER 17

The Swiss Alps
(Tuesday)

OLIVER sat waiting for Zak in the village café. It hadn't changed much since he was last here a few years back, it was just as he remembered, warm and snug. The lady looking after him, Käthi, appeared to have remembered him also, as she asked after his 'wild' Rose, which amused him no end. How right she was about his wild Rose! He'd had breakfast and wished Zak would hurry up. Olly knew that his Swiss friend was living with his brother, in their family hideaway at the top of the mountain. Zak and Pieter often took private parties skiing in the winter months to supplement their income and would ski down early in the morning. But Olly was just feeling impatient for some action. 'It's alright for some,' he muttered to himself.

A few minutes later Zak came sauntering in, bringing with him a blast of cold air. Grinning from ear to ear and looking thoroughly fit and well exercised, he ordered a coffee from Käthi as he passed by the counter.

"*Grüezi.* Hello Oliver." Olly knew that when Zak used his full name there would be something important to relate. He grinned back.

"Good morning Zak. Good ski down?" Olly bent forward to pull out the chair next to him. Zak nodded, took off his coat and scarf, shook out his mass of unruly dark hair, scattering a few icy pieces stuck to his outer collar all over the floor; then sat down with a satisfied sigh. Käthi brought over his coffee and glanced with mild disapproval at the puddles around his feet. But she smiled with affection and ruffled Zak's hair before walking away muttering something which Olly thought might be a German version of 'naughty boy'!

"Well come on then, out with it, what's the news?"

Zak, annoyingly, grunted and took a couple of sips of his coffee, taking his time before speaking. Then he put the mug down, grinning again.

"You are so impatient my friend! Yes of course I have news and quite a lot actually." Käthi interrupted them again by bringing across two delicious warm pastries which neither had ordered.

"For my boys, yes?" She patted Zak on the shoulder chuckling and then went back to her counter to serve another customer.

"As Pieter has already discovered, our Russian is here with his family in one of the best hotels, the new one at the top, looking down over the town. He's here until early Friday morning. Then he returns to Geneva and flies out on his father's private Bombardier, due in tomorrow; back to Talinn the same day. Pieter has been briefed on the flight details by his friend at Geneva airport. The family are fabulously wealthy and spend money like water, but they are not at all popular. At least they aren't here as, apparently, they are causing a few problems." He stopped to take a breath, drink some more of his coffee and gauge Olly's reaction.

"Good Heaven's! You and Pieter really have discovered quite a bit in just a few short hours. Why are they so unpopular, what have they done?"

"They are demanding, rude and think that money can buy them anything. We Swiss don't like their attitude or their manners. Not at all. We have old fashioned values, particularly up here in the mountains."

"And quite right too." Olly agreed.

"But that's not all and this will really make you sit up."

"Go on." Olly was now intrigued. "What else?"

Zak took his time and glanced around to make sure that no one was within earshot, but the other customers were in deep conversation with Käthi, over the far side of the room.

"It's the girls!"

"Oh no! What about them?"

"Both Marc and Alicia have been in touch." Oliver appeared concerned and Zak knew he'd have to relate the next piece of information carefully as it would not be welcome.

"Well, you'd better brace yourself as it looks like the girls might be coming out here." Olly stared back at Zak.

"What do you mean they're coming here, not here literally? They can't be. You must be joking. They can't come here, not with this thoroughly dodgy ongoing situation. It's not safe. Who on earth has organised this?"

"Hang on and I'll explain. My liaison in the Federal Intelligence agency in Bern says that your boss back in London wants to be sure as he can be, that our man out here is the same person that took your friend Ellie: I am told there have been serious repercussions since the abduction. He could be involved in a lot more than kidnapping for money. There are worrying implications on the political front apparently centred on the relationship between Estonia and Russia. The whole operation has moved up to another level. They know that your barman at the restaurant in London recognized him, but the only one who can identify this man for certain is Ellie. Alicia thinks she's recovered enough from her own ordeal to do just that." He paused for a minute, rubbing the stubble on his chin, before continuing, "As we know all our friends seem to be far away from home at present, are they not?"

"Yes," said Olly. "Even Jake, Ellie's boyfriend, who you haven't yet met. He's new in the force. I too am wondering exactly where they all are. It seems I'm not to be told anything much and only used for surveillance. So what do you know? What about the girls? Who is coming and when?"

"*In ordnung* Ok! Marc has been taking care of things in London and he's organized the travel arrangements. They'll probably arrive tomorrow evening and it will be Alicia, Rose and of course your young friend who was taken; Ellie."

"Well, needless to say it would be my wife and Alicia, wouldn't it? They're always bloody well up to their necks in everything that happens, but I just hope that the poor girl Ellie will be able to cope with it all. After what she's been through, she's had one hell of a shock."

Olly put his head in his hands and looked downcast for a moment at the thought of his beloved Rose putting herself in the firing line yet again. Zak noticing, tried to reassure his friend.

"London is adamant that it's really important that they catch this guy and Alicia is apparently quite determined."

"Yes, she'll have everything under control. She always does," answered Olly, good humour returning once more. "She should be in Special Ops herself, working with Guy. Jesus! can you imagine?" Zak laughed, shaking his head.

"Yes I can imagine, she'd run the whole show. But you needn't worry they'll all be safe with us here, up the mountain. As you know it's our job, from time to time and we're good at it… the best, actually and life has become a bit boring of late, so it's good to see you and I shall look forward to welcoming the girls as well."

"Yes I know you're the best and it's good to see you too," replied Olly a little dismally, giving his old friend a gently punch on the arm, "but I don't like the girls being involved; especially my wife and poor Ellie. Bloody hell Zak this has to be something mega important doesn't it?"

"Yes, it's something involving several countries I suspect. I have also been told by Bern that identification of this Russian takes precedent over everything else at the moment. There must be a bigger agenda. There's just one other thing Olly." Zak hesitated and cleared his throat, Olly sat up knowing there was something coming which he wasn't going to like.

"I have been asked to tell you to stay right away from the girls and not to let them know that you are here, as it could compromise matters. I'm afraid I am the one who has been asked to run this part of the operation." Oliver let out an expletive followed by a heavy sigh.

"Ok, I knew there was bound to be a glitch, yet I do understand... I suppose, but what exactly is the plan? I have to know with my wife involved and about to arrive?"

"The girls will fly in tomorrow evening, Wednesday. Pieter and I will settle them up at the safe house and I'll brief them as to what is required. Meanwhile we will watch our man's movements so that on Thursday, at some point, we will find a way for Ellie to identify the bastard. Probably the hotel at the top, when the Russians have settled in for the evening, will be the best bet. It's big and there are a lot of people around; easy to watch and observe discreetly."

"After which, when the bird has flown off to Talinn, presumably our job here will be done and normality can be restored once more. Hopefully I might even get in some skiing with Rose and the others," Olly said cheering up.

"Yes, *Gut*! Let's hope we can all go skiing together again. You'll stay on at the hotel in the village, as before?"

"Yes, of course. It was great to see Hélène again. But she couldn't understand why Rose wasn't here with me. So I booked a double room and said that she would be following me out shortly. I'll have to go carefully there as Hélène and her husband don't miss a thing. Their hotel is the most efficient I've ever been in and it runs like only a Swiss clock can. You'll have to keep the girls well out of sight."

"I know, that's no problem. It's only for a short time: Thursday is the key day. Once we know the Russian movements, for sure, we'll make a plan for Ellie to get a good view, so as soon as he is gone, they can come down to the hotel."

"Meanwhile we'd better make the best of the time we have now and see how and where our man spends his day. But Zak please make it clear to your liaison that my wife and the other two are not to be put in danger, so we have to work on a fail-safe plan for the identification." Zak placed a reassuring hand on Oliver's shoulder.

"We will certainly do that, don't worry, but you must help with the details. You know I wouldn't let Rose or any of the girls come to any harm. Pieter is on watch at the hotel until we get there. His girlfriend is on reception which makes things a lot easier. So we'll have another coffee and discuss how best to progress."

Zak caught Käthi's eye and made a sign for some more coffee.

❉   ❉   ❉

CHAPTER 18

The Girls
(City airport to Bern, Wednesday)

ANOTHER day doing nothing but sit around and worry: Ellie, recovering well from her ordeal, was fed up to the teeth with being cooped up inside. She was unable to go to the office and had completely lost her independence. Apart from which they had still heard nothing, not a peep from the men, which meant that they were seriously occupied with their alarming mission.

Rose had been in constant touch with both Alicia and Emma by email and mobile. Since Ellie's arrival they'd all met up for coffee in the mornings to discuss the overall situation.

Adriana had also joined them the day before, but she had her own problems after being told at her last doctor's appointment that, although all was well, she must understand that having twins meant that she had to take things a little bit easy for a while. This annoyed Adriana as the others could see; she said that she felt fine and wished to be informed and included in everything. After all Julian was away and she also had no idea where he was or what he was doing.

On Wednesday morning Alicia appeared in Rose's flat on her own and earlier than before. Rose could tell instantly that something was up.

"Your looking very chirpy this morning! What's happened?" Hearing the door slam, Ellie came hurrying out of her room along the passage, desperately hoping for news. Alicia hated having to disappoint her.

"Ellie! Hello! I'm sorry, but no news from the men as yet, but…" Alicia continued quickly, noticing Ellie's smile fade and giving her a reassuring hug, "as I said before Ellie, remember: no news is good news. It just means that they are busy and can't get in touch for the moment. Meanwhile guess what! I've had a brilliant idea!"

"What? What is it?" demanded Rose and Ellie together catching the excitement. Rose had a feeling that Alicia had been planning something when they'd spoken earlier.

"Well – there is one place we can all go where Ellie can recover, have some space and… be safe!" she paused for effect, watching their expectant faces.

"Alright, go on then, where? Where can we go?" Rose was impatient.

"Rose, you remember Zak, up in the Swiss Alps?"

"Yes, yes of course I do, the safe house where you went before you were married, when Guy had disappeared off the face of the earth on yet another ill-timed op," she turned to Ellie. "Zak was the lovely man who helped us all during our last and never to be forgotten skiing holiday. How could I possibly not remember him? We all had a bit of a thing for him." Ellie looked thoroughly confused. Alicia sat down on the sofa and patted the place beside her.

"Let's all sit down and I'll explain it all to Ellie. Ever since that troubled time Guy has always told me that, if he wasn't around and if one of us was in any kind of danger needing to move in a hurry, there are two particular places to go, to be safe. Well, this is one of them." Ellie's jaw dropped with amazement.

"You mean this place up the mountains is a real Secret Service-type safe house? Are you serious…?" the other two nodded, "...about us going there I mean, because if I'm honest I don't feel at all secure outside here, even though I'm not on my own. I can't help but think there's someone following ready to pounce or that I'm going to bump into one of those terrible people around every corner. Also, forgive me Rose as you have been wonderfully caring, but it is a bit boring and despairing being cooped up inside and not knowing what the hell is going on with the men."

Ellie's face lit up, "Would we really be allowed to go, even perhaps for a long weekend!"

Alicia grinned.

"Yes, we would be allowed to go and nobody and nothing can touch us there, not in Zak's safe hands. His place is easy to get to as well, although it is completely hidden. We can fly from City airport to Bern where we will be met, looked after and taken up the mountains into that lovely pure air and away from the rest of the world." Alicia broke off for a moment savouring some memories with a faraway look in her eyes. Then she continued, now thoroughly excited herself.

"Yes, yes! It's all organised. You see it's one of the men's perks for having an 'out of the ordinary job'... their big bosses always have concern for the wellbeing of their other halves..." she trailed off, her face aglow with the thought of Zak and his parents, who had nurtured her before when she'd needed it most.

"But can we just upsticks and go there without the men knowing?" Rose asked trying to be practical. She stared hard at Alicia determining whether or not there was a hidden agenda: this seemed to have already been meticulously well arranged.

"Of course we can. After all we have done it before. Anyway, the men will know exactly where we are, they always do through their 'oh so very secret' channels. Marc is helping liaise things. Rose can you spare the time? Work-wise I mean?"

"Yes, no problem, so long as I have my computer and mobile."

"Right then, if everybody is happy with the plan we'll leave in a couple of hours! I'd like to get there before dark." Well pleased with herself, Alicia waited for the expected surprised reaction.

"Good Heavens Alicia! It's as if you're also an undercover agent. How can you organise everything so fast?" Ellie remarked, extremely impressed with Alicia's capability for resolving what had seemed to her a complete impasse, with her temporary living arrangements.

Rose ran her fingers through her wild curly hair. Alicia could certainly move things along at a moment's notice although she knew well that Marc and others were behind her. There had to be a hidden contrived plan: she was sure of it. Good! She couldn't wait to find out what it was.

"Hmm, I always rather fancied Zak, our lovely mountain man – before Olly proposed of course!"

"Come on, we all did." Alicia laughed good naturedly.

"But what about Adriana? She'll want to come, as will Emma if she can get her mum or sister to have the children."

"No," Alicia replied firmly, "not this time. Emma and Marc have already done their bit, haven't they Ellie?" She nodded, smiling in agreement. "Arri hasn't that long to go and probably with the twins on board shouldn't risk flying anyway. I wouldn't want the responsibility; besides which someone has to keep the home fires burning, so to speak. Also, don't forget, there is a very good reason for getting Ellie away, out of London."

'Um,' thought Rose. 'She's quite safe here with me and there's somebody outside also keeping tabs on us, so there definitely is more to this than Alicia is admitting'.

*

After a quick visit to Ellie's flat to collect her passport and more suitable clothes, the girls flew out of London City airport for Bern. It was a quick flight and with the wind behind them took only a few minutes longer than Geneva. Zak met them in the arrivals hall, where he stood grinning with pleasure, waiting for Alicia and Rose to spot him. He then drove them all up into the mountains in his reliable well fitted jeep and on into the Gstaad valley. Zak had to pick up some supplies, before taking them to the new cable-car which would whisk them to the very top of the mountain. He left them in the four by four at the station while he went about his errands.

Alicia was happily prattling on about Zak's parents; relating some of the funnier stories that had occurred when, one summer, she'd been here hiding out at Zak's farm with Adriana; describing the difficult time that she and Arri had making themselves understood. They had dreaded being left alone with the elder people, when Zak was outside with the animals, as his lovely parents couldn't speak a word of English. Alicia and Adriana had felt embarrassed not to be able to speak much German.

"I actually got quite good at milking and Adriana, when she followed me out, loved collecting the eggs. She insisted on giving each chicken a ridiculous name." Alicia chuckled with the memory.

The scenic Panoramic Express came in from Montreux and from the warmth of Zak's jeep they watched the people alight, feeling the cold as they stepped from the heated train.

Suddenly Ellie let out a muffled cry of alarm and ducked down beneath the window.

"Oh my God! Oh my God!... It's him!" She raised her head and peered warily out of the window. "It is him... no it's not... this man's got a limp!"

Alicia in front, swivelled around, quickly touching the central locking device as she did so.

"Ellie, Ellie! Look at me, it's alright the doors are locked and the windows are darkened, no one can see in. Now quickly show me, who is it and where?"

Ellie with one hand covering her mouth and the other pointing was now staring with horror out of the window. A good-looking, well dressed young man was about to get into one of the smarter hotel's private limos. Rose and Alicia, realising that this was something crucial, took in as many details as they could of the man who had obviously featured somewhere in Ellie's recent ordeal. The man was talking to the driver, then he hopped into the back of the vehicle placing his briefcase carefully on the seat beside him. The chauffeur shut the door, regained his driving seat and drove off.

They watched as the expensive limousine disappeared around the corner with the satisfying purr of an immaculately maintained engine. They both turned to Ellie who was now sitting bolt upright in the back, wide eyed, but with a puzzled look on her face. She seemed to have pulled herself together, although her hands were shaking. Alicia unlocked the car, got out and went to sit beside her in the back, re-locking the doors after her.

"Now Ellie, it's alright, honestly. You're quite safe – now tell me who was that man?" Ellie raised her head to look straight at Alicia. Rose watching, caught a meaningful glance from Alicia and her suspicions were confirmed. They were definitely here for an undisclosed purpose.

Ellie had recovered and wanted to talk.

"It's really odd. I thought for a moment that it was the man I met in the bar that night whilst I waited for Jake. You know, the one who drugged me first, then took me out of there to that dreadful place where they locked me in." Her eyes were bright, the pulse in her throat visible: her hands tightly clenched in her lap. "But it wasn't him," she continued, a frown creasing her pale forehead. "Although they look alike, this man was shorter, somewhat stockier and he has a limp. Still it's strange that they are so very similar."

"I'm so sorry Ellie, what a horrible shock. That's all you needed, isn't it?" Ellie smiled bravely.

"It's alright, don't worry. I'm Ok and it's just my imagination, I suppose." Rose couldn't help but catch Alicia's eye again, with her head slightly on one side as if in question. Then she put her arm around their young friend.

"Well I'm sure that I would be terrified of seeing the bloody man around every corner after what you went through," Rose announced trying to lighten the atmosphere. Alicia made a mental note to tell Zak of the incident in private and to remember the name of the hotel advertised on the side of the man's welcoming limo.

"Here's Zak, he's coming back." Rose, on the other side of Ellie, couldn't help but heave a sigh of relief.

"Good." Alicia glanced out of the window and saw the man with a beard she'd noticed earlier, propped up against a ticket machine, walk towards Zak. They exchanged a few words then the man went off disappearing inside the station. Alicia realised that they hadn't been alone not for one single minute and that the bearded man had been put in place to keep an eye on them whilst Zak was collecting his supplies. He put the bags down by the car and knocked on the window. Rose unlocked the doors.

"Sorry we locked it while you were gone!"

"You needn't have worried," Zak replied amiably stowing the goods. He got back into the driver's seat and turned to look at the girls in the back. He winked at Alicia and she was quite sure that he already knew all about the man with the limp.

"What's up?" he asked calmly "You all look as if you've seen a ghost!" he joked.

"Well I think perhaps Ellie may have seen rather a significant ghost, actually." Rose retorted slightly indignant.

"Ok tell me all while I drive to the lift. Let's get going and get you up to the house." He glanced at Ellie in the back mirror as he drove. "You are quite safe here Ellie, I do assure you," he added in the confident comforting way that Alicia remembered so well.

❊ ❊ ❊

CHAPTER 19

The Silence of Snow
(Wednesday night)

ZAK and his brother Pieter saw the girls safely up to the top of the mountain, where Alicia quickly commandeered one of the waiting snowmobiles.

"This is just great," she cried with undisguised enthusiasm and delight. "I haven't been on one of these since we were last here together Zak, back in that coldest winter of all."

Rose stood beside her and stared out across the lovely unspoilt snowy vista below them, then she pointed upwards as movement caught her eye. Silently they looked up above. In the fading light one of the eagle clan glided on the thermals, mewing to its mate, as the pair rose slowly in ever increasing circles, out and away over the valley.

Ellie, wrapped in her hooded fur-lined jacket, also was standing still, watching, entranced by the beautiful pristine winter scene laid out before her. Not another soul in sight.

The lifts were long closed to all but the people running the two topmost hotels, which at night catered for the most serious skiers and early rising climbers. Their supplies were usually sent up first thing in the mornings, but for this evening Zak had requested a late gondola. The lift attendants were well-aware that, on occasion, even though the animals were now all based down in the village, Zak sometimes needed access to the family farm hidden away off piste. It was higher than all the cable cars and far away from prying eyes, but nobody ever asked questions.

Zak stood with his brother observing the three young women enjoying the twilight scene before them. The youngest, who he'd just met, attracted his interest. While he knew, from past experience, that Alicia and Rose were both strong and competent, Ellie appeared vulnerable and tense after what had happened. Hardly surprising: she was slight and small framed, yet he had been told that she'd been extremely courageous under duress. Ellie would need special care so he must arrange things sensitively. He looked to the summit, then at his watch. Alicia had now turned to him and was smiling, waiting to be off. Pieter had stowed their small carry-on bags onto the snow machines, securing them with leather straps. He saw that the girls had learnt to travel light. Their supplies were stowed in the fixed aluminium boxes. Zak grinned.

"Ok! Let's go." He glanced up at the sky again and felt snowflakes flutter down onto his face. "It's going to snow again. Ellie, come with me please."

Rose was already asking Pieter to let her drive. Alicia started the engine and positioned her machine between the other two. Ellie flung her leg over the seat behind Zak wrapping her arms shyly around him; he gave her hand a quick squeeze for re-assurance. With a soft chuckle he said, "Hold on tight then!" And they were off. Ellie, with Zak on the front snow-mobile was mesmerised by the alpine scenery. It must have snowed since Zak had last been up here as there were no markings on the track, only recent prints of some small wild animal and the odd bird. As they reached the crest of the mountains, Zak stopped for them all to take in the breath-taking views on both sides. There was no sound once the engines died: just complete silence deepened by the thick blanketing of pure white. '*The silence of snow,*' thought Ellie in wonder. She could just see the tiny twinkling lights of the villages far below down in the valleys on both sides of the narrow path; it was a sight she would never forget. With her sensitivities so raw and without realising what she was doing her arms instinctively clasped tighter around Zak's warm comforting body.

Little did Ellie know that Jake also had been riding one of these same snow vehicles, just a short time ago, but far away in an unfriendly country and in very dissimilar circumstances. Zak felt her vulnerability again and turned his head slightly so that only she could hear.

"You really are safe here with me, Ellie." She leant in closer against his back.

"Thank you," was all that she could manage, in a gentle muffled voice, then they moved on again. Here was someone who could read and understand what she was feeling and in these beautiful mountains she felt reassured.

✳

Rose and Alicia shared the main twin-bedded room with its own bathroom. Ellie was given another, up a small flight of stairs in the attic, with a bathroom between her room and Zak's. It was a lovely cosy bedroom, all pine beams and wood panelling with, Ellie was told, the very best view of all. Pieter slept in a downstairs room beside the sitting room; off to one side was a shower room housing all their outside winter gear and skis.

The elderly parents now lived down in the village in the valley in wintertime, but they'd sent up a good supply of food that only needed heating up. The only other occupant of the old farmhouse was Merida, a big, beautiful mountain dog. She was only two, but would do anything that the men asked of her and had apparently already proven her worth by finding a lost skier one night, lying immersed in a snow filled gully, with a broken leg.

As darkness fell, completely isolating the safe house from the rest of the world, the five people sat around the log fire drinking hot *gluwein* and eating delicious *boeuf stroganoff* with hot potatoes, prepared by the men while the girls were settling into their rooms.

Ellie looked tired yet somewhat revived and elated by both the spectacular journey up the mountain and the mulled wine. She at least had colour in her cheeks again, thought Zak appreciatively. His brother caught his glance and unseen by the others smiled and merely shook his head just very slightly. Zak nodded with a grin and quickly bent to ruffle Merida's ears.

Ellie was off limits he knew and already spoken for; but he would protect her with his life if he had to, as with the others in the past. It was part of his training. He was well aware that he needed to curb his natural instincts of attraction for this brave yet vulnerable girl, with whom he'd felt an immediate affinity.

He wondered what Olly was doing down in the town and – looking at Rose – could she sense his nearness? She was staring into the fire with a faraway look in her eyes.

Pieter was now eating again and Alicia was chatting without pause. She was the perpetrator of most of the girls' adventures. 'The organiser', he had privately named her.

"What do you think Zak?" she was asking him now: he immediately returned to the conversation.

"What do I think about what exactly, Alicia? Sorry. I was having a bonding moment here with Merida." The dog stared up at him in loving agreement.

"Well, two things really; first – may we go skiing tomorrow? And the second is could we possibly go dancing at the new hotel's night club in the evening? I'm sure it would cheer Ellie up."

"Yes to the skiing, where there's new snow at the top. Pieter will take you but you stay together. I need to go down tomorrow to do a few things in the town and if you really want to go dancing, that's something I have to think about. So let's see what the morning brings as you English say! *Wenn das in ordnung ist?* Ok?"

"Oh yes that's absolutely fine Zak, thank you and it's really good of you to have us all, isn't it Rose?"

"It certainly is and it's wonderful to be somewhere safe and sound, but I miss Olly: he should be here." She appeared wistful for a moment. Zak was certain that Rose and Ellie had no idea why they were here. It was quite obvious that Alicia hadn't told them yet. Rose was now fixing him with a slightly steely glare.

"The thing is that when I try to send him my thoughts from here, I am sure as anything he feels them landing. It's almost like he's down there somewhere not far away. I suppose it's because we really are on the same wavelength and also as we've been here together." She laughed, appearing rather embarrassed for a moment and called the dog across. The atmosphere was electric: Zak didn't dare look up from studying his fingernails. Rose was astute as ever and how was it possible, he thought incredulously, for two people to be that close? However, a plan was forming in his head. Alicia quickly broke the loaded silence.

"Well, funnily enough, I can sometimes sense Guy blanking me out. It's because, I think, when he's out in the field doing something particularly dangerous, he can't be distracted by thoughts of me. So I try not to worry and leave him alone." She sent a meaningful look across at Rose, "It's odd though, isn't it?" Rose understood and was quiet.

"I think that's rather wonderful," said Ellie unaware of the real meanings behind the telepathic messaging. "I don't feel I know Jake well enough to have such ESP, but it must be very special when you do." She glanced at Zak, saw understanding and felt his empathy. She turned her face to the fire not wanting anybody to notice her heightened colour.

"Let's have an early night, travelling is exhausting," Alicia suggested, getting up and stretching.

"Good idea and I've got a great book," answered Rose, impatient to get Alicia alone.

"I think I'll just sit by the fire a little bit longer, if that's alright?" Ellie said quietly. "It's so lovely to be here and to feel safe and sound again." For the first time since her abduction she began to look more relaxed and peaceful.

"That's fine, now don't worry about a thing. Here we really are in the best hands possible." Alicia kissed Ellie on both cheeks and gave her a hug. "Thank you Zak, thank you from all of us."

"You are very welcome, have a good night's rest, there's no hurry in the morning; breakfast is organised." Alicia and Rose started up the stairs. They turned halfway up to call goodnight again but Zak was busy putting another log on the fire and Ellie was just gently smiling as she watched the flames. A very cosy picture they made Alicia thought.

Rose shut their bedroom door firmly behind her.

"Right now Ally, tell me what exactly is going on?"

❈   ❈   ❈

CHAPTER 20

A Clandestine Meeting
(Estonia)

GUSTAV was flown up to the Narva border base in a military helicopter. Accompanying him on the flight were the Commander of the Estonian Defence force, a Major General, an admiral, an Air Commodore and three general staff, one from each branch of the Defence Forces: all were well aware of Russian movement along their Eastern frontier. The balance of safety on the borderline had been problematical ever since the Russians last withdrew their troops from Estonia in 1994. The country still felt extremely vulnerable, with Russian movements constantly under close surveillance at all times, by air, land and sea.

As soon as it was confirmed that their adversaries were once more amassing troops, a land force was immediately sent to take up position on the Estonian side, from Narva all the way South to Vasknarva and Lake Peipus. The navy sent out light combat craft and coastal patrols, with their support vessels, along more than 3,500 kilometres of the Northern coastline; a huge feat with all the numerous bays, straits and inlets to police. The naval island bases and the Baltron squadron had also been briefed and instructed to raise the alarm level status to high. The Baltron squadron had the responsibility for overseeing Naval defence and security between the Baltic States. The Ämari Air Base was put on red alert: Nato had also been fully informed of the latest developments.

The emergency meeting scheduled at the Narva border included the Estonian and British Special Operations Force together with the Estonian high command, who had already been made aware of the British mission under way. Gustav had voiced his opinion that the location of Irina's estate was likely to be especially relevant, particularly as she was acting out of character and remained out of touch. The main telephone lines, in her area, which had been affected by the storm, were now up and working again, but there was still no connection to either her house or to the hunting lodge, which was suspicious in itself.

Guy and Julian had been flown up to the border earlier in the day and were waiting with the Estonian special force, well out of sight in a building behind the Narva frontier kiosks and barriers. Guy had received a message from Jake that morning, giving him the confirmation and the details they most needed which he had read with some relief. Both Jake and Irina were holed up in the hunting lodge unharmed but quite obviously right in the middle of an international incident, with the Russians about to walk into Estonia again, after infiltrating Irina's land and taking up residence in her hunting lodge.

They all heard the distinct noise of a military helicopter approaching. Guy got up and walked over to the window.

"Good! They're using a British Wildcat reconnaissance helicopter. Now let's hope that these Generals speak good English," he said turning with a grin to Maksim his Estonian counterpart. With an amused chuckle Maksim answered.

"I think that you will find their English better than your Estonian my friend!" Guy laughed in return.

"That wouldn't be difficult!"

Everybody stood as the new arrivals marched in. The special op's leaders were immediately asked to join them in a separate, private room on the far side of the complex.

It looked as if this building was often used for secure investigations and interviews. The three staff, with various pieces of machinery, telephones and computers, sat at a table at the end of the long room primed to record and document the discussions.

Gustav made the introductions before they all sat down. Guy was much relieved to find a civilian amongst the elite Estonian group with excellent English, who could translate if necessary. Large detailed maps of the area were then laid out on the table between them. Gustav made sure that he sat next to Guy. While the others were settling themselves and coffee was being served from a small kitchenette off one side of the room, he quickly explained his relationship with both the Estonian elite army and his longstanding friendship with Irina and her grandson Jake.

As the Commander opened the meeting they all stood and bent to peruse the maps. There was no doubt about it – Irina's large estate was in a prime location. The Major-General showed them where the multi-national land forces were positioned and pinpointed the Russian forces.

The Admiral then explained the role of their small Navy and it's difficulties in making all of their coastal waters secure. The Air Force base, South of Lake Klooga at Ämari, circled in red on the map, was a mere twenty nautical miles South-West of Talinn. Guy was then asked to enlighten them about his role in the situation. He did so, bringing the senior men up to date with the details of Ellie's abduction, his flight into Russia and with the known location of his colleague Jake. He finished by saying:

"And so Sir, there is no doubt in my mind that the Russians are intending to invade Estonia once more by literally walking in over Irina Gregoriach's land comprising many kilometres across. Troops are in place to either side of her forestland, as you will see on the map. Because of the thick forest making it well nigh impossible for manoeuvring tanks or even trucks, her land I understand, is not seen to be vulnerable."

Guy stopped for an instant to let this last sentence sink in. The Major-General didn't look happy but said nothing. So Guy continued.

"It is interesting that one of my team, Jake Nicholson, was forced not only to help bring out very substantial funds, but also I imagine to persuade his grandmother into succumbing to the Russians' catastrophic wishes. I realise that by now your resources by land, air and sea are all on full alert and that shortly you may be negotiating a stand-off with the opposing side. May I just ask for a short time frame, with your own Special Op's, to secure the release of both Irina Gregoriach and my colleague, her grandson Jake Nicholson? There are three Russian officers in the house, all who must be taken into custody and who will have much to tell us. There is a small unit on guard outside which we can easily overcome, but there is one key man, we are waiting for, who also will prove to be of great interest to you and whose return to the hunting lodge we believe to be imminent." He looked at Maksim for support. "We shall find a way to infiltrate the house..." at this Gustav raised a hand and stood up to speak.

"I have a suggestion, if I may?" The Commander waved for him to speak.

"As it turns out, depending on the timing, I think we have a way in." Gustav paused a moment to make sure that he had everybody's full attention.

"A group of the Roma come here for a month every year, at this time. They have been working for Irina in her forest. On this coming Friday these people will bring their musicians and dancers to perform for her, to thank her for their employment before returning home to their families. They collect their money on the last night after the

162

entertainment. These Romanies are a tough breed: I know them well. They are loyal to those who are good to them. The Contessa had already been informed, by their leader, a formidable man named Gunari, of recent unusual movement along the borders of her land. On a couple of occasions, to my knowledge, she has passed on these facts to the Defence Department. No doubt you will have heard of these incidents?" Gustav paused again for this last fact to be confirmed.

The senior men all nodded and the Commander once more looked annoyed, but other than raising an eyebrow declined saying anything to interrupt. Gustav half smiled at Guy, took a breath and kept going.

"I am also expected as a guest, to be entertained by the Roma, at the lodge on Friday night. I have no idea of the situation within the hunting lodge as yet, but I am quite certain that Irina will already be working towards having this event go ahead as planned if at all possible. She will be thinking, as are we, that it would be a good way in for us and that it could turn the whole situation to our advantage..." he trailed off. Guy nodded at Maksim and raised his hand again, Maksim indicated for him to go ahead.

"This sounds like an excellent way for us to go in, Sir." Both Julian and Maksim raised their hands in agreement.

"I just want to explain more about this particular man we are after. We already want him for kidnap, embezzlement, money laundering and fraud. We have it on good authority that he, or most likely his very wealthy Russian family, are behind this whole latest episode with Russia, which has, as well you know been brewing for quite a while. The man has been in London; he was in Irina's hunting lodge and now, I have been informed, is on his way back here via Geneva. He will no doubt be banking the very large amount of money which we had to put up for the release of the girl,

Ellie Maundsley…" he hesitated aware of the disproving stares, "in view of the bigger picture you understand."

Here Guy paused while Gustav quickly translated what he had said: the Admiral was looking a little puzzled trying to keep up.

"I'm sorry Sir. I'll slow down. Ellie Maundsley just happens to be my colleague Jake's girlfriend, which can't be a coincidence. I repeat we need this man badly as I think you do. We need to find out exactly what part he and his family are playing, their political leanings and where they are based." Gustav began again to translate but was waved down as this time they'd all understood.

The trio of senior men then continued a discussion, low and in their own language, with much nodding and shaking of heads while Guy, Julian and Maksim exchanged views in English on the number of men they'd need for this next part of the mission. The Commander of the EDF then addressed the whole table once more. He and the others all agreed that the Special Forces be given the time to get Irina and her grandson out and hopefully catch the all-important Russian at the same time. They all knew Irina and were concerned for her safety. In particular Gustav, Julian noted. He was quite obviously much more than just a long-standing friend. Guy then asked for permission to take the Gypsy leader into their confidence with the help of Gustav, who agreed wholeheartedly.

"By all means." The Commander then stood abruptly, indicating that the meeting was over and he was ready to leave. *"Jah,* get Irina and her grandson out of there but at the same time it is of paramount importance to apprehend this young Russian man. I'd like very much to know who is responsible for our present situation and their political aims above all else. I want this whole incident wrapped up as quickly and discreetly as possible, before it blows up in our faces. Meanwhile we will try to maintain a normal congenial conversation with the Russian ambassador, but all forces will remain on full alert until the end of the week. That's all the time you have. Gentlemen, *Aitäh!* Thank you and Good luck, *Edu."* He fixed Maksim with a meaningful glance, stepped around his chair and pushed it in with a quick short shove.

They all rose to their feet. The Commander strode off towards the door indicating for the rest of his people to follow, turning one last time to say, "I await to hear of your success, *nägemist,"* before exiting through the steel door.

"Well," said Guy quietly, turning to Gustav, "the Major General wasn't too happy with our remarks about the Contessa's land being left unmanned and vulnerable, was he?" Gustav smiled at the younger man.

"No, especially as it has already been highlighted before on more than one occasion!"

They all sat silent until the sound of the eminent group's footsteps had receded. Guy was awaiting confirmation, from Jake, that the evening's entertainment on Friday was to go ahead before a coordinated plan could be made for Guy's team to infiltrate the house with the Romanies. Maksim's force were to deal with the Russian unit in position outside with the tanks and army vehicles comprising about a dozen soldiers.

Guy and Julian just hoped that by then the young Russian would have returned from Geneva. Meanwhile they would go to introduce themselves to the gypsies.

❊ ❊ ❊

CHAPTER 21

A Risky Business
(Alpine hideout: Scotland)

OLLY sat by himself in the hotel dining room, toying with a plateful of rösti and a rare beef salad. He was missing Rose beyond everything, particularly as he'd now been effectively taken off the job and found time to be on his hands. Knowing his wife to be up in Zak's hidey hole at the top of the mountain was almost too much. She was so near and yet so far. Zak had just called to tell him of the girls' safe arrival.

Little did his Swiss friend and colleague know that Olly had seen them for himself, in the car parked by the station, after Zak had brought them up from Bern airport. He knew exactly how to see and not be seen, lurking in the shadows and merging with the crowds. He was confident that he was exceptionally good at it. He'd even seen the man, with an uncanny likeness to his quarry, being met off the train and taken away in the smart Limo advertising clearly the name of his hotel.

Olly thought over the situation and the plan Zak had in mind for the following evening: he wasn't at all happy; yet Zak had said that he would take no chances and if he didn't feel that Ellie was up to the identification ordeal then he would cancel it, no matter what his superiors ordered. Zak reassured Oliver that he would not have any of the girls put at risk. Olly agreed vehemently.

Oliver decided that he must insist on being near at hand whatever the plan. He'd talk to Zak in the morning when he came down the mountain. Meanwhile he could pop out and survey the possible identification location for the following night. Just for his own peace of mind he'd like to give it the once over.

Helena came across to Olly's table. "I have to say Oliver that you look distracted or are you just lost without your wife? When is Rose coming out?" Olly knew his face looked anxious. He must cheer up and not give anything away, otherwise Helena would guess that things were somewhat awry. The dining room was quiet. It was late and most people had left, so she sat down in the chair opposite. The chair which should have been Rose's, Olly thought, not able to help himself. He smiled at the attractive hospitable face in front of him. He could see that Helena was upset for him; she was such a caring thoughtful hostess. He and Rose were both fond of Helena and her husband.

"Yes, you're right Helena, I am a bit lost without my gorgeous, gregarious wild Rose. It's just that we both love being here together, you know that and it doesn't feel right for me to be by myself in our usual room with the balcony and that spectacular view! But she's coming soon she assures me. She had to tie up a few loose ends in the office when a late job came in, which I suppose they couldn't afford to turn down. Hopefully, she should be here by the weekend. You know what Rose is like Helena, she insisted I come out first and not waste any of our planned holiday."

Olly hoped that his forced bravado and enthusiastic smile would alleviate the worry on Helena's kind face. She couldn't bear for one of her guests to be in any way downhearted. She and her husband and all the staff worked so hard at making sure that everyone was happy. Yet she thought it a bit odd that Oliver had left it so late to book their lovely room. It was just lucky that it had become free unexpectedly when the Austrian couple had rushed home for the birth of a grandchild.

"Well it's going to be a sunny day tomorrow and the snow is good, so Olly you should ski and get some practice: I am well aware of just how good Rose is! If she lived here she'd be competing in the winter Olympic team, I think!" Oliver laughed, his good humour restored at the thought of Rose ordering all the Swiss ski athletes around.

"Yes, that's a good idea Helena you're right, Rose is extremely hard to keep up with so I do need to get in some practice; now I might just take a stroll through the village before turning in."

"Good idea, but it's pretty cold out there at minus eight, so wrap up warm and I'll say goodnight." She got to her feet as did Olly and kissed him on the cheeks three times according to the Swiss custom. "Sleep well Oliver, please send my love to Rose and tell her to hurry up!" Olly chuckled, "I'll do just that." He followed her out of the dining room, then went on up to his room, collected his wallet, car keys, coat and scarf and set off for the most prestigious night club in town.

❄

Amidst the noise and crowd surrounding the dance floor it was easy for Oliver to check out all the relevant exits from the night club to the washrooms, behind the bar and the emergency fire doors. Then he went to locate the bar in the main hotel and ordered a whisky. He was supposedly off duty so felt he'd earned himself a nightcap.

Sitting in the spacious, comfortable sitting area with his late-night drink and a newspaper, Olly was also able to study the guests as they wandered past. Most were well heeled. They would have to be he decided judging by his bar bill. The elder people were smartly dressed whereas most of the younger generation didn't look to have bothered much. It seemed to be the trend these days Olly thought; rather sad for the hotel staff who were so immaculate themselves and took such an enormous amount of trouble looking after their guests.

He was disturbed by a crowd of loud speaking people who had just appeared, to one side of him, from what must have been a private dining room. Russian: they are speaking Russian, Oliver realised with a jolt. Given the situation he couldn't help but think what an unmelodic, guttural language it sounded. But this might well be the family of such interest to them.

Alert and focused, Olly felt the adrenalin kick in as he observed the party wandering slowly past. The father figure, leader of the pack, was exactly Olly's idea of an oligarch, dressed in an expensive suit, close cropped hair and hard cold features. Beside him strutted a very heavily made up lady with dyed flaxen hair, a good if voluptuous figure, wearing authentic but vulgar flashy jewellery. Her clothes were over the top and too young for her age as she looked around her making sure that she was noticed, expecting admiration. The wife Olly decided, gently ducking his head down a little and adjusting his paper so he appeared to be reading. Oliver suddenly experienced another shot of adrenalin. At her far side, walked the - good-looking man he'd been following, smartly dressed and talking earnestly to his father. The two men seemed to be having an intense conversation whilst heading for the night club.

Just behind them tottering unsteadily, came an attractive dark blonde, long-haired girl, the daughter he guessed as her features were a younger version of her mother. She was dressed in a short tight black dress: little wonder she could hardly walk in her pair of unbelievably ostentatious high heeled and expensive looking red shoes. Her legs went on for ever, Olly couldn't help but notice. She was presumably with a husband or boyfriend, the way she was hanging onto the arm of the man beside her. He couldn't quite see the rings on her hands, they were waving around too much. The way she was swaying made it obvious that they'd both overdone the alcohol at dinner.

Probable grandparents followed; the older lady was walking with another well turned out young man with a limp, the man Oliver had spied earlier at the station. He had a very elderly white-haired man on his other arm. Except for being stockier and shorter, the young man bore a marked resemblance to his brother, the man in front who Olly had been tracking.

Then came a couple more men who took up the rear of the party. Oliver decided they were most likely minders; their clothing had little taste yet fitted reasonably well. Their shoes, in a cheap imitation of their employer's, were at least clean. One of the men had a definitely suspicious looking bulge to the left-hand side of his jacket. They were efficiently scrutinizing the hotel guests, including himself Olly noted, glancing down at his paper again at the appropriate moment. He would not wish to come up against these two heavy and unattractive individuals with pock marked faces. Without doubt these were the people that Pieter also had under surveillance.

The barman appeared at his side.

"Would you like another Sir?" indicating the whisky and removing the empty glass.

"No thanks," Olly answered, "I think you have other customers." Out of the corner of his eye he'd seen the inebriated younger pair heading towards the bar.

The barman looked over his shoulder.

"*Ach je* – Oh no, not again!" he muttered with a fleeting frown, then smiling once more politely wiped the table where Olly's glass had left a slight mark.

"Are they here for long, do you know, that particular group?"

"Long enough," the barman answered quietly. "It's the same every night. They follow a definite routine." Resigned he stood up and looked towards the bar. "If there's nothing else Sir, I think I'd better go and encourage some coffee before those two hit the night club again!"

The barman gave a long-suffering sigh, grinned sheepishly at Olly and moved off.

Right thought Oliver, Zak needs to know about this. The darkened night club was the obvious place for the final identification. Let's just hope I get permission to be included at least for outdoor surveillance purposes. There would need to be plenty of back up: this lot were a formidable bunch with their own well armed arsenal of personal security.

Olly sat long enough to watch the young man with the limp return from escorting the elderly people up in the lift and re-join the other two at the bar. Then when they all set off to follow the parents into the night club – he waved a goodnight to the barman and made his way back out to his car and his own hotel. It would be difficult to sleep with tomorrow's agenda uppermost in his mind, but he could rest; the TA had taught him how best to relax when faced with dire situations out in the field. He would just pray that he was allowed to take part in this crucial piece of the action. After all it was his own wife and friends in the firing line.

*

172

Marc, bearing a tumbler of his favourite Scotch whisky with ice and a large glass of Pinot blush wine for Emma, strode towards their snug sitting room. As he reached the open doorway he hesitated; he could see his wife looking somewhat glum and more than a little exhausted after putting their two busy, spirited little girls to bed. She was sitting in front of the television staring at a gardening programme lost in her thoughts, quite obviously miles away. Bath and bedtime for young mums was always the most tiring part of the day: Marc was often late back from the hospital and so unable to lend a hand. Tonight at least he'd picked up an easy take away dinner for them and… he had a plan which he hoped would be appreciated.

"Here we are darling! I've tucked up the little monkeys and read them a story. Dinner is organised." Emma jumped; she had been away in another world. She leant over to grab the TV remote to turn down the sound.

"Oh dear, I'm so sorry. I was just thinking about Guy and Julian and of course Jake. I just hope to God they are all alright."

Marc hadn't missed her brushing a tear away. She was really worried about their friends.

"I talked to Adriana this morning and this is the longest time ever she's had with absolutely no news of Julian. What with the babies well on the way now she must feel so lonely. I know I would be."

"Yes I agree she must feel a bit abandoned, but I have a plan." Marc sat down on the sofa beside her and took her hand.

"I think that Alicia and Rose may be taking Ellie out to Switzerland, where they'll hole up with Zak for a bit. Ellie's feeling very claustrophobic in Rose's flat and it's difficult for her to go out much given the situation."

"Oh Heavens! Is that a good idea? Are you sure, I talked to Rose early this morning and she didn't say anything?"

"Yes, I think it was a sudden decision, but seems like a good idea to me, especially for Ellie." He took a gulp of his drink and sat back with a satisfied sigh. Emma wasn't happy he could see.

"Poor Adriana will be even more bereft with only us around and what with you at the hospital and me here mostly with the girls, I haven't much time or energy left for her, poor thing."

"No, I know darling, but listen to my plan." Emma watched his dear face light up, as he began to voice his idea.

"Uncle Alec rang me during my lunch break. He's having trouble, up there in Scotland, with some foreigners staying in the lodge at Glencurrie. Russians apparently." Emma interrupted.

"Russians? Good God! I hope they're nothing to do with what's going on with Guy and Julian, wherever they are?"

"No! No! This lot come from London. They live here, he's a diplomat; with the Russian ambassador, his right-hand man or something. Anyway, Emma just listen for a minute please."

"Sorry!"

"It's alright, I know you're feeling a bit frazzled but just let me finish." Emma, contrite, turned towards her husband, to concentrate on what he was saying.

"The thing is one of these wretched people has shot a red deer stag, out of season, which is causing Alec a problem and he wants to get rid of his tenants, but they are refusing to budge. So I said I'd go up. He then suggested that you come with me."

"But..." Emma interrupted.

"Wait darling, wait a minute while I finish. The other telephone call I had today was from your mother who asked if we would let her have the children for half term. Your sister is going to be there also, with your little niece Sophie. You need a break and I think that, as Alicia and Rose are quite likely also going to be away with Ellie, we should gather up Adriana and take her and her large tummy with us. We'll go by train, Alec will meet us and we can hire a car if we want. Some time ago Julian asked me to keep an eye on Adriana if he was ever away and I'd like to do that. So – what do you think?

"Well," answered Emma immediately cheering up, "you have been busy! If Mum and Beccy are really happy to have the girls, then I think it's a lovely idea and I'm sure that Adriana will agree, she's getting really browned off."

"She does agree, I've already checked and I've booked our tickets too!"

Emma's face was now alight with excitement.

"I can't wait!" was all she said. Marc, delighted with Emma's reaction, took another swallow of his drink and let out a deep chuckle.

"Good!" he muttered then leant over to kiss his wife.

✳ ✳ ✳

CHAPTER 22

Close Connections
(Switzerland: The Scottish Highlands, Thursday)

THE following morning Olly sat in the same café in the village at the same table. Käthi quickly served him his coffee, efficient as ever. More impatient than he'd ever been, he waited for Zak to put in an appearance.

Last night they'd had a late conversation to discuss Olly's observations at the Castle Haute Hotel with its Russian guests and suitable night club location. He'd had a horrible night afterwards. He was all fired up and couldn't help imagining Rose, with the others, in Zak's safe hidey-hole up the mountain. So near and yet so far away. Eventually Zak appeared, he was grinning as usual.

"Entschuldigung! I'm sorry. My lady guests, your wife in particular, all wanted *rösti*, eggs and ham for breakfast. Now they have gone skiing over the other side with Pieter, so I am freed up for a bit."

"Right," Olly replied dismally. "It's certainly alright for some! How are they all?"

"Yes, they're good, but now we have a plan for tonight," enthused Zak. Noting the despondent look on Olly's normally cheerful face he continued, "Thank you for the info last night, but I hasten to add that I did not mention to my boss in Bern that you were actually in the Castle Haute Hotel. As you know London has specifically given instructions for you not to be involved. You're too closely connected Olly. You must realise that?"

Olly looked up, an unhappy look of resignation beginning to form around his eyes and mouth. He didn't say anything but merely acknowledged Zak's caution with a subdued nod. Zak gave him an encouraging pat on the arm.

"*Kein Problem!* Don't worry my friend. I have already insisted that we need you, at least for surveillance outside the building. There are just too many exits for the small team we have to cover. Also you and I are the only people, other than Ellie, who actually know what this guy looks like. His brother is quite alike and it's of paramount importance that we target the right one." Oliver's face lit up again finding that he was to be involved after all.

"The brother has an obvious limp. He's shorter and more solid in stature too. It shouldn't be hard," said Olly, waving to Käthi enthusiastically for another cup of coffee.

"*Nein,* it shouldn't be difficult, but I'm worried about Ellie. She's been through hell and even to be in the same room as this man is going to be pretty *furchtbar,* disturbing I mean. She's brave, yet she's still vulnerable."

"Yes, I agree but she'll have both Alicia and Rose with her. What a nightmare. How did she react to our plan for the night club?"

"Good, *Sehr gut* considering her state of mind must still be fragile. Now she's recovered a bit from her dreadful experience she's angry at the man and determined that he gets his just deserts but..." Zak trailed off.

"What is it then? You're worried about this particular job, aren't you?"

"I am because I realise that it's part of a bigger agenda. Ellie's kidnapping, I'm sure, was just the beginning. Neither of us are being told exactly what's going on. It must be something really serious to claim the attention of our most senior supervisors."

"That's not unusual," Olly answered. "I have a mounting suspicion that our close colleagues are most probably in Mother Russia herself. Marc is receiving snippets of info back in London but nothing concrete. Yet there's something else as well isn't there Zak?" He fixed his friend with a knowing stare. "I can see what's happening my friend – it's Ellie isn't it?" Zak looked away then waited a moment while Käthi served them fresh coffee.

"I just said she's vulnerable, that's all."

✳

Marc, Emma and Adriana left London Kings Cross, by North Eastern Rail, at 10am precisely on Thursday morning, heading for Inverness. It was a long leisurely journey. They were due to arrive in Scotland at about six-thirty in the evening, in good time to catch the local train a further half-hour North to Dromvaar. There Marc's uncle Alec would meet them at the station and drive them into the Highlands and on to Glencurrie.

They had a relaxed lunch in the train buffet car and plenty of time to catch up on each others' recent news. Adriana regaled them with hilarious stories of Julian's antics when he had insisted on accompanying Adriana to one of her pre-natal baby classes. It was to be the first and last time that he was to be persuaded! Emma couldn't help but pass on what she felt might be helpful pieces of advice to Arri regarding the impending birth. At this point Marc bowed out and sat back to read.

After they passed Durham, the train had mostly deposited the many businessmen with their noisy mobiles and the atmosphere quietened. As soon as Adriana found an empty seat beside her, she stretched out as best she could and went fast asleep. When she woke the two girls sat each at a window, silently peaceful and enjoying the beautiful scenery before it became dark. Where the line bordered the seashore, the water seemed inky blue against the brilliance of the setting sun. They watched spellbound as it crept ever lower in the sky towards evening. A lighthouse and swooping seabirds formed a silhouette against the spectacular coloured backdrop.

As they neared their destination small villages flashed past in the slowly fading day; the twinkling street and house lights defining the roofs of houses and an occasional church. The last part of the journey to Dromvaar would be completely in the dark as it was only a small village in the heart of the countryside.

Marc spent the time deep in thought, wondering what the other men were doing and assessing Adriana's present state of health in view of her impending twin birth. She looked physically well, but must be quite worried with being out of touch with Julian for so long and at such a time.

He had been in constant touch with his invisible contact, gleaning little information except for his orders relating to the other girls' trip to Switzerland. The man had seemed somewhat concerned, which was odd considering the three girls couldn't be safer in the care and protection of the capable Zak.

He had called his elusive secondary superior before leaving London, to announce his movements with Adriana and Emma. He was told that Olly was also already somewhere in Europe and would be his liaison if and when there was information to pass on. As both a doctor and close friend Marc, feeling responsible for Adriana's health and happiness, requested that he be informed whenever possible on Julian's location as well as notice of his intended return.

London had been non-committal as to the men's whereabouts, so Marc's suspicions were strengthened that the operation was both complex and enduring. As they progressed Northwards he couldn't help but remember the last time they'd all been in Scotland together in Alec's lodge. It had turned into an enormous adventure and the beautiful Adriana had been so desperate for a child. Now miraculously she was expecting two. What would the babies be like and who would they take after? Neither she nor Julian had wanted to know if they were boys, girls or one of each. Apparently, they were already of a good size. As he looked at Adriana now, staring out of the window and unaware of his scrutiny, he thought that although she seemed frustrated by her forced inactivity, she was looking more than comfortable in her role as an expectant mother. She was brave and strong and however difficult the birth might turn out to be, she'd handle it well and as her doctor in charge he'd feel thoroughly proud of her.

As far as the world was concerned Arri only had a couple of months to go now, but the twins might well come early. Marc wasn't worried, he'd delivered many babies, including two pairs of twins one year, when he and Emma were in Greece. But with Adriana he felt more than usually responsible. Theirs was a long standing and committed friendship and he must make sure of a successful delivery and happy outcome, should it happen on his watch. Sitting opposite, Emma was now deep in her book, but Adriana as if she sensed Marc watching her, turned away from the window to give him one of her knockout smiles. His stomach flipped at the memory of that extraordinary day they had spent together in the Scottish Highlands the previous year.

"I'm hungry again!"

Emma looked up at her smiling friend.

"Honestly Ari, these babies are going to be born eating!" she said, getting a cheese and ham sandwich out of the bag beside her. "Thank goodness Marc suggested a picnic basket for tea." Marc laughed.

"No doubt, with you carrying these twins, Mrs H will be cooking for us as if we were an army." He was looking forward to an evening whisky and to catching up with his uncle.

"I know your poor uncle Alec doesn't know what he's let himself in for." She took the sandwich and bit into it with relish.

"Well as long as you don't have them up here," Emma said with feeling.

"Oh, I don't know," replied Marc chuckling. "I'm sure Mrs H would be a great help!"

"Well, I'd rather they weren't too early, yet I'm not fussed so long as Marc is around. But I would prefer Julian to be at home when our children choose to put in an appearance!" Looking directly at Marc, Adriana said. "You will let me know as soon as you have any news, won't you?"

"Absolutely, of course I will! As from tomorrow, I'll have Olly liaising with me and as you know he's very well aware of your situation, so you needn't worry."

"I'm not." Adriana answered. "I'm not in the least bit worried as long as we have a competent doctor in the house!" Emma looked across to smile at her friend, thankful that they both had such great confidence in her 'doctor' husband.

* * *

CHAPTER 23

A Welcome Return
(Alec's Scottish home)

ALEC Neilson was fed up to the teeth with the insensitive Russians. They had only been accepted for a week's stay at the lodge, with two days included for the late hind culling. They had only paid for one week. The stag stalking season was well past. Alec was certain that the diplomat son's friend, who he'd disliked on sight, had every intention from the start of bagging a stag with a good head for himself. The young man had been sent back to his family with his tail between his legs after concocting every possible ridiculous excuse for shooting the stag by mistake.

Now all that Alec wanted to do was get rid of the whole lot, but they wouldn't go; making out that the diplomat's wife had a temporary bout of bad health. He couldn't wait for the arrival of both Emma and his nephew Marc and of course he was also looking forward to seeing the vivacious Adriana again. He got up from his chair in the study and advanced into the hall. It was time.

"Mrs H!" he called up the stairs, "are you all ready for the invasion? I'm off to the station now, giving myself plenty of time. Do you need anything on the way? The village shop will still be open."

Mrs Haddington smiled to herself and leant forward to look down over the bannisters, from the first-floor landing. "No thank you Colonel, we're fine, no need to fuss, everything's ready. I just wish we had the little ones coming up as well."

"I know but it'll be a break for Emma and we'll have our hands full enough as it is; we'll need to look after Adriana because we don't want her dropping the twins while she's here, do we?"

"Nothing to worry about there, Colonel, not with our doctor, young Marc, in the house." Alec laughed, full of good humour at the thought of his favourite family and guest about to arrive.

"Right. I'll be off then Mrs H. We'll be back in plenty of time for dinner. That'll give the girls a chance to settle into their rooms and do whatever girls do, before we sit down at eight thirty or thereabouts, if that suits you?"

"Yes, that's guid, now you go steady in that great big barouche of yours Colonel Alec, it will soon be dark! It's freezing already and I hear there's more snow on the way."

As Alec drove slowly across his land towards the main road, he watched the sun go down in all its splendour. As the mighty globe dropped from an aqua sky sheathed in fast approaching grey night clouds, a skein of geese flew silhouetted against the last red and orange rays of the sun. He braked hard as a black grouse flew low across the track, in front of the car, giving its own unique call, 'get back, get back, get back'. As he drove on towards the station, Alec chuckled to himself, remembering past adventures with the three lovely people he was soon to greet. With Marc's support the bloody Russians hadn't a hope, they'd be gone from his house in no time flat and they'd all be able to relax.

✳

Alec was standing on the platform, his face wreathed in smiles as he greeted the three beaming young people. He'd already organized help with the luggage.

"Emma, how marvellous to see you and as for you Adriana, Good God! What's happened to that sensational figure of yours?" He laughed delightedly, embracing both girls before giving Marc an affectionate hug.

"Come on now, Mrs H has cooked a sumptuous dinner and everything good awaits you all. How absolutely lovely that you are here again."

He put his arm around Marc's shoulder and following the ancient porter with the luggage cart, they headed for the small station exit. Marc drove them all back to the house as it was so dark now and very icy: Alec had admitted that his eyes weren't as good as they used to be.

Mrs Haddington was waiting at the door as they climbed out of the ancient vehicle. The girls were sent in while Marc and his uncle saw to the luggage. Half an hour later, when the girls were upstairs in their rooms getting ready for dinner, Marc sat with Alec in his study, each with a glass of whisky to hand beside them.

"I've really been looking forward to this." Marc picked up his drink, took a sip and sat back with a sigh, watching the rich amber coloured liquid glinting against the ice as he gently turned the glass in his hand. He was glad they'd come back to this lovely place: he was very fond of his uncle.

"Now tell me what's been going on?"

Alec smiled, taking a thoughtful sip of whisky himself, then raising his glass before answering.

"It's really good to have you all to stay again Marc, especially in view of what has been going on up here recently! You know while I was in the army, when I was in touch with Intelligence matters, I learnt to trust my innermost feelings, my gut instinct. Once you have it, you never forget that intuitiveness. It never quite leaves you, no matter how old you are and over the years that sixth sense has stood me in very good stead." He chuckled looking at his nephew with affection. "From previous experience during the adventures we have had together, I believe that you have that gift too. So, when I tell you that I have a bad feeling about these Russians, or about one young man in particular; I know that you will understand." Marc nodded.

"Go on," was all he said. Alec related what had recently occurred and described each of the foreigners involved.

"The trouble is that, as you know, I am a magistrate so the young man, who is responsible for the dastardly deed of shooting the stag out of season, has to be seen to be dealt with in the proper way. We are still quite old fashioned up here in this part of the Highlands. He has to come back to face the music, so to speak. But there we have the problem." He stopped to pick up his glass and take another sip of the fortifying liquid.

"So where is this man?" Marc asked.

"Unbeknown to me he flew the nest; to somewhere in Europe, I think. I don't know which country and according to this diplomat, who is in residence in the lodge, the fugitive is refusing to return." Marc sat up.

"What do you mean he's refusing to come back? He'll have to. Do you have a name for the culprit? A description, any more details? We need to know where he went? Did you say he is a friend of this diplomat's son? They must know where he went. Who is the diplomat?"

"Well the diplomat, Mikael, is really quite charming, as is his son, Luka. The wife is alright too. They are unusually discreet and quiet living people. I would imagine they come from good families and have been educated partly in the West, most probably here in the UK. Although Mikael may not use the language much, he speaks better English than he lets on and he definitely understands it, as does the boy Luka."

Taking another sip of his whisky Alec continued… "but the man is being extremely unhelpful as regards his boy's friend who committed the atrocity. Mikael is anxious, I think, about any publicity which might get him into trouble when he returns to London or even back to Moscow. I expect that's why he's lying low and making the excuse to stay, using his wife's health, hoping it will all calm down. I don't think it's anything to do with worrying for the boy. In fact, he doesn't seem at all concerned for his son's so called friend, neither does Luka. I distinctly got the impression that they don't even like the young man and they were pleased to be rid of him. So why on earth did they have him here at all? It's odd."

"I see, well Mikael will have to take responsibility to get his son's friend back. Would you like me to go and speak to him?"

"Yes, I would. I'd really appreciate your help Marc and your thoughts regarding these people. Don't get me wrong: I like Mikael and his son, they seem to be really likeable, decent human beings. God knows I'm not being paranoid, but I am suspicious. There was something decidedly sinister about that other young man." Alec looked relieved having unloaded his concerns.

"Mikael will probably try to pay us off. Money is obviously no object. But there's something else…" His uncle hesitated a moment. "I just have this gut feeling that the missing young man is not only thoroughly bad news and not to be trusted, but I wonder what shenanigans he might be up to. I can't put my finger on it, although I had the distinct sense that he had another hidden agenda."

"Even Hamish, our game keeper, said that his mind seemed to be elsewhere a lot of the time, so why was he here? As I said, I disliked him on sight, as did Mrs Haddington; do ask her. Also talk to Hamish who will not hold back in expressing his opinion and who of course has first-hand knowledge of the incident. He just said to me that it was obvious the young man had handled a gun many times before. He said that despite the boy having a slight handicap, it had been an incredibly difficult shot, but the young Russian was an excellent marksman, straight through the heart it was. What's more; at the end of this conversation with Hamish, he said to me, 'do ye ken Colonel, that unfortunate shooting incident; well... it seemed to be premeditated to me and sent chills down my spine for some reason, cold blooded murder I'd say it was. Ay that was it, murder, no more no less as they say!'

"So you must understand Marc that although Hamish is very straight forward and forthright with his thoughts on the matter, I am not alone with my suspicions."

"No you're not, obviously, I can see that. I'll talk to Hamish with pleasure." Marc, knowing perfectly well that his uncle was neither a scaremonger nor prone to imagine things, felt relieved to be able to help him.

"If you give me all the details of the diplomat and family, I'll check out the whole scenario."

"Good!" said Alec. "Thank you. But one last thing... Mikael, although polite and apologetic, absolutely refuses to give me the young man's family name."

"He'll have to," answered Marc indignantly, "but I wonder why that is? Sounds like they have something to hide doesn't it? I know someone who'll put the fear of God in him if he doesn't tell us – don't worry!"

"Excellent," replied Alec, "your contacts are very much better than mine these days. My lot are all too old now or even retired!" Emma appeared in the doorway to announce that dinner was ready.

"Who is too old now? Not you Alec. You'll never be old." She went up to him and kissed his cheek as he stood up. "Come on now you two, it's dinner time and Adriana is unsurprisingly starving."

They followed her into the dining room. Alec was looking forward to dinner and was feeling much relieved to have discussed the unsettling tenancy problem with his nephew. This gut instinct wasn't all bad; he could feel the slight adrenalin rush of excitement, just like it had been in his covert military days.

After dinner Alec had an unexpected telephone call. He appeared back in the snug sitting room where the others were all enjoying relaxing by the fire. They all looked up as he walked back in.

"I'm sorry to break up the party but Marc, I'm afraid this concerns you. We need another chat." Emma looked at Alec's unsmiling face and made note of her husband's reaction. Marc, seemingly unsurprised grinned happily at the two of them before getting up from the sofa to follow his uncle out of the room. Adriana and Emma knew straight away. Something was up and quite obviously they weren't to be told.

"Here we go again!" Adriana sighed. Emma gave a nervous laugh.

"I just hate it when we aren't involved, don't you? I loathe being kept in the dark."

"Don't worry I'll text Alicia. She'll tell us if there's anything afoot that we need to know about. She might have heard from Guy by now, in which case he's bound to have news of Julian. Apart from which I'd like to know how Ellie is," Adriana patted her stomach adding, somewhat disgruntled, "lucky things to be away skiing in the Alps with Zak."

"Yes, I agree, but it wasn't right for you to fly, it would have been madness, an unnecessary risk. You're much better here with us. I can't help thinking that Marc would rather like to deliver your babies, then Mrs H and I could assist. Wouldn't that be fun?" she giggled. "But we'll have some fun here too Arri, I'll make sure of that."

Adriana made a face. Emma burst out laughing. Although missing her two small daughters, she was relishing the grown-up spell they had before them. Adriana had no idea what she was in for once these twins arrived. They'd better make the most of the time they had, she decided determinedly, after all the babies could well arrive early.

❄ ❄ ❄

CHAPTER 24

The Roma
(Irina's Estonian forest, Thursday)

GUSTAV knew his way into the gypsy encampment and had already been in touch with Gunari the headman, warning him of the urgency of the meeting. They were well acquainted over the years. Guy and Julian both noticed immediately that the camp was well policed. Gunari was waiting to meet them long before they would normally have been heard. Guy had noticed a slight tell-tale sound of discreet movement from time to time, to one side of the track or the other. Only somebody trained and alert would have sensed that they had concealed company, as they crunched their way along the icy winding paths, through the forest leading to the well-hidden Romany lair. The first real sign of life as they neared their destination was the smell of woodsmoke. The snow-laden tree branches provided a protective tunnel-like ceiling.

Only the heaviest snow would penetrate through to the paths below where they walked, unlike the surrounding flat treeless landscape, where there was no protection from the howling winds and drifting snow.

Eventually they came upon a large clearing. There was a small, simple woodsman's slatted log cabin, surrounded by various traditional covered wagons and caravans all set in a circle. At the centre was an open fire-pit with a huge cauldron hanging from a large hook supported by rods of iron. Weathered brown faced elder women were sitting nearby, attending to the cooking, wrapped in fur-lined coats with hoods and thick boots. Beside the cabin was a long lean-two protecting three ancient US Jeeps and an old Land Rover. Not a child or a dog in sight, Guy noticed thankfully. These people were used to travelling light and living discreetly.

Tucked away from the outside world, the settlement area felt several degrees warmer, shielded by the closely packed trees and with the fire at its midst. Gustav, so much older and nowadays unused to clandestine adventures outside a well-heated house on a cold winter's morning, welcomed the warmth. But he was fired up, eager to hear the latest news from the Romany leader. He was dead worried about his dearest Irina, who never went out of touch for more than a couple of days at a time. Gunari would know of any recent activity surrounding both her house and the hunting lodge. As they approached, Guy, Julian and Maksim studied the headman walking towards them, with interest. Gunari was dark skinned, stocky and strong looking, with dark curly hair and a moustache running into a heavy beard. As he came forward to greet them, you couldn't miss the friendliest of faces, the very whitest of teeth and a pair of twinkling black eyes. Gustav had already told the Englishmen that Gunari was the toughest of men and had the courage of a lion; at one time in his extreme youth he had fought as a mercenary. The experience, tempered by good humour, showed. The man offered a firm and dependable handshake and then encouraged them all to the fire, with a special greeting and a slap on the back for Gustav.

"Hello – *Pa-dru-ga*. You are most welcome my friend and you have saved me a journey. I was preparing for a visit to the city, to see you and your army friends! Come, sit please."

Six other men had appeared from behind the encroaching trees. All probably armed, but they each nodded a friendly greeting as they positioned large logs around the fire for their guests to sit on. The women moved off and disappeared into one of the caravans. Julian knew that several more pairs of black eyes would be studying them from the safe confines behind the dark doorway of an old but freshly painted *vardo,* a Romany horse-drawn wagon. It was well in use with smoke billowing out of its chimney, but with no sign of a horse. No doubt this particular vehicle remained in Irina's forest, for the following year, when the group returned home. He could hear lowered voices coming from inside. These temporary homes were well concealed and protected from the harsh weather. An unbidden enemy wouldn't leave this place easily and no stranger without an escort would find it. This part of the forest was dense and impenetrable for most adventurers.

Maksim introduced himself to Gunari as did both Guy and Julian. Everybody sat, while hot acrid coffee in tin mugs was handed around. Gunari then waved the coffee bearers away and without more ado turned to Gustav with a worried expression.

"The Countess is in trouble. This is why I was on my way to see you. Some Russian soldiers are in the lodge holding both she and her grandson captive inside." Gustav already aware of his beloved Irina's predicament tried to remain calm. Guy cleared his throat.

"Yes, this we know already as my colleague Jake has managed to get a message out. We also know how many soldiers are in situ outside and what armoury they have." Gunari appeared both surprised and impressed.

"Good! We can double check that with my man on surveillance duty nearest the lodge." He noted the barely concealed anxiety on Gustav's face. "Don't worry, I already know that both Jake and Irina are in good health and no doubt your indomitable lady friend will be giving the

Russians a hard time! The Countess is a very strong lady."
He then caught Guy's attention and grinned.

"Gustav may have told you, I also have known Jake for many years. He came here as a young boy and befriended one of my nephews and his cousins when they were children." He looked again to the two Englishmen.

"Gustav tells me you will need our help and that is why you have come," he spoke to Guy, rightly sensing that he led the small group of visitors. "Yes" he continued, "I have had my eyes and ears open here in this dark forest and therefore have knowledge already of Jake's resolute character under duress. I have every confidence in his ability to support us from the inside. Friday is the day to go in and together we will make good arrangements. I understand that the Countess and Jake are aware of how crucial it is for the plans to remain as they are. The Russians must have no reason to believe that our Romany entertainment is anything different from any other year."

"There is much movement on the border along Irina's land." Gunari continued, "The Russians are getting themselves ready to walk into Estonia again, of this I am quite certain: this time they'll cross the Contessa's land where the borderline is at its most vulnerable. The Multi-National surveillance troops are concentrated only at the more obvious border crossings. The men are positioned to either side and some distance from these so called 'impenetrable' forests: an elite task force such as the Russian *Spetsnaz*, with determination and the right equipment, will find their way through even the deepest parts. Once across the frontier with a well-equipped arsenal they'll merely force entry everywhere."

Gustav let out a long sigh. "I suspected as much."

"You have done well Gunari. You have given us just the information that we need," said Maksim.

"Also thanks to you and your people, we have the way in," added Guy. "The musical distractions tomorrow night must go ahead and as you say we certainly do need your help."

"But of course, I have my beautiful dancing girls, who are the best distraction you will ever see! And my best musicians are also well proven fighting men."

"Good, then let us discuss the evening schedule."

Guy was pleased that the Romanian spoke such good English, understood Russian and seemed well informed. He'd had years of learning the forest layout. He appeared to be a great character; he and his men were certainly well trained and seemed both mentally and physically fit. Gunari was obviously fond of both Irina and her grandson. Guy was in no doubt that he was to be trusted and could be relied upon. Gustav's input also was extremely helpful as he'd attended all the previous musical evenings and was able relate details and timing of the expected performance and describe the internal layout of the house. Guy nodded with satisfaction.

"It must be as it's always been. I would suggest that Julian and I should join Gunari and his people going into the lodge, under disguise of course, which we need to discuss. I imagine that you Maksim and your force can deal with the contingent in place outside the house. You'll have back up from above. Jake is already aware of our intentions to infiltrate the lodge with Gunari's musicians. He's one of my elite team and was already on a mission when he was taken. He's managing to get messages out via a small new type of covert device. It's the first time we've used it and it's been a tracking and communicating God-send in these extreme weather conditions."

"*Asta e bine,* that's good and that's my boy," chuckled Gunari thankful and strangely proud that Jake was so well informed and admired by the Englishmen. "I taught him everything I knew when he was here with us in the camp." His eyes crinkled with genuine affection. "The Countess sometimes used to let him spend all day and the odd night with us in summer when he was growing up. She used to say that he needed to come out of his gilded cage and learn to live simply, in case one day he found himself to be in difficult circumstances! It seems that time has come. In return he taught me my excellent English." He laughed deeply from the stomach.

Guy grinned to himself, no wonder Jake was so good at his present job. He was born to it and at an early age had learned to live rough. He allowed himself a satisfied smile and turned to hold both arms out encompassing the whole group.

"Thank you Gunari, I am confident that we have the best possible team to wrap up this whole unsettling mission and bring it to its proper conclusion. We are only a small part of a much bigger picture. There are plenty out there on permanent alert, waiting to deal with the Russians for once and for all and to put paid to their unsavoury intentions towards Estonia."

"Good," replied Gunari. Maksim, Julian and Gustav were all nodding their heads in agreement. Gustav laid a hand on Gunari's shoulder.

"Just one thing my friend; after processing all the information I have been given over these last few days, I agree with you. I also am in no doubt whatsoever of the Russian intention of making their move and crossing the border over Irina's land. I too think their intentions are imminent and most probably this Friday night, when they know she and her household are otherwise engaged, they might well begin their invasion. The intended evening's entertainment is a perfect smoke screen."

"Yes," Guy replied. "I think you are both correct. We are all of the same mind."

"Yes, it is most likely." Maksim looked thoughtful for a moment. "Do the Russians know that you are here in the forest watching their every move?"

"No!" answered Gunari adamant. "I assure you that they consider us Romany people a gaggle of gutless *Tigani;* scum who live rough, chop trees, sing drink and play the guitar. That's all. I can't wait to show the dirty *Ruska* just what we are actually made of!"

Guy chuckled. "Well you'll certainly be able to set matters straight my friend. You'll find that extremely satisfying I feel sure."

Gunari appeared thoroughly pleased and was quite obviously looking forward to confrontation with the Russians. He raised his hand and instantly one of the caravan doors opened.

"Good!" he said again. "Now we'll eat and finalise the more intricate details."

'He's certainly done this sort of thing before,' thought Guy admiring the Romany way of proceeding.

It had been an early start and they were all hungry; no doubt they'd be walking back with all their plans in place for the weekend and with their stomachs well filled. He grinned at Julian, happy in the knowledge that he was working with such a superb team. He'd just have to be careful that these new friends didn't get too carried away once they got their hands on the Russian soldiers. They must make for a hot-headed bunch: he needed to discuss this privately with Gustav who knew the Romany leader the best.

They left the encampment in the early afternoon to head back to the border at Narva, where a building had been allotted to them for the duration of the operation. Another meeting had been set up with the Roma leader for the next day, when communication equipment would be left for Gunari and his men. They could then liaise throughout the whole venture. Guy sent a further message to Jake telling him that they'd met with Gunari, that everything was in place for the next evening and to be prepared.

Later that night Jake managed to confirm back that once more he had received the message. All was ready. Now all they could do was wait and report back to HQ at home.

Guy intended to find out the latest movements of the others involved elsewhere; the girls, for instance, who always managed to discover a way of getting in on the act: whether intentionally or not he had yet to find out. He needed to speak to both Oliver and Marc, to assess how Ellie was faring. He'd been busy and no doubt there would be more updates since he'd last checked in.

❋

Irina sat by the fire, in her hunting lodge, wondering how the following night would unfurl. It would be dangerous, she knew, but she had confidence in her friends in the forest and also in her grandson with his crack team on the outside who, he informed her, had managed to liaise with Gunari. She just prayed that the treacherous Russian, Nikolai, would be back well in time for the party. She couldn't wait to be in command of her life once more and see that young man put firmly in his place. In fact, she found herself feeling more excited than she had for a very long time!

Jake on the other hand was worrying about how on earth he was going to keep Irina and her maid safe and out of the way of the inevitable skirmishes ahead. He knew that his old friend Gunari and his men were well up to outwitting the Russians but if only he felt better prepared himself inside the house. After all he had no weapon of any sort whatsoever to hand; there was merely a kitchen knife perhaps, which he had no way of either extracting from the drawer, where they used to be kept, or concealing on his person. A dash of something potent perhaps added to the pungent traditional drink would certainly do the trick. He would talk to Irina. She might well have sleeping pills in her bathroom cupboard and it would make matters a lot easier for everybody if they could at least slow down the soldiers in the house. It wouldn't work with Nikolai. He'd be too alert and most likely would prefer to drink Irina's excellent champagne, rather than the Romany's preferred plum brandy or Russian vodka. He'd likely have a fairly refined pallet, Jake thought.

Although anxious about the armed men in the house, Jake remembered the effect that the Romany dancers had made on him as an adolescent and even on Irina's male employees. The Russians really had no idea what they were in for. He glanced across at his grandmother sitting quietly beside the fire. She was smiling as she stared into the flames. The Russian guard were out of the room for the moment.

'My God my grandmother seems almost to be enjoying herself,' thought Jake with admiration and feeling a surge of adrenalin and the inevitable thrill of coming action at last. He was quite sure that his grandmother's hidden thoughts matched his own.

✻ ✻ ✻

CHAPTER 25

Painful Recognition
(Gstaad, Swiss Alps)

UP the mountain in the safe house Alicia sat Ellie down, wanting to make absolutely certain that she was feeling confident enough to do as she'd been asked; identify the young Russian Nicholai Peronovich.

"Yes, yes I want to do it. They have to get this man before he does something awful to somebody else. You'll all be there, so it will be fine… I only have to glimpse the bastard's face, just once, as I shall never forget his smarmy good looks or for that matter his voice, as I passed out."

Ellie frowned at the memory, then her face set determinedly as she listened to Alicia launch forth.

"Alright then! The plan is that we will be having dinner in a restaurant nearby and we stay put until we hear that the Russians are in the Castle Haute night club. Then we move. We meet Zak in the huge reception area of the hotel. By then he'll know exactly where the group are seated in the club. The two brothers don't dance; apparently they talk intensely to their father and appear just to be keeping an eye on their outrageously out of control sister. The family settle themselves at the same semi-circular corner table, which they book each night, mostly just to drink. There's quite a big seating area around the bar where the minders hang around at a discreet distance, away from their employer."

"Ok! That all sounds good," answered Ellie, quite enthusiastic now that they were to take some positive action.

"One last thing Ellie... Zak says for you to dress with care, preferably something dark and not too eye-catching! When giving me his instructions he also added... 'because Ellie is quietly captivating and could easily draw attention'. Those were his actual words!" Alicia watched Ellie's face as she tried to disguise her colouring cheeks. She couldn't resist adding quietly, "And I can see that you like him too." Then quickly, before Ellie could reply, "Come on then let's get dressed and get this thing done so that we can relax and have ourselves some fun!"

✳

They met as planned behind the hotel reception. Zak had commandeered a table where Ellie could sit facing away from people walking from the main hotel down into the night club.

Alicia and Rose had taken a lot of care in changing Ellie's hair and make-up. Nicholai had only seen her in an office suit with a completely different hairstyle, so it was unlikely that even up close and in the dark he'd recognise her after this transformation.

The Russian family were already occupying their habitual place in the night club. Oliver, after successfully insisting he was needed, was lurking over the far side of the room with the dance floor between him and the Russian group. He was so relieved that Zak had managed to arrange for him to be on hand, just in case anything should go wrong.

"I need to go to the washrooms before we go in," announced Ellie heading off to follow the discreet not far distant sign.

"I'll go with her." Alicia jumped up and they went off together. Zak moved to sit closer to Rose.

"Rose, please remember what I said when I briefed you and Alicia up in the mountains…" Rose immediately interrupted him.

"I know, it's alright Zak. We've done this sort of thing before, haven't we? So I know what to do. I'm to stay perfectly calm and to show no surprise whatever happens. I just hope that you have plenty of support around should anything backfire."

"It won't. I have two extra people in the night club and a car outside the nearest exit. Everything is covered." Rose waited, wondering if there was more. Zak was non-committal and wouldn't quite meet her eye.

As Alicia and Ellie were returning, Alicia suddenly saw the man with the limp who'd frightened Ellie so much at the station. He appeared from the direction of the men's washrooms at exactly the same time. It was inevitable that their paths would cross and there was nothing they could do about it.

Alicia leant to whisper quickly in Ellie's ear, to warn her. She looked startled, just for an instant, yet managed to pull herself together swiftly enough to laugh, as if they were enjoying a girl's joke together.

The Russian stopped politely letting Ellie cross in front of him. As he did so he looked at her with appraising eyes, said something, indicating where he was going, then moved on looking back once. The girls kept it together and answered, equally polite and smiling.

"I can't believe our luck," sighed Alicia as they regained their places on the sofa." She looked at Ellie. "I think that was the man at the station with the limp that startled you so much yesterday?"

"Yes," she answered. He must be a brother: They are so alike." She gave a little shiver, circled her shoulders and looked to Zak for guidance.

"Well done!" replied Zak looking intently at Ellie. "You did that very well indeed. What did he say?"

"He wanted us to join him in the night club of course," Alicia answered for her.

"Alright, stay here with Pieter. I just have a quick phone call to make. I won't be a minute." Zak picking up his mobile walked away to a quiet place in a bay with French windows. Olly picked up immediately.

"We have a problem." Zak spoke without hesitation.

"Already, what the fuck has happened?" Oliver couldn't believe that their carefully made plan was going awry almost before it started.

"The brother with the limp was here in reception and hit on Ellie. She handled it very well, but he'll be looking out for her in the night club." Olly felt a rush of adrenalin as he thought quickly.

"Right, if he starts to make a move, you be there, don't let Ellie move from your side, she's your girlfriend. Dance close with her so she can identify the other brother Nicholai, if you get the chance. I'll look after the other two but warn them before you come down. I don't want Rose to openly express astonishment at finding me here."

The phone went dead before Zak could reply. He turned around and walked back over to Pieter and the girls, trying to conceal his amusement. Olly was assuming command of this particular part of the operation. Zak understood, in Oliver's place he would have felt the same. Olly adored Rose, they had an especially close relationship. It was almost as if Rose knew to whom he'd been talking. How could she possibly know, Zak thought, taken aback. She couldn't possibly have heard any of the conversation, he was too far away. He sat down again and leaned over towards the others so that they could all hear what he had to say. He couldn't resist glancing at Rose first, before he began, giving her a discreet nod and a wink.

"Now listen well. There's someone down there who you both know; Rose in particular... you mustn't show how surprised you are to see him, just play it naturally." Turning to his brother, Zak continued, "Pieter stick close; Ellie you're with me as if we are, as I think you say in English, 'an item'. If it's possible for you to identify the man from a distance fine. If not don't worry we'll think of something else. But you must stay right beside me. Pieter walk with Rose and Alicia." Zak took Ellie's hand and felt a slight tremble in her fingers; he squeezed her hand in return.

"It's Olly, isn't it Zak?" Rose perked up, sitting very straight. "I know it's him downstairs, I can feel him near." Zak grinned.

"Yes, but remember, no surprise, you're here together on holiday, we all are, but I'm your off piste guide if anybody wants to know. Oliver will have found us a table in a good position. He's been down there a while so everything is organised."

"Can we go and get this over with then?" asked Alicia smoothing her blonde hair, standing up and straightening her skirt. She was feeling responsible and anxious about putting Ellie through yet another trauma, thought Zak, smiling at her and mouthing 'don't worry'.

"Yes, let's do that." Rose jumped up full of energy and trying, but failing, to damp down her excitement, her dark curls ruffled and her cheeks glowing pink not just from skiing all day. She looked great thought Zak, bubbling over in a cream silk top, with tight black jeans and high heels.

Olly was a lucky man. He turned to Ellie. "Ready?" he asked.

"Ready," she announced standing up, yet not letting go of his hand.

❆

As soon as they entered the night club Zak saw Oliver waving from the furthest corner and they went cheerfully forward to greet him, just as if they'd all been together earlier in the day.

The setting was perfect, crowded and dark, plenty of flamboyantly dressed girls, groups of people on holiday and the odd businessman relaxing.

Noisy, loud music, an exuberant atmosphere yet discreet enough should you want a dark corner to hide away. A waiter had followed them over to take any extra drink orders. Oliver already had a bottle of prosecco on ice for the girls and beer for the men, should they prefer it.

Alicia, Ellie and Zak all sat down on the half circular seating around the table. Rose couldn't wait to be in Oliver's arms again and insisted on taking him off to dance immediately. Pieter sat on the other side of Ellie and watched Rose and Olly take to the floor. Olly was whispering in her ear and Rose was laughing.

"Hello, my darling, now first and foremost I need your help. Without looking until I say, when we achieve the other side of the dance floor I want you to glance over towards the bar and the furthest table in the corner on the left. Then I want you to tell me exactly when you can get a good enough look at the two young men around that table to be able to identify the man we're after, if you were Ellie. Luckily they are both facing this way."

"Ok, I'll do my best, but how are you and how long have you been here for heaven's sake Olly? I knew you were near. I felt it as soon as we arrived."

"Later. Later I'll answer your questions, but first we want to get this job done and Ellie out of here," he whispered in her other ear. As they moved around closely together, the music had slowed to give everybody a breather. Olly knew he must disregard Rose's body straining against him.

"Behave!" he chuckled.

The clever lighting rotated slowly around the dance floor and Rose waited until it had passed over her to glance across at their target. The two men in question were talking animatedly to an older woman opposite them, perhaps she was their mother, who had her back to the dance floor. Rose got a good look at the men. As she turned back to Olly, one of the two suddenly got up and started to look around as if searching for someone.

"I can see both clearly from here but one of them has just got up. He's obviously looking for someone and is beginning to wander," Rose spoke softly. "He's the guy we saw at the station and just now in reception. The one with the limp. He might well have seen us come in."

"Right back to the table, to warn the others... just in case he's heading our way looking for one of you," answered Olly, noticing the man as he began to circle the dance floor. They arrived back at the table. Oliver quickly explained to Zak where the Russian family were seated.

"Rose could see well from the far side, just choose your timing with the lights. The one with the limp, we think he's headed this way so cosy up tight to Zak, Ellie!" Ellie leant in towards Zak while he put his arm around her whispering,

"It's Ok, don't worry, I'm here." He glanced sideways as the lights continued to beam their way around the raised wood stage casting a rainbow of colours over all the excited young faces." Yes, I see him and he is coming this way, probably to ask you to dance, so I shall beat him to it. Come on Ellie."

As they got to their feet and reached the floor with their arms already around each other the man arrived in front of them. He looked at Ellie with a question on his face. She smiled a polite 'hello' again as she began to glide away, enveloped in Zak's arms.

"Well done, that was just right, now let's get this thing done Ellie. I'm going to hold you very tight and move around the floor until you can get a good enough view of the brother. I'll tell you when... Ok?"

"Okay!" Ellie pressed her face up against Zak's reassuring soft stubble and held onto his hand, as tight as she was able, leaning into him for all she was worth. His other hand was around her waist, the music was slow as he guided her around the crowded dance-floor surreptitiously looking to where the conspicuous Russians were seated.

"About here, if you look towards the bar and to their table, which is the furthest left of the bar Ellie, that's where he is and he should be facing this way, talking to an older woman with very bright coloured hair. His father has cropped hair and is beside him, can you see where I mean?" Zak kissed her cheek tenderly. Her hand gripped him more tightly.

"Yes."

"It's Ok, the lights are just coming around again; now take your time and have a look if you can. Just one peek and you'll be able to tell."

Ellie leant a little to one side, looked and saw. Zak felt her tremble and kissed her again. Ellie responded by kissing him back, then whispered, "Yes, that's him. No doubt whatsoever. How could I ever forget that smarmy face?" She muttered, really trembling now. Zak held her firmly feeling a tear slide down her cheek as he pressed his face against hers.

"Right, well done, brave girl! We'll return slowly to the table, finish our drinks and get you out of here."

He turned her around so that she had her back to the bar once more and they worked their way around to their table. As they approached, to Zak's horror, the man with the limp was standing waiting for them. He stepped forward offering his hand politely to Zak and staring with open admiration at Ellie.

"Good evening, may I ask the lady to dance?" he asked in perfect English without trace of an accent.

Zak pulled Ellie to his side but answered for her, equally politely.

"I'm so sorry, please do forgive us, but my girlfriend isn't feeling too good, it's early days, she's having a baby and I think my darling…," he looked lovingly at Ellie, which wasn't at all difficult, "we do need to get you home."

Ellie slowly raised her free hand to her flat stomach saying with a sad sigh. "Yes, I'm afraid I do need to go home, otherwise of course I would have been pleased to dance with you; but thank you for asking me."

"My apologies," the immaculate man answered, "then I'll say goodnight and wish you both well."

Ellie noticed that the same false smile never reached another pair of the very coldest eyes. As he turned to leave they were fixed on Zak with a piercing glare of undisguised dislike. He glanced at Ellie one last time and moved off. The man wasn't used to being turned down thought Zak.

Ellie shivered and let out a relieved sigh. Her hand felt cold as ice. Shock, Zak concluded.

"Can we go?"

"Yes of course," still holding Ellie's hand, Zak taking back command, spoke quietly to the others.

"All done. I'll take Ellie back up. I suggest you all take your time to follow when you are ready." Turning to Rose he added, "I imagine you'll stay at the hotel now with Oliver?" Rose nodded enthusiastically. She wasn't about to let Olly out of her sight. Zak grinned.

"Ok, can you manage tonight without your things? I'll get them down to you first thing in the morning?"

"That'll be fine, thanks Zak, I have all that I need for tonight," she said looking longingly at Olly.

"Pieter will stay until you are ready Alicia, then he'll bring you back up to the farm. I'll see you there."

They went out hand in hand, with Ellie walking on the far side of Zak hidden from view from the bar and all its seated customers. Without speaking they retrieved their coats and left the hotel. The waiting car drew up outside. Zak helped the quivering Ellie into the back, jumped in after her and tucked her warm scarf more securely into the neck of her coat, leaving his arm protectively around her.

"*Es ist fertig,* all done," he said, to the driver.

They set off back to the lift. Job well done thought Zak thoroughly relieved, taking his mobile out when he was assured that Ellie was comfortable and no longer shaking. All it needed was one short sentence to his boss.

"Mission accomplished, exactly as we thought, identification affirmative."

Zak then concentrated on trying not to show his rising excitement at the prospect of having Ellie to himself for a while, far away up at the top of the mountain.

❄   ❄   ❄

CHAPTER 26

The Power Of Love
(Mountain safe house)

ELLIE didn't speak the whole way back up to the farm. She just nodded and smiled gently when Zak asked if she was Ok. The cable lift had once more been galvanized into action: it had remained open exceptionally late on this particular night, for Zak's enigmatic visitors about whom the attendants knew better than to ask questions. When they regained the snow-mobile at the top for the last part of the journey, Zak could feel Ellie's arms clasping ever tighter around him, trembling slightly as her body strained against his back as if she'd never let him go. Ellie had been much more frightened than she'd let on. Before they set off for the final run down to the farm in the hidden valley, Zak turned around and kissed her on the cheek.

"It's alright Ellie, you really are quite safe here with me. It's over. I won't let anybody harm you. That I can promise you."

She just kissed him back, then laid a bare hand on his cheek before putting her glove back on again. He understood what she was feeling, while Ellie could read the confirmation of his own thoughts in the dark pools of his eyes lit by a revealing moon as he had turned around. It was a bright cold night, particularly exhilarating for two people already in the throes of an adrenalin rush from the drama they'd just experienced. They left the snow-mobile under cover in the barn and trudged through the snow hand in hand to the house. 'This has nothing to do with Jake', thought Ellie shivering uncontrollably. 'I'm just so thankful to be alive and what I am feeling? It's just inevitable and natural. I have no intention of putting a stop to it.'

They removed their coats and boots, then Zak led Ellie over to the sofa by the fire. He sat her down then bent to attend to the fire. When he turned around, Ellie was sitting almost completely still, but he noticed she was still shivering. She wasn't cold now; he knew that. She was just watching him. As she raised her gaze to meet his, he stared deep into her huge dark navy blue eyes with a longing that he knew to be reciprocated. Then she smiled and stretched her arms out to him. For the first time in his life Zak was completely and utterly lost.

Zak was determined to be gentle; somehow to take it slowly. She'd been through so much. But as he began to kiss her face and neck Ellie's lips found his with an unexpected intensity. She drew him close until she was enveloped in his safe strong arms. He could see the fluttering pulse in her throat exaggerated by desire; he smiled as he laid her back against the cushions, while she lifted her arms for him to remove her dress. Then she wriggled out of the rest of her clothes pulling a bright coloured rug off the back of the sofa around her. Her slight figure was perfection, as he knew it would be.

Ellie watched as Zak removed his clothes then lay down full length beside her, stroking her body with meticulous care. How could somebody so strong and brave be so gentle, yet she knew this was how it would be. Ellie pushed Jake to the back of her mind. She'd never wanted anyone so much as this man, almost a stranger yet he saw into her very soul. The sexual undercurrent had been there from the very beginning. Instantaneous, it had been; now the strength of that attraction would not be denied. She'd lived through an horrific ordeal; fright seemed to have merely heightened her yearning. Extreme emotion mingled with the physical anticipation was beyond them both. There was no awkwardness, just an immediate understanding of each other's needs.

Zak moved over her, reading her open and honest invitation. Without preamble he gently entered her hidden depths, staring into her eyes drinking in the shining, emotive affection he saw firmly reflected there, together with the urgent desire. Giving himself completely and utterly, savouring every moment, Zak took her with him up to the summit of that powerful, surging tidal force. Then, relishing its glory for an exquisite unstoppable moment, they spiralled together over that ultimate pinnacle of no return, down together into the rippling pulsating waves of sensual abandonment. In the aftermath of ecstasy, as their breathing and heart rate began to steady, they lay together unable to speak, yet revelling in the magic and rejoicing in the luxurious wonder of it all.

✼

By the time Alicia and Pieter appeared back Zak had tucked Ellie up in her own room and left her, promising to return when the others had gone to bed and the house was quiet. She was sated and peaceful after their lovemaking but exhausted from the identification mission in the town. He could hardly bear to leave her.

"That was wonderful Zak," Ellie whispered, "as I knew it would be. Thank you for keeping me safe. I have never experienced anything like that just now. No matter what happens to us in the future I shall always cherish tonight." Her face was flushed and her eyes were swimming with barely contained tears. She sighed contentedly, turned over and was asleep almost before he'd left the room.

Zak had then settled down beside the fire with the dog and a book to await for the others to return. An hour or so later he heard the snow-mobile arriving. Alicia bounced in. She was in a high state of excitement; Pieter had let her drive. She looked beautiful and exhilarated, with her blonde hair and glowing cheeks. They had accomplished what they'd set out to do.

"That all went so well Zak. I'm very glad and so relieved for everyone. Now tomorrow we can have some fun. How is Ellie?" she asked, Zak just managed to stop himself from saying 'Ellie is wonderful!'

"She's alright, very pleased it's over I think; tired of course but asleep by now I imagine." Zak's brother Pieter looked at him quizzically.

"You're looking very relaxed, were you asleep as well?" he asked with a distinct twinkle in his eye."

"Well, yes I might have nodded off I suppose, it's been a long day, but a successful one. Now you're back I'll let the dog out and get to bed."

Zak rose to his feet yawning and went to the door with Merida at his heels. The dog ran out and he stared out after her, at a perfect moonlit night with the stars appearing to shine brighter than he'd ever noticed before. He had never fallen hopelessly and helplessly in love. He wondered where this mystical dawning romance, which had so suddenly overwhelmed him, would take them both. There was Jake to consider. Ellie lived in another country. Zak's natural inclination was to let things alone for the present and relish the union of two like minds: what will be will be. This house at the top of the mountains and under the stars would now always hold the most treasured memory. Whatever the future, nothing could change or spoil what had happened between himself and Ellie this evening, even if it was to be a once in a lifetime shared secret.

Merida came back in wagging her tail as if in agreement. Zak locked up, saw the dog to her bed and made his way upstairs. As he walked past Ellie's room he saw that she had left the door very slightly ajar. She must have woken when she heard the others come in. He waited until he was sure that the others had settled, then quietly made his way back down the passage to Ellie. Zak was determined that the rest of the night was yet to be savoured, whatever the future might hold. They must make the very best of their time together. Memories to make which might have to last them a lifetime.

* * *

CHAPTER 27

Compiling Evidence
(Glencurrie Manor, Scotland)

MARC went across to the gamekeeper's bothy first thing in the morning. Hamish had cleaned his gun and polished his brogues meticulously, as he did every morning and was now busy making tea. When at home he always made the tea. He said his wife Bridget couldn't make tea or porridge properly because she wasn't a true Scot, only half. Her father's family came from the other end of the British Isles, Devon farmers they were, a county best for its dairy herds and scones with clotted cream, he would say, with a chuckle.

At present Bridget was away in Inverness to see their children. Marc was sorry to miss her but laughed to himself: Nothing would ever change Hamish's early morning routine. It had always been the same. He smiled as he approached the ancient cottage to greet his loyal friend and confidant since childhood. The man who'd taught him to shoot straight, to understand, enjoy and respect the wild Scottish Highlands with it's indigenous animals and birds. The man who had covered for many youthful misdemeanours.

He stepped through the open door which was never shut in the daytime. Fergus, the old dog, came straight to him wagging its tail with pleasure. Hamish looked up from what he'd been doing at the kitchen table and his eyes lit up with delight. He looked just the same Marc thought, comforting and dependable in his solid sturdiness; with his soft red beard and twinkling blue eyes. A man who didn't look right in anything other than a kilt, tweed cap and jacket above his pair of heavy brogues.

"Marc, hullo, guid mornin'! I heard you were coming and wondered when you'd be up for a blether." Hamish ambled over to Marc grasping his hand, giving him the usual bear hug. As always, the older man was happy to see his protégé. "I was just seeing to the guns in case you wanted to come awa' with me up the hill."

"Hello Hamish, it's good to see you too, it's been far too long and yes I'd love to come out with you, but first I need to ask about these tenants of yours that are causing such problems at the lodge." Hamish put the gun down and with his big hands now in his pockets turned to face Marc.

"Ay the situations naw guid, I'm that worried for the Colonel."

"Yes we need to get rid of these people, they're obviously bad news, or at least one of them is. They've overstayed their welcome. As you know Hamish, there are new people renting the house shortly. What can you tell me about the young man who shot the stag out of season?" Marc stepped back to half sit on the heavy table on which he'd always perched as a child.

"Ay he's the one that's a bad lot. The family members are naw so bad, quiet and polite, quite gentlemanly; but that one... there was something about him. I can't put my wee finger on exactly what it was that raised my hackles, dae ye ken?" Marc couldn't help but smile at the thought of Hamish having a 'wee' finger!

"Tell me about the actual shooting incident."

"The boy's a fair shot right enough, too guid I'd say as, in his well-schooled English, he admitted to me that he'd had no teaching in the actual sport. So, he must have learnt to shoot in a very different environment; if it wasn't for sport, then I dare not think what that activity might be.

We'd had a difficult stalk after the hinds, with the deteriorating weather and mist. Even if it had been the right time of year and with all my experience, I wouldn't have taken that shot to the stag myself. But given the lad's disability, he still shot it clean through the heart. In no way could it have been a mistake as he knew full well we were only after hinds and that it was too late for the stags. There's no avoiding it… come what may he meant to have that beast."

"Right," said Marc. "Well, he'll have to come back to face the music and I'll have to somehow persuade his host to help. I don't suppose you have any idea where the young man flew off to, have you Hamish?"

"Ah dinnae ken, but he did say something about skiing with his family, though how he'd do that with the disability I canno' imagine."

"What was the matter with him?"

"A bad limp, after an accident he told me."

"Well that's all very helpful Hamish, thank you. But don't you worry I'm going to get that young man checked out. First I'll go and see what the diplomat's family have to say about the incident."

"Guid, their English isn't so guid mind and the Mrs is a nervous creature; you'll see. The son has been well educated also, he seems a nice lad and I canno' think what he was about befriending the other youngster. Noo two peas in a pod those two, dae ye ken?"

Marc gave Hamish a reassuring pat on the shoulder and changed the subject to ask about his family.

After finishing his mug of tea and a couple of Bridget's excellent shortbread biscuits from the same aged old tin, Marc set off for his uncle's lodge determined to set matters right after this latest upset with the Russian tenants. Alec deserved a trouble-free retirement. He'd led a busy fairly fraught life, sometimes working undercover for the protection of the country he loved. Losing his wife some years earlier had been a tragic event after which he had worked even harder at his clandestine job. Although he was now an older man, his instincts were still spot on and Marc was more than ever resolved to get to the bottom of his present predicament.

Hamish's sister Catriona opened the door to his knock.

"Och Marc it's good to see you. Come in." She opened the door wide and then hurried him around the corner towards the kitchen. Once the door was shut she turned to him. "Have you seen Hamish?"

"Yes Cat," he answered, using the pet name he'd used as a boy. "I have seen Hamish, so I'm up to date with what's been going on."

Catriona loved any form of gossip or excitement and always made sure that she was on the front line of events. Her cheeks were pink like rosy apples from the cold Scottish air and her soft brown hair wavy as ever. But Marc could see just a suspicion of white appearing at her temples and her figure was definitely just a little more robust since last they'd met.

"Ay but there's a wee bit more to tell." She was almost whispering. Marc looked uncertainly towards the door. "Dinna fash, don't you worry. I've just taken more coffee in; they won't be moving from the room just yet. Now," she clutched Marc's arm, "listen to me: there have been many phone calls of late, some in a foreign language, Russian I believe, Luka also makes calls in English and I made sure that I could hear a wee bit, when the hoover wasn't too busy of course," she added with twinkling eyes. "Do you want to know where I think that wretched young devil went?" Cat paused for effect.

"Well go on then Cat don't keep me in suspense. Where do you reckon he's hiding out? What exactly have you found out with your sleuthing?"

"He's in the Swiss Alps, that's where he is and I think it will be in one of those beautiful posh places." Her eyes took on a faraway look. "Where all the stars hang out on the street as well as in the sky and people go around in horse drawn sleighs." She sighed as she returned from being transported into another world. "But that young man has too much money for places where people are sophisticated and discreet, he'll stick out like a sore thumb alongside all the proper smart people. He was always showing off and flashing his fifty-pound notes around. There that's what I think," she finished importantly; the intrigue making her cheeks even pinker and her eyes shining ever brighter.

Switzerland! Marc felt a sudden lurch of alarm. Good grief Catriona was probably right. He needed to get this latest information checked out fast.

"Ok Cat! Agatha Christie would be thrilled with you! You've been a great help: Now can you introduce me to the family in the sitting room?" Cat grinned with pleasure.

"Right then Marc, my bonny boy, I'll announce you, then show yer in." She began to march off then stopped to turn around pointing her finger at him, "And ask Adriana and Emma to come up to see me when they can; mind you, tell Emma to bring pictures of those bairns of yours as well." She strode off again purposely, down the passage and into the hall, with Marc almost running to keep up.

The Russian diplomat spoke reasonable English. He was well-dressed and appeared quite mild in manner. But once the polite introductory niceties were achieved he managed to manoeuvre things so that whenever Marc asked a key question he made out that he couldn't understand.

The son, in his mid-twenties, spoke very well and was both good looking and polite. Yet every time he tried to help his father answer, he was shut up immediately with a very diplomatic wave of one hand. This silenced the boy: Marc would have especially liked to interview him, as he appeared friendly and might have proved more helpful than his father.

The supposedly 'frail' mother merely sat with her feet on a stool, her legs covered with a cashmere blanket, silently sniffing into a lace handkerchief. She was attractive in a rather delicate way, composed and far more alert than she appeared. Mikael diplomatically apologised for his wife being slightly indisposed.

Marc tried several times to obtain the information he needed but with no success. He was aware that his questions, when repeated and translated into Russian by Luka, were continually being met with no positive response. He wondered how it would be discussed once he'd left the room. He had to be firm for his uncle's sake. So, he addressed Luka one last time.

"Luka, if your father doesn't understand, will you please explain again what I have to say. It is important. I know that your father, as a diplomat living in the UK, will want to do the correct thing. Nobody wants a fuss or bother about this incident but your friend, whoever he is and wherever he is, needs to come back here. He has to deal with some straight-forward legal procedures regarding the illegal shooting of the stag, out of season, off this estate. Unfortunately, as my uncle is the local magistrate, this has to be done properly as otherwise it means more trouble with a police investigation which will involve everybody and could be extremely embarrassing for both your Dad and my uncle. The local police won't just let up and let the crime go unpunished, however small a matter your father may consider it to be. So, I really do need to know of your friend's whereabouts and his family name."

Marc waited studying the expressions of both Luka's father and mother, as what he had said was being translated. Marc was quite sure that Mikael understood much more than he let on, after all if he was a diplomat, he would have to be able to speak pretty good English. The man was playing for time. As Luka appeared to emphasize certain points, his father looked on, at first politely disinterested, then wary, then finally slightly annoyed, saying something which sounded quietly dictatorial and conclusive to his son. The aloof wife sipped at a glass of water shaking her head without speaking as she continued to flip through a glossy magazine. Luka looked rattled. Turning to Marc he stood up straight and apologised for the language problem which Marc felt to be exaggerated. The diplomat understood perfectly well what was at stake. Of that Marc felt quite sure.

"My father says that he is very sorry for what has happened and is happy to pay for the stag and to compensate for any misunderstanding and extra expense. But my friend comes from an important family and is reluctantly forbidden by his father to return to this country at present. His good name also has to be protected. That's all I'm afraid." Luka finished, appearing rather embarrassed and avoiding looking anymore towards his stern faced father. He merely glanced at his mother, then down at his feet.

"Thank you Luka. Please tell your father that sadly this situation isn't just resolved by money. I also have important contacts who will be called upon if necessary. I have no more to say at present, but I suggest you all return to London as soon as possible as my uncle has new tenants arriving, as I am sure you are aware. I do of course know where to find you. I wish you all a safe journey and I'll be in touch, most likely through your embassy. I'm sorry to have met in such unfortunate circumstances. Good day."

Marc went across to shake the diplomat's hand. Oddly enough the man had a good firm grip and an unexpectedly warm smile which lit his face with a glimpse of concealed humour. Luka walked with Marc to the door, where he held out his own hand saying quietly,

"I am so sorry for all this mess. I never liked Oleg; he was stupid to shoot the stag. He was a bully at school and the accident to his leg was all his own fault. Your uncle, Hamish and Catriona have been very kind. If I had my way I'd like to settle and live here. I also apologise for not being able to say anything else, but it is more than my life is worth to give you extra information. I hope you understand. I am hoping that my mother and I can persuade my father to return to London in the next day or two so that we cause no further trouble."

"Thank you, Luka. I do understand how difficult it must be for you. I wish you luck and a happy future. Feel free to get in touch should you ever have the need." Marc handed over his details; the boy stuffed the card in his pocket, gave a little bow and fled.

As Marc walked back to Glencurrie and his uncle he was thoughtful. Luka, the poor boy, was trapped in an impossible world. Particularly difficult after living here in the West, for a private education, away from all the obvious constraints of a communist country. However, he had enough information now to check out both the family and Luka's elusive friend, Oleg with the significant limp. He must be found. Things were on the move; he was looking forward to another quiet chat with Alec but first he'd get the investigative checks in motion. He wondered, not for the first time, if pushed, these people would claim diplomatic immunity. He imagined they would, yet he felt there was something just a little puzzling about Mikael.

To where exactly in the Swiss Alps had the young man absconded? Was the elusive young Russian holed up somewhere just too close for comfort? No! Surely not where the girls were now based? There were plenty of other smart ski resorts in Switzerland. Nevertheless, he felt a twinge of apprehension and an uncanny but very real sense of 'déjà vu'.

❄ ❄ ❄

CHAPTER 28

A Double
(Glencurrie)

EMMA sat opposite Adriana, pretending to read the paper. Adriana was intent on some baby book and busily making notes. Later they were all going to the pub for lunch to give Mrs Haddington a bit of a break from the kitchen. Marc had gone to see the Russian tenant; after which he'd be looking in on Alec to tell him about the meeting. So, Emma and her close friend were quite alone, sitting in the unexpected sunshine in the conservatory.

Adriana had always put on a brave face in times of difficulty, as she was doing now. It must be hard having Julian away on some secret mission when she was getting close to the end of her pregnancy, but she seemed to have absolute faith in Marc's ability to cope, should the twins arrive early. Apart from their being friends, they obviously had a good doctor patient relationship. Emma couldn't really imagine having such a close male friend involved in the birth of her children. He was taking such good care of Adriana; she'd noticed Marc studying her friend closely sometimes when Adriana seemed unaware. If if wasn't for the fact that her husband was a doctor and Adriana was now huge, Emma couldn't help but feel just a tiny bit anxious about their obvious closeness. Just a tiny twinge of jealousy perhaps, which she thought was ridiculous and quite uncalled for. After all they were such good friends and had been through much together in the past. Nevertheless, Emma couldn't help but hope that these babies took their time to put in an appearance, waiting till they were all safely back home in London with Julian.

Adriana smiled to herself as she felt a kick and then another. She sat up straighter and gently placed her hand on the protruding bump with a little pressure until it withdrew and settled again. Emma, sitting in the window seat on the far side of the room, seemed deep in the newspaper, so Adriana indulged in the happiest of memories from the last time they were all up here together in the Highlands.

Never in her wildest dreams had she even considered that she'd come back from that particular holiday with not one but two babies on board. Now here she was just waiting and longing for her children to appear. They were, she'd been told, well grown and on schedule for their due date, three weeks away yet. She'd assured her friends that it was unlikely to happen for at least a month and they were bound to be late, otherwise Emma would never have let her travel North with them.

Adriana's gynaecologist had actually said the opposite, that he thought they'd come early which was often the case with twins. He saw no reason why she shouldn't have a perfectly normal delivery as the little ones were already in a good position. But she was healthy and well and he'd been quite happy for her to travel up North, by car or train, with a doctor friend in the party. In the unlikelihood of a complication he had even given her the name of a gynaecologist in Inverness who happened to have been to Edinburgh university with Marc. In the Highlands, helicopters were well used to transporting women in labour, stuck out in the back of beyond in mid-winter, to hospital. It was well organised and took no time at all by air.

So, Adriana felt quite content to have told her friends a few fibs and was perfectly at ease with the whole situation. Secretly she would have loved to have given birth up here with Marc in attendance. She had absolute faith and trust in his ability and knew that he would feel more than privileged to take on the task. Julian was away, involved in some devious secret operation, no doubt, but Adriana sat back, knowing that there was no point in worrying about him. With Marc here, alert to her every need, Adriana felt well and truly comforted. She looked up to find Emma, having relinquished the paper, watching her with obvious amusement.

"Are you uncomfy? Are the little darlings having a wee punch up?" Emma asked, grinning.

"Yes, amazing isn't it, the way you can gently push back a foot or a knee. Sometimes I wonder if they are going to be born fighting! It's exhausting!"

"I know, it's these last weeks when you just long to go into labour and get them out; once you know that they're 'cooked' so to speak! But they're not due yet Arri and I'd rather you wait until you are safe home with Julian, if you don't mind!" Emma said without thinking. "Seriously though, do you feel that they might be getting near? I did wonder about the journey. It might have just hurried things along a bit?"

"No, they're fine, just a bit rampant, at present. Anyway, with your husband, the good doctor watching my every move, I'm not in the least bit anxious." She looked across at Emma. "I bet he was brilliant when the girls arrived, wasn't he?"

"Yes, he couldn't have been better, but really Julian needs to be back so I say just hang in there a bit longer!" Emma laughed. "Come on then Arri, let's get ready for the pub. I have no doubt you're starving again and I said we'd meet Marc and Alec there."

As she got up Adriana did feel a twinge, was it the babies or was it something else? A certain look from Emma which left her feeling just a little uneasy. No, she was being paranoid; she wasn't going to worry as Emma couldn't possibly know. Nobody knew. Nobody except Marc, of course, her temporary doctor; only he knew of her most private and innermost secret.

❋

Marc put his head around the door to see Alec sitting at his desk deep in thought, his elbows on the leather blotting pad and his hands steepled under his chin. He raised his eyes to the door as Marc knocked and entered.

"Come in, come in; sit down Marc. I know you have been up at the lodge, but brace yourself my boy for I've just had a call from an old friend in London." Marc looked at Alec with interest. The man could quite obviously hardly contain himself. He was like he'd been in days gone by, literally, alight with excitement. Marc was impatient to hear the news his uncle had to impart.

"Let's hear it from you first then," was all he said.

"Alright, are you ready for this as it will be a shock to say the least?" Alec's eyes were sparkling.

"Go ahead!"

"Right then... the diplomat, Mikael... he's a double and he's one of ours!"

"Good Lord! And neither of us had the slightest idea. But why on earth didn't they warn you when he first came up here?"

"Because the man had an agenda."

"I suppose that agenda has something to do with the son's unlikely friend who shot the wretched stag and then scarpered, most likely to Switzerland?" Marc prompted.

"Yes, how did you guess?" Alec raised an eyebrow before continuing, "I have a feeling that matters everywhere are going to suddenly converge." Marc sat for a minute realizing that his uncle probably knew as much as he did, if not more. So he decided to update him on the information he had regarding the girls in the Alps.

"Alec, I suppose you know that the girls, Alicia, Rose and our young friend Ellie, who you haven't met, are all in Switzerland? But they're safe in the capable hands of Zak, a reliable colleague of both Guy and Julian. Actually I have already ordered checks on the diplomat's family and the sons friend called Oleg. It's only a matter of time before we find out exactly where he is."

"I already know where he's gone and where the operation centre appears to be at the moment. It's as you suspected, Switzerland and as you say the girls are, once more, right there in the middle of it all. But this time, I am reliably informed, their journey and location was intentional."

"I suspected that. When I set up their travel plans, my guy, behind the scenes, seemed more than happy for them to go to the mountains. He said something about it being the best and most helpful place for Ellie to be. I asked what he meant exactly by 'helpful' and I was palmed off, 'Oh that was just a turn of phrase' was all he said. It had appeared to be Alicia's idea to go there in the first place! I felt it impulsive and wondered at the time, if someone else altogether had suggested it and she'd been told to keep it quiet."

Alec went on to tell Marc all that he'd just been told. The diplomat had been lying low in Scotland. He had been given the job, with Luka's help, to get to know his son's classmate, from the boys' days together at university and to find out everything possible about his family. Luka had been reluctantly persuaded to invite the young man for a visit. Alec paused for a moment to let Marc absorb all this information before once more fixing Marc with a meaningful stare.

"Not only is Oleg's family of great interest to the SIS but the girls, particularly Ellie, also have an extremely important role to play out there in the Swiss mountains."

"Oh my God," was all that Marc could reply.

❅ ❅ ❅

CHAPTER 29

Friday
(Irina's Estonian Estate)

IRINA busied herself with the arrangements for the evening's entertainment. She was well aware of what had been planned. Unbeknown to their captors Jake had been in constant touch with his colleagues outside: he'd managed to get messages both in and out on his concealed mobile, now hidden under the floorboards, in the bathroom next to his bedroom. Irina thought that he was acting his part, portraying merely an anxious and caring grandson, exceptionally well. He was certainly fully trained in the covert world. She felt extremely proud.

Irina knew that she must make sure that everything appeared to be going ahead normally for this yearly event. Secretly she had to admit to herself that she was rather enjoying being involved in the clandestine drama as life, over the last few years, had become quite mundane. She considered the Russian officers in the house; they were all of retirement age she thought and hopefully past their tendencies to violence, probably relishing such an easy job. She wondered if they actually knew what their superiors were up too; possibly not. It was only the young man, Nicolai, of whom they had to be very wary. He was a man of another calibre altogether, as were the soldiers outside. They were of a different class, no question about that, she'd seen them through the window; focused and efficient, menacing even, with frighteningly up to date weaponry by the looks of it. But luckily those outside were not their problem. Inside the house Irina knew that her imminent future prospects were in the hands of Jake and his capable colleagues, somewhere out there in the vicinity in her deep dark forest. Jake had assured her that the whole operation, both inside and out, was meticulously well coordinated.

Along all the Estonian borders and vast coastal regions Jake had told her that movements were being well monitored. Many nations had secretly responded to the delicate situation. The US 2nd fleet was in the Baltic, where it had been for some time because of ongoing provocation by the Russians. Goodness only knew what intimidating sea power lurked beneath the water. Nato's Air Ops centre on Uedem was on high alert, ready to provide surveillance, air defence and backup. The multi-national ground forces along the borders were also all on standby. These troops had been deployed to counter the risk that the Russians might make another attempt to invade Estonia.

Irina's little Estonian maid who had bought all the supplies across from the house, was in a state of complete disarray, poor girl. She was absolutely terrified of the Russian soldiers in the house and couldn't understand what was happening: Irina was having a difficult time calming her down. Although it was an extraordinary predicament in which they all found themselves, Irina knew that she must remain focused while keeping the evening's plan for their deliverance to herself. Her maid would never be able to control her nervousness if she got an inkling of what was really going to happen.

Irina did feel rather in her element: after all she had always known that it was only a matter of time until the Russians made another move on her beloved Estonia and her country wouldn't have it; not if she had anything to do with it. She had complete and utter confidence in those outside the house and in her own grandson, now intent on employing the soldiers to help move some heavy furniture around to make room for the dancing. They were doing as they'd been asked, but with a certain amount of grunting and heavy breathing. Irina chuckled to herself: Jake was managing to manipulate them very well indeed; little did the men know what they faced later on.

In spite of the strange situation Jake had achieved a reasonably friendly relationship with two of the officers. The third man, Colonel Bobrinsky, seemed a little more suspicious and ill at ease, even though at times his compatriots tried to reassure him. Jake himself gave the impression of a resigned calmness. Eventually they all seemed to be entering into the spirit of preparations for the evening, just as Jake intended; they'd finally given up playing cards.

Periodically Colonel Bob, as Jake privately referred to the man with the most pips on his shoulder, went outside to smoke and to see what the Russian special force soldiers were up to. Each time he let in a draught of freezing air which irritated Irina to such an extent that she let out an obscene oath making the other two men smirk, yet nod in agreement, if they happened to hear.

Jake also took the opportunity to glance outside whenever he could. There were two light tanks and two army vehicles, left some distance away, in a clearing off the drive. This had been confirmed by his colleagues. The two jeeps immediately outside the building hadn't moved since they'd arrived earlier in the week. Judging by the young soldier's radio equipment uniform and weaponry, Jake knew them to be men from a special reconnaissance counter force, part of the highly trained Russian *Spetsnaz*. He'd recognized their uniform and had already relayed this info to Guy. His friends needed to know approximate numbers and what type of opposition they faced.

It must have seemed an easy task for the mature Russian soldiers, being ordered inside on a cold winter's day; with hot drinks made available and put in charge of a harmless old woman, her amenable civilian grandson and one terrified maid. Jake had to smother a grin; nobody else had any idea of the capabilities of his grandmother. As a small boy Jake had once seen her take on a would-be burglar. The man had run for his life, pursued by an irate Irina brandishing a scalding hot fire iron. Also, although his appearance was somewhat hidden underneath his grandfather's ill-fitting clothes, Jake himself was fit as a fiddle after training with the best. The two elder guards in the house and their senior officer wouldn't be a problem. Two had a tendency towards fat and Colonel Bob was obviously too fond of his vodka. The man had a small flask in his pocket and Jake had noticed it's constant use. Their weapons had been discarded and left on the hall table. They weren't expecting any trouble.

The young men outside were a different bunch altogether, lean and aggressive, armed with modern weaponry including submachine guns. But Guy would have every eventuality well covered by now: he also had the very latest equipment and a force of silent stealthy men, used to both jungle warfare and extreme cold. They would be more than capable of silencing the military group, before the alarm could be sound. They were trained to operate in every type of territory and climate. Jake's main task and concern was Nicolai.

Irina's maid, Renata appeared at Jake's side for reassurance as much as for practical matters, he decided. The girl had a mere smattering of English, but Jake couldn't be heard to speak Estonian.

"Renata, don't worry it will be alright," he whispered quickly, then louder to catch the Russians attention, "why don't you get our friends here something hot to drink?" He gesticulated with his hands. "They've been working hard moving all the furniture around." Irina stood up and rubbed her back.

"Good idea," Irina called. "I'll have some tea too Renata and bring some of that cherry cake as well, we can all have a piece." Renata scuttled away, looking surprised that her employer should be offering her cake to the dreadful Russians. They in turn merely smirked and saluted their thanks.

The tea arrived and Jake noted the unapproachable Colonel once more surreptitiously adding his own tipple to his mug. The other two were seemingly uncomfortable and inexperienced finding themselves in such opulent surroundings, but they obviously appreciated the tea. Jake realised that he must keep working at making them feel relaxed. He glanced at his watch, still no sign of the elusive Nicolai. It was imperative that he return for this mission to be successful. Whilst waiting, in between sips of his tea and mouthfuls of cake, with as much camaraderie as he could muster, Jake set about describing the Romanian dancers and their attributes in the hope of putting all three Russians at their ease.

*

Meanwhile outside in the forest Gunari with his men, the British special ops force and Maksim with his team, were all ready to go. For once it had stopped snowing. They were merely waiting for the woman and the musicians to don their traditional gear.

The men sat around the fire drinking the hot acrid coffee; then two elderly women brought out a large carpet and spread it on the ground as one after another the gypsy girls appeared from the caravans. All had alluring, voluptuous figures, with long silky black hair and beautifully made-up faces. They were moulded into wonderfully bright coloured dresses cut seductively low at the neck. The newly arrived group of men couldn't help but stare. The girls hurried to cover themselves in the cold, throwing thick shawls around their bodies, whilst slipping their feet into high warm boots.

Suddenly Guy sensed someone behind him and spun around. One of the girls had crept up behind him and was standing theatrically graceful, absolutely still with her hands hiding her face. She lowered her arms and to Guy's astonishment he found he was gazing into the beautiful smiling face of his air hostess Katya, made up and in traditional dress. She was absolutely gorgeous.

"Katya! Good heavens! What on earth are you doing here?" he exclaimed. Gunari answered for her.

"Katya is my niece and she is part of my team. She trained in these forests and remembers Jake. She is my crown jewel. She is essential to this mission. This young Russian Nicolai won't stand a chance... he is her target." Guy was speechless.

"I had to do something to help, poor Jake," Katya explained. "Luckily he didn't remember me on the plane, but we played together here in these forests as children." She laughed and added, "I was also a little plumper then!"

"Well I have to say I am suitable stunned." Julian appeared equally astonished as Guy leant forward and kissed his airhostess on both cheeks. "It's wonderful to see you again Katya, but..." he looked towards Gunari who gave another of his deep rumbling belly laughs.

"Don't you worry my friend, Katya is very able to take care of herself. She has a job to do. She can dazzle any man and she knows exactly what is at stake, so have no fear for her. She has won many awards for her dancing, we do need her tonight and she will employ all her talents."

"Well, all I can do is say 'Aitäh'... thank you both and all your people, what more can I say?"

"It's nothing, there's no need," Gunari got up to pat Guy's shoulder and kiss his niece on the cheek. He introduced Katya to Julian; then she greeted Maksim with another dazzling smile before sitting down quietly beside her guardian to listen. He grinned happily. Guy could see that Gunari was in his element.

"Come, let's go over everything one last time."

✳

An early ural owl flew across the clearing calling to its mate, somewhere from within the forest depths. Julian felt a slight sense of foreboding which he determinedly shook off. For a fleeting moment Adriana and the unborn babies came to his mind, as she was nearing her time. But thoughts of home must now be banished, so he threw himself back into work mode as he'd been taught. Nothing more needed to be said; each and every one of them knew exactly what they needed to do. The timings had been sequenced. The night was drawing in, Julian checked his watch once more and nodded as Guy caught his eye. Guy had received Jakes message confirming Nicolai's arrival. The Russians outside had removed themselves from sight. Everybody was ready. The dye was caste. It was time.

✳

The musicians and dancers, with Guy and Julian in their midst, were to enter the lodge first. They would be looking no different from the others and would slip in to take their places at the back of the room, well concealed from the audience. At the appointed time, when the enemy would be distracted by the music, with support from above,

239

Maksim and his special task group would take out the contingent of Russians in the clearing outside. The operation would commence at seven o'clock precisely. Gustav was to arrive at the Hunting Lodge half an hour earlier.

❊

Gustav sipped at his whisky as he changed for the evening. He couldn't wait to see Irina, to see with his own eyes that she'd come to no harm at the hands of the boorish Russians. Despite a predictably violent evening ahead, he was also looking forward to seeing Jake again and how he handled himself in these present dire circumstances. He'd been a mere boy when last they'd met and now he was part of this English special force: It was hard to take in, but Gustav wasn't surprised; as a child Jake had always been mature for his age, strong-minded and keen on physical fitness. Gustav was very fond of Irina's grandson. They'd kept in touch over the years, communicating mostly by email and by telephone when Gustav was with Irina.

Gustav looked at himself in the old mirror in his bedroom. This evening he had to handle things to the very best of his ability. Whilst Jake concentrated on the young Russian Nicolai, his job was to keep Irina out of harm's way. This he would do, at any cost, for he had loved this woman since their very first meeting many years before and, no matter how old they both were now, that would never change.

❊ ❊ ❊

CHAPTER 30

Apprehension
(The Highlands)

ADRIANA felt a strange dropping sensation to her lower stomach. Realisation dawned with the unfamiliar shifting of weight pressing under her diaphragm to her pelvic region. 'Great! The little tykes are getting into position.' She hadn't dared let on that she was actually only a couple of weeks from her due date, not several as the others all thought. What's more, at her last scan she had been told that the babies were big and were very likely to be early. As she wanted to have them naturally it would be better for her if they were! Anyway, there was no point in worrying. She knew from her reading about the whole birthing process that the babies could drop a while before they were born. Emma looked up from the opposite sofa and noticed Adriana's grimace as she changed position uncomfortably.

"What's wrong Arri, are you feeling Ok?"

"Yes! yes, don't worry: there's just a bit of a war going on. They're bound to be boys!" Adriana laughed, "Maybe it would be better if we knew, then at least I could have bought some blue or pink baby clothes instead of all this white or cream coloured stuff!"

"I know, but actually it is more fun not to know. Let's go up and have a bath before dinner: you could have a bit of a lie down. You didn't have a proper rest today and you do look a bit pale. Marc will soon be back from filling up the car. He says he needs another session with Alec before dinner, so we have plenty of time. They do seem to be meeting privately a lot those two, don't they?"

Emma was sure that there was something more going on that they didn't know about. But she didn't want to worry her friend in her vulnerable condition. Adriana hauled herself up.

"Marc's very fond of his uncle, isn't he?"

"Yes, he is. I suppose that's it. They just have a lot of catching up to do, as well as the fact that Marc wants to help Alec get rid of the tenants who seem to be a bit of a problem."

"Yes, that's most likely what is taking so much of their time. Ok then, I'll go and put my feet up for a bit then have a good soak; though I have to say that I have plenty of energy today and don't feel nearly so lethargic as I have been!"

Emma studied her friend as she waddled off towards the door. Adriana did look heavier than ever and she could have sworn that the shape of her tummy had changed. She did look ready to drop the babies at any minute. 'Oh Heavens!', thought Emma, 'it might be intuition, but I could swear that Arri is very near her time: maybe they've got the dates wrong'. She'd better warn Marc of her suspicions as soon as he returned.

Emma put her head around the kitchen door where Mrs H was hard at work preparing a sauce for the meat. That was her culinary speciality, sauces as well as puddings.

"Hello Mrs H, can I help at all?" Mrs Haddington looked up smiling, her face glowing with her efforts at the stove.

"Och noo thank you my darling. Just a wee bit of parsley from the tub outside the back door would be great, if you'd be so kind. I don't want to stop stirring." Emma opened the door and quickly grabbed a bunch of the herb from its little sheltered hiding place.

"Phew! The snow is early this year. It sure is cold out there. Shall I chop some of this for you."

"Ay that would be kind dear, the knife's by the board there on the table." Emma set to work, deliberating whether or not to say anything about her suspicions.

"Mrs H…"

"Yes my love…, I ken what's troubling you." She turned around and glanced quickly at Emma whilst still circling the wooden spoon.

"You and I have both had bairns and I also think your friend is near her time."

"Oh no! So you agree? Can we manage, do you think, if it happens up here? I mean supposing it's in the middle of the night and we can't get her to hospital with all this snow. Poor Marc what a responsibility and it's not exactly his thing… doing the midwifery bit, you know." Mrs H took the saucepan off the stove and set it on the side then turned to Emma, with a resigned look on her face and a soft sigh she refastened her apron.

"Now look dear. Marc mentioned this possibility to me only this morning. He is well aware of the situation and has everything he needs in an emergency already in place here. He is the best doctor in the whole area, there is nothing he canno' do. He was delivering babies before you two were even married. There will be noo drama, noo drama at all. I have assisted at many a birth as well, in the village up the glen. I am quite able to do my part should the babies decide to put in an appearance early. So get away with ye up to have a bath and stop yer fretting."

"Alright…, thank you Mrs H. I feel much less worried now. You're right, of course we'll manage if necessary." She pecked the older woman on her warm pink cheek and went upstairs somewhat relieved. But she'd feel much happier if someone could get hold of Julian.

As Emma lay in the bath she decided to try Alicia's mobile once more. After all they were just having fun out there; or so she thought. It was unlike either Rose or Alicia not to answer. Not even a text: she would have liked to share her anxiety about Adriana.

Emma had a definite sense of events taking place elsewhere which, at present, were to be kept from herself and Adriana. She was also determined to talk to Arri about her actual due date. She'd said very little about her last doctor's check-up appointment before she left London. Emma also fully intended to try to get some information out of Marc when they were next alone together. She would relay her own suspicions on Adriana's condition and see what he really thought. Arri's behaviour was slightly odd, she really didn't seem that fussed about Julian being completely out of contact. After all Emma reasoned, she is having twins, but she seems to have such faith in Marc; it's almost as if she wants to have her babies up here with us. There just was something, about the whole event, on which she couldn't quite put her finger.

Emma lay back in the warm water swirling it over her shoulders and breast and thinking of how lucky she was with her own family. She missed the girls already and she couldn't imagine giving birth without having her husband beside her. Emma wriggled her toes, she'd been in the water long enough; she was hungry and looking forward to one of Mrs H's special French dishes, 'Pheasant a la Normande.' She got out of the bath and had just wrapped herself in the warm towel as she heard Marc come into the room. Her heart lifted with anticipation and the usual comfort and joy of just being together again. She determined not to worry about something that was out of her control and the twins might not choose to arrive early. What was it they say? 'Live in the now and don't worry about something that might not happen anyway'.

* * *

CHAPTER 31

Battle Stations
(Estonia)

JAKE sneaked a glance at his watch. Everything within the lodge was ready. The food and the layout of the room was perfection, as it always had been, under his grandmother's control. She was one of the great entertainers.

It was time: the two jeeps with their men aboard had moved out of sight of the imminent visitors. When Jake had gone up to change for the evening ahead, he had managed to inform Guy of the vehicles approximate new location. This relocation had been immediately confirmed. So, his colleagues were up to speed, thought Jake thoroughly relieved. All the *Spetsnaz* vehicles and men were now together in a hidden clearing to the left of the drive up to the house, near enough, yet completely concealed from the hunting lodge. It had snowed hard on and off all afternoon so there was no trace and no tracks to be seen. They were in a perfect spot for a strike from above.

Gustav was due at any minute and in spite of the circumstances Jake was looking forward to seeing the older man, who had in some ways replaced his long-gone grandfather. They'd always had a good relationship and Jake knew that Gustav would remain calm and reliable however things unfurled tonight. He'd had plenty of experience with army operations in his younger days. The only thing that worried Jake was that he himself had no weapon, except for the possibility of a basic kitchen knife.

As Jake primed his mindset and sought to steady his impatience to get things started, he took a moment to admire his grandmother as she swept down the stairs, in a long dark green velvet dress with pearls at her throat. She was beautifully made up; her maid had obviously helped with her hair and although from another era, she looked ready for anything.

"Hello darling!" she said as she approached: "you look very smart in your late grandfather's smoking jacket. It fits you quite well. Now I don't see our minders, where are they?" she muttered under her breath, looking towards the hall.

They're in the kitchen, hoping for a quiet quaff of vodka, I think." Jake said making no effort to hide his disdain. "They're certainly getting more into the party spirit."

"Hm, it's a pity I don't keep sleeping pills, they could help, but let's have some champagne now... shall we offer it? I have made sure that we have plenty and hopefully they'll not be used to it, so mixing with vodka and luck on our side, they might be rendered legless rather quickly. What do you think?"

"Yes possibly, but they are well used to the hard stuff; they have strong heads these Russians. It'll take a lot of alcohol to do the trick. I'll go and organize it myself. Gustav will be here at any minute, so you stay put here by the fire." Jake found Renata in the kitchen in a dither trying to get rid of the soldiers, who were getting under her rather small feet.

Nicolai was looking impeccably turned out. Anybody would think they were having a bloody dinner party, Jake thought, as the man turned towards him smiling.

"This all looks wonderful Jake. I can see that your grandmother is a past master at entertaining. These men..., my men," he corrected himself, lowering his voice, indicating the three officers who were now congregating in the hall as Jake appeared, "aren't used to seeing such a feast."

"No, I can imagine," Jake shrugged his shoulders, "but I suppose as it is a party they can have something to eat and drink with us for once. After all we are here together, stuck inside, in a pretty extraordinary situation. But..." he looked up with a mere flicker of a smile, "I can promise you that this music and dance troupe are absolutely spectacular."

"So my men have been telling me. They said that what you had described sounded sensational." He laughed. Jake took a bottle of champagne from the bucket.

"Will you have a glass with us or are you all forbidden, even on a cold night such as this? My grandmother and I will certainly have a glass with her friend Gustav, we are treating ourselves to one of the very best years tonight, in spite of our enforced incarceration," he said with a wry smile, studying the bottle, before pouring.

"Of course I must join you, I wouldn't wish Irina's guest to think me rude, ill-educated and unused to fine dining. I loved my time in England." He placed a hand on Jake's arm. "I rather wish we'd met in different circumstances," he said. "However don't even consider your getting us inebriated tonight my friend, for I am used to the very best champagne. My father has a vineyard in France. As for my soldiers, their staple diet is vodka and they can drink anybody under the table, but just one drink will be enough for us, whilst on duty, thank you."

There was a loud rap on the door.

"Excuse me," Nicolai said, "I think that must be Irina's friend. I'll send my men back into the kitchen for the moment." He set off for the hall. Jake placed a comforting hand on Renata's shoulder.

"Don't worry Renata, just do everything I say, now go to the door as normal, then bring the champagne please, he whispered pushing her in front of him. Jake followed, then hovered in the doorway ready to welcome Gustav.

Both Irina and Gustav played their parts to perfection. The older man behaved as if there was nothing unusual and Irina was as pleased to see him as she always was: no more no less. Gustav was delighted to greet Jake; after such a long time they really were thrilled to see each other. Jake noticed Nicolai standing watching and introduced the Russian to Gustav as an old school friend, as he'd been told to do.

"Ah so you were at Rugby too," and with his usual charming smile Gustav shook Nicolai firmly by the hand. "I dread to think what you two got up to at school." Nicolai had the grace to look slightly embarrassed and Jake chuckled. He looked up at Nicolai trying to put him at his ease.

"Gustav came to my rescue and got me out of a few scrapes as a boy. I tried to forget the incidents, but he never did!" They all laughed. Renata came around to fill up their glasses. Gustav and Irina accepted, but Jake and Nicolai had hardly touched theirs. Jake suggested quietly to Renata, as the others talked, that she might offer some more to the officers in the kitchen. Renata again looked horrified, but when Jake gave her a private wink, she returned a slight nod of understanding and moved off.

"I can hear men's voices talking out there in the kitchen... who is there?" Gustav asked seemingly perplexed and covering for Jake. Nicolai answered smoothly.

"I'm afraid I have a driver with me these days and he has a couple of relations with him. We rescued them on the way here, from the train station which isn't operating because of the storm. They live not too far away, so I agreed they could be dropped off later on our way home. Irina kindly said that Renata would give them something to eat and that perhaps they'd like to stay for the entertainment too. Your grandmother is very generous." Nicolai bowed towards Irina with another guileless smile. Irina merely raised an eyebrow at her abductor. Jake had to admire the man's perfect English.

Polite conversation ensued for a little longer. How long, Jake wondered, would they have to keep up this farcical situation in front of Gustav, who unbeknown to Nicolai, was perfectly aware that they were all being held captive in Irina's own hunting lodge. His old friend spoke to Jake with his eyes as well as his voice and nodded reassurance whilst the others were turned away.

Jake chuckled at something Gustav said and patted his arm warmly to reaffirm both his friendship and confidence in the imminent deliverance from their predicament. Once more he glanced discreetly at his watch. It was time. Jake's well-trained ears first heard the sound of several engines approaching before anyone else. Soon there followed a slamming of car doors and footsteps crunching on the frozen snow. A loud knock on the door announced the arrival of the Romany troupe.

Jake knew everything to have been well prepared and there was no more time for prevarication. The operation was under way and pray to God that by the end of the evening the meticulously laid plans would have been carried through with success and without loss or harm to any of those most dear to him.

Gunari, in all his finery, with a twinkle in his eye and a smile on his face, came in with a flourish leading seven musicians. He bowed low over Irina's hand, surreptitiously squeezing it for reassurance. Gunari shook hands with Gustav, then nodded a delighted greeting to both her grandson and the other well-dressed young man who, for all his contrived Englishness, Gunari knew to be the Russian interloper. The double doors through to the dining room had been opened and he set about organising the musicians in their allotted places to tune and prepare their instruments.

Jake noticed two familiar figures at the back of the group. They looked no different to the Romanies, except for the slightly characteristic loose-limbed movements of one of his colleagues, known to him so well. Guy had a fiddle and Julian a woodwind instrument, which he held as if he knew how to play, Jake realised thankfully. Knowing that now he was no longer alone he experienced a surge of adrenalin warming him against the blast of cold air from the open door. So far so good, everything was well organised and going according to plan.

As Gunari settled the troupe, the dancers began to spread out and to take their positions in the middle of the room. Poor bewildered Renata was called upon to refill the glasses of the audience. Barely concealing her nervousness and with shaking hands she had some difficulty, with so many people now crammed into the room, not to spill the expensive nectar. Once again Jake noticed Nicolai decline, but one of the Russian soldiers standing half hidden in the doorway leading to the hall had definitely helped himself from the kitchen. Jake could tell by the colour of his face. He must tell Renata to again make sure that the vodka was made easily available.

It was then that Jake noticed another girl, heavily veiled, standing slightly apart from the rest of the group, across on the far side of the room. Her clothes were of a different calibre to the rest: sophisticated Jake thought, how strange, maybe she was the star of the show. But there was something about her, he turned to look for Gunari and as he did so Nicolai came into focus. He too was staring quite openly at the alluring figure of the veiled girl in the corner of the room. She, quite simply, oozed sex appeal. Then Jake caught

Nicolai's eye as he dragged his gaze away and turned towards him. With a raised eyebrow the Russian raised his glass, nodded as if in agreement and they both smiled.

❉   ❉   ❉

CHAPTER 32

Action On All Fronts
(Scotland: Estonia)

BY six-thirty in the evening, after Adriana had achieved the steep climb up the stairs to her room, she had no doubt that the babies were thinking about arriving. She ran a bath, adding delicious smelling lavender oil, undressed and carefully stepped into the luxurious old cast iron tub, making sure that the large fluffy towel was well within reach. Marc was in the study with Alec. Emma was a mere shout away, also changing for dinner. Mrs H was adding the finishing touches to another fantastic dinner and Adriana's husband Julian was... well, God knows where. She wished they could have at least spoken, before it all started.

Adriana was neither fussed nor frightened. The babies, she had been told, were well positioned. She was healthy and strong and quietly confident that, with Marc's help, she could bring her children safely into the world with no big drama. She lay back in the fragrant water, with a rolled towel behind her head and studied her heavy breasts and enormous stomach. She was certainly having contractions; mild as yet and intermittent but her body was preparing for the huge task ahead. Adriana watched with fascination as her tummy tightened; grimacing with the pain until it lessened. She knew how to breathe and what to expect as things progressed. She wanted Marc to deliver these babies and she decided that she definitely needed sustenance before the real ordeal began. Dinner wasn't long off and she must eat something for energy, but she'd lie back for a little while in the warm comforting water and relish these last few precious moments of peace. Her life, as she knew it, was about to change in the most miraculous, yet painfully exhausting way.

✳

Mrs H was in the dining room when Emma came downstairs. She was arranging a couple of soft cushions on Adriana's chair.

"Hello my dear, did you have a nice bath?"

"Yes thank you Mrs H, can I do anything to help?"

"Aye you can arrange this towel, out of sight under these old cushions on Adriana's chair, just in case... dae ye ken?"

"Oh Good Heavens Mrs H! Do you really think it's all about to happen?"

"Aye, she has that certain look my dear; but don't you worry now, we'll manage perfectly well with the doctor here." Marc had just walked into the room. He was smiling catching the end of their conversation. He bent to kiss his wife.

"Come on now darling Adriana's not ill: she's just having a couple of babies: if she has them while she's here it's really not a big problem."

"What's not a problem? I hope you aren't all talking about me," Adriana wobbled into the room smiling. "I'm starving Mrs H, is it ready? What's for dinner?"

Marc laughed. "You have a great appetite Adriana and that's good." He went to kiss her on the cheek. "These babies are going to appear well nourished." Emma patted Adriana's chair.

'Look we've made you a really comfy place here, so you sit down and I'll help Mrs H bring in our dinner. It's your favourite… pheasant and yes, it is ready and we're all starving!"

"Good, I'll go and dig Alec out from his study then," Marc winked at Mrs Haddington and went out humming. She was the only one to know that he had discreetly examined Adriana earlier in the day. The babies were indeed imminent.

Adriana sat down carefully, glad that dinner was about to arrive. She wondered how long she was going to manage to sit still; the pains were every twenty minutes now but so far perfectly bearable. She'd managed to catch Marc on his own earlier in the day and while he'd checked her over, had admitted to having kept quiet about her true dates. But Marc had been brilliant and assured her that he was actually one step ahead and that he'd been well aware of her condition, just by looking at her. He had already spoken to her gynaecologist in London that very morning. He was, Adriana surmised, in his element and well prepared. She believed that he wanted to deliver these babies himself: after all they were extremely special to them both.

At dinner, Alec seemed very hyped up over his Russian lodgers. He obviously liked the diplomat and his son; so Emma couldn't quite understand what the problem was with the other young man they'd had staying. But she soon realised that there were certain things, relating to the current situation, that neither Marc nor his uncle wished to discuss with herself or Adriana! She looked across the table at her friend. Arri was scooping up her leek and potato soup with relish, but then Emma noticed her screwing up her face slightly as if she had a pain then, after a minute, her face relaxed again. Adriana shook her head slightly and made an 'it's Ok' face across the table, before putting down her spoon. Emma grinned back encouragingly. 'Oh well,' she thought, 'I had several false alarms before the girls were born, let's hope it's just one of those'.

But Emma was uneasy. Perhaps they shouldn't have brought Adriana with them as her proper doctor was in London and twins could well be born early. Yet it was odd because it was almost as if Arri wanted to have her babies up here with them and in the back of beyond. She seemed unusually unflustered about the whole event. She looked around the room. Marc, totally at ease, was talking about going up the hill with Hamish one day. But Alec caught Emma staring across at the lovely portrait of his dead wife Caroline. Alec smiled at her.

"She was lovely, wasn't she?"

"Yes Alec she was beautiful and Marc always says that Caroline had the warmest and kindest character as well," Emma replied.

"She did," agreed Marc, "and we all loved her dearly and wish we'd had her with us for very much longer." Alec looked far away for a moment, then Mrs Haddington came bustling in to clear away the soup plates. Emma got up to help.

"It's pheasant next in a delicious sauce uncle Alec: would you like me to dish it out for a change?"

"Yes please, that would be great." As Emma followed Mrs H out to the kitchen, Marc and Alec heard a strange sound. Adriana was sitting bolt upright in her chair. Her face was pink with embarrassment.

"Oh my God! I'm so sorry Alec, but I think I've ruined your chair! My waters have just broken!"

✳

Maksim and his team waited, well concealed from both the house and the Russian unit. As ordered by Nicolai, all evidence of the Russian intrusion had moved off, down the drive, into a hidden clearing to one side. The snow had continued to fall thickly blanketing their tracks. The Russian group were well trained, there was absolute silence and now that it was dark, no light whatsoever could be seen to show their whereabouts. But Maksim knew exactly where they were.

Stealth, Maksim knew to be of the utmost importance. His unit were also highly skilled in both hunting and killing in silence. They would attack on schedule at eight pm, when the music inside the lodge was at its loudest and the killer drone was positioned above. He could just hear Gunari's musicians beginning to warm up, tuning their instruments. Maksim had absolute confidence in the gypsies with their unique skills inside the house and in the British with backup from the sky. He liked their leaders. He had the utmost trust in his own men who he had mostly trained himself. So he knew that every one of them could be relied upon. They were well aware of what they were up against. They'd had plenty of skirmishes with this particular force before.

Jake had managed to keep them updated with the arrangements being made inside the lodge, letting them know exactly how many enemy they were dealing with outside. Now that Guy, Julian and Gunari were already inside the building, the covert mission had begun.

Earlier, Maksim had seen the young Russian in charge arrive back. He had watched Nicolai get out and enter the house with a driver and another passenger. It was a very dark night with no moon, perfect conditions he thought with satisfaction. His men knew the forest as well as Gunari's people. They had laid traps for any Russian slinking away during the imminent attack. The Estonian leader checked his watch once more. The music was becoming ever louder.

The drone targeting the tanks and army trucks was due overhead in exactly ten minutes. He raised one hand, the signal passed on immediately down the line, from man to man. The last check that his men were all in place.

❄

Inside the lodge the atmosphere was electric. So much going on everywhere, Irina realised, largely within one room and so much to be covertly achieved. She couldn't tell which were Jake's colleagues, they blended completely with the male dancers and musicians who all seemed to be fully involved in the entertainment. She couldn't quite see the four men with their instruments right at the back of the room. The infiltrators most likely would be placed out of the limelight and they'd be well camouflaged with darkened faces, in their borrowed gypsy costumes.

The spectators had moved back, spilling into the hall, while the music and dancing began. The women dancers in the foreground, were both sensual, lithe and athletic. Together with the music they were mesmeric. The Russian soldiers couldn't take their eyes off the swirling hips and alluring figures. Because of their jobs they were probably sex-starved, thought Irina. Good: this was the very best scenario to distract the soldiers. Renata had told Jake that Nicolai had now removed the vodka bottles from the kitchen table. Irina had twice seen the third brutish Russian officer secretly refilling his hip flask at the beginning of the evening. He obviously had a drink problem, but they all appeared relaxed now and perhaps slightly intoxicated, their guard down. Irina couldn't help but wonder what poor, sad lives they must lead.

Renata looked much more at ease now that she was so busy; at Jake's request, she had made sure that there was plenty of champagne replacing the vodka in easy reach of the Russian men. She must have realised by now that something unusual was afoot. The more the soldiers drank, the redder their faces became visually slackening their features. With all the activity and roaring open fire the large room was becoming warmer by the minute.

Great, thought Irina, everything was going according to plan. So far so good. She hadn't felt so alive and excited for a long time. It was wonderful to be trusted with such secret, dangerous knowledge allowing her to anticipate and relish the capture of the smug Nicolai and his men. She knew also that there was major surveillance along Estonian borders and coastal regions, with many nations involved.

The Russians were in for a surprise if they thought they could just walk into her country, let alone take over her house. But there were bound to be skirmishes and some casualties at the very least. Jake had reassured her that the main house and occupants would be safe and she was not to worry about what went on outside. She was so proud of him. He was playing his part perfectly; polite and seemingly entering into the spirit of things, but with just the right amount of reticence. Irina had told Nicolai that she resolved to host her party in the same way as she had done every year and that she had no intention of letting his presence spoil any of it it. Nicolai with a raised eyebrow had nodded charmingly.

Gustav, Nicolai and Jake all stayed close to her as the entertainment began; Gustav had managed to squeeze her hand and wink encouragingly when Nicolai's attention was diverted, whilst he stared at an intriguing girl on the far side of the room.

As the musicians finished the first part of their schedule, Irina found it most interesting to discreetly observe both her grandson and Nicolai watching the same beautiful veiled creature waiting in the wings to one side of the troupe. The stylish young woman had a powerful magnetism and was quite obviously the star of the entertainment. Irina had never seen her before; she would have remembered. On this occasion this girl must be crucial to this evening's plans. She had already attracted furtive glances from all of the men. Clever of Gunari, thought Irina. These Russian soldiers were quite obviously deprived from the company of women and the girls had really gone to town with their outfits this time: they were sexier than ever.

The music was hotting up and the fascinating creature on the side lines began to gyrate, swinging her hips seductively as she slowly circled the troupe until they made a path for her to the centre of the room. Once there she stood still, with her arms raised elegantly for a minute while the others continued to dance outwards to create more space. All eyes turned towards her as the music became ever more frenzied.

Jake glancing at his watch, managed to swivel his head slightly, just enough to mouth 'seven mins' to Gustav. Then as the others moved out of her way, the girl suddenly threw her arms high up in the air emphasizing her whole body. She hesitated for a moment then began to dance in earnest. They all stared: mesmerised by the bewitching fluidity of her lithe body.

*

"God Almighty I'm glad you're here," Adriana gasped through clenched teeth. "It hurts like hell you know. You should have warned me long ago!"

"I know it hurts," Marc answered grinning. But you're doing fine and just think what you are going to get; two little menaces instead of one. No pushing just yet though.

I'll tell you when. It won't be long." Mrs Haddington appeared at the door, pink faced with barely subdued excitement.

"Anything else you need Doctor?" she asked in a comfortingly calm voice.

"Not at the moment, thanks Mrs H. We're doing fine. Where's Emma?"

"Unpacking Adriana's baby case and getting everything ready for the little mites." She hastened out to help.

"Ok, that's great. I'll shout when we need you," he called after her and turned back to Adriana, placing his cool hands on her swollen tummy." Honestly Arri, I can't believe how dishonest you've been with your dates. I guessed just observing you on the train, you know. I imagine that you came up completely prepared as well, didn't you?" he chuckled. Poor old Julian, have you misled him too?"

"No not really. I was just a bit vague about the dates. I think he's so terrified that he'd probably much rather not be here anyway. Actually I can't believe that for such a brave man, he's such a wimp regarding the baby business... Ouch, there's another one coming. Bloody hell! No one tells you quite how bad it is, do they?" She grunted as the pain took control again. Then recovering, "I am so sorry Marc but I really wanted you to be with me, if Julian was away. I know you promised him that you'd look after me if the time came on your watch. So, I'm afraid you have drawn the short straw. Heavens! I think I want to push, where's Emma! Emma! Mrs H. Please come!"

Emma appeared beside her in one of Mrs H's white aprons. Adriana grabbed her hand crossly.

"Good God! What have you got on? you look like some starchy old Matron." Emma giggled nervously as Marc got seriously busy down the far end of the bed while Mrs H stood quietly waiting at the door.

"Hold on tight then and squeeze my hand as hard as you like," said Emma holding her friend's hand firmly and looking to Marc for guidance.

"Alright Arri you can start to push. I can just see the first head, lots of hair, everything is as it should be, it won't be too difficult as the second baby is helping push out the first. Twins are usually impatient when the time comes. Now push with each contraction... and shallow breathing in between, just like you've been taught. Mrs H can you come in please and bring more towels, as we're nearly there with the first."

❊ ❊ ❊

CHAPTER 33

Double Victory
(The hunting lodge)

AT eight o'clock precisely, as the music was reaching its exhilarating climax, Maksim with his keen hearing sensed, then caught a glimpse of the drone overhead. He dropped his raised hand as did the others all down the line. Each man in his protective clothing and head gear dived for cover, as the pre-programmed, autonomous weapon released its lethal load from the sky.

At the same moment as the targeted tank and vehicles blew, Katya was moving seductively towards Nicolai her arms open in welcome. The Russian was totally under her spell: hypnotised. Hearing the blast, Jake sprang on the man from behind. Gustav had pushed Irina out of the way, back into a corner and stood his ground protectively in front of her. The Russian officers, their attention riveted on the dancers, hadn't noticed the three male musicians circling the room to discreetly stand behind them. The explosion shook the whole house, the three Russian soldiers in an anticipated state of shock never stood a chance; they were completely taken by surprise. Only one put up a fight. As Jake held the squirming, swearing Nicolai in a fast expert grip around the neck the other Romanies came to help, knives held aloft.

Katya backed off breathing hard with barely controlled anxiety and at that moment, as she and Jake held eye contact for one fleeting instant, he recognised their beautiful air hostess from the horrendous flight out of the UK. But there was also something else about her, something familiar. No time to wonder, he looked quickly around him to make sure his colleagues had secured the other three Russian soldiers.

Gunari, Julian and Guy quickly hand-cuffed the officers. Then they all heard a piercing scream. Two shots and the sound of shattering glass came from the kitchen. At the same time the front door burst open. Maksim entered followed by two men. Renata ran from the kitchen covered in blood. Irina was there in a flash trying to calm the blubbering woman who thankfully appeared to have suffered only minor cuts from some breaking glass.

One soldier from the *Spetsnaz* unit, located outside the clearing, had managed to creep away to bushes just outside the kitchen window when he was efficiently dispatched by one of Maksim's team. As the man fell one shot had shattered the window in front of which Renata happened to be standing: with fright she'd dropped a bottle of champagne which had also exploded.

The tank, the army trucks and jeeps had been taken out by the drone, together with five unsuspecting men who happened to be inside the vehicles. The other six men, positioned on the outskirts of the targeted area were easily captured, disorientated from the blast, only suffering superficial burns and minor injuries. The man shot outside the kitchen window was badly wounded, writhing on the ground, being attended to by one of Maksim's men with his medical bag.

Two Estonian army trucks, followed by a jeep and two medical vehicles, roared up the drive coming to a spectacular sliding stop outside the lodge, spraying snow everywhere. Several more of Maksim's team leapt out, ready to take over from the British.

Guy, Julian and Jake, Gunari and Maksim marched the Russians out of the house, watched from the doorstep by Irina, Gustav and the shaking Renata covered in a blanket. The ambulances were quickly dispatched to deal with the dead *Spetsnaz* soldiers in the clearing. The Russian officers were bundled into one of the trucks to join the other surviving members of the unit. Irina could see their pale stunned looking faces staring out of the back of one of the vehicles. Poor things; she couldn't help but think of their dead colleagues' families. Nicolai, with an Estonian soldier either side, was about to climb into the jeep.

"Just a minute young man!" Irina called regally, beckoning for him to be brought before her. Nicolai, still holding himself erect and proud turned to remount the steps to stand in front of the Contessa. Jake remained at the bottom. Nicolai raised his eyes to hers. Irina held his gaze.

"Have you anything to say to me?" Irina asked quietly adding, "for you don't seem to me to be a bad man, just hitched up with the wrong sort I imagine and got in out of your depth, was it?" Nicolai bowed and offered her his hand. "I am truly sorry for the inconvenience," he said. "You are a truly great and brave lady. I merely wish that we had all met under different circumstances." He bowed again, then turned to salute them all before nodding to his captors and returning to step into the jeep.

Guy, Julian and Maksim took their leave to set off by helicopter back to their base at the border, to where their prisoners would also be taken. They could all hear the big bulky army transport arriving overhead, waiting for the departure of the Estonian force before touching down on the large sweep of the cleared driveway. Jake was ordered to stay with his grandmother and to report to the border at Narva the following morning.

Gunari collected up his people ready to set off back into their forest retreat. Before leaving he turned to Jake, with a wink, saying that he was sure that both he and Katya would enjoy helping to restore the lodge to its former glory. Irina gave Gunari the money he was owed for the Romanies' work in her forests. Once they'd all gone on their way the rest stayed outside for a few minutes watching the night sky, which was alight with activity.

Sporadic gunfire could be heard somewhere along the frontier behind Irina's house but that was all and thankfully it looked as though a major incident had been averted. Guy would be calling Jake again when he reached their base. They would know by morning what had happened elsewhere, after all the reports came in.

✳

Irina, as ever the impeccable hostess, had Renata serve hot drinks and food for the weary houseguests. The young maid, beginning to smile again, had managed to clean up the kitchen and wore fresh clothing. The cuts she'd suffered were just superficial: Jake, Gustav and Katya returned the lodge to it's former state. By the time they'd finished it was late and Irina was unsurprisingly exhausted.

"Well," she said, "Gustav and I are ready to drop," so we'll leave you young people by the fire. Katya it was an absolute pleasure to meet you, what a brave beautiful young woman you are: no wonder Gunari is so proud and loves you so much. You are welcome here at any time and please of course stay the night, there's plenty of room and Renata will see you have everything you need." Katya smiled and replied in perfect English.

"It was my pleasure to be able to help, it's wonderful to catch up with Jake again after that dreadful flight we had together." Irina noticed Jake was still intrigued by Katya, almost as if he was puzzled by something. The girl spoke

268

excellent English and Irina wondered where she had come from. There was something vaguely familiar about her. Somewhere in the past Irina remembered Gustav telling her of a story, about a little girl, that Gunari had once told him. Perhaps Jake had met her a long time ago with Gunari, but he obviously didn't remember. Irina couldn't help but notice how comfortable they were with each other. There was a very definite attraction; hardly surprising, the girl was both lovely and fearless. Irina kissed them on both cheeks, winked at Jake, then went upstairs with Gustav, followed by Renata.

"Let's have a nightcap, "Jake suggested. "I'm off duty at last."

"I think you deserve it," Katya replied. "What an ordeal you have been through since last we met."

"Yes, that was a pretty horrendous flight, wasn't it?" Jake poured them each a whisky, from the drink cabinet, added some ice and took the glasses across to Katya to where she was sitting on the sofa which they had moved back beside the fire. Then there was silence except for the gentle tinkling of the ice and an odd electricity in the air. Jake threw a couple of logs onto the blaze, then went to sit beside her. He ran his fingers threw his hair and turned to gaze into her bewitching face once more. Neither spoke.

"Katya," he touched her cheek gently. "You have such courage and were wonderful on the plane, but tonight you were just sensational, simply stunning, with an extra special magic about you. I can't quite put into words what this mystical thing is," he turned to peer into the flames for a moment slightly confused before adding, "because there is something else too, that I can sense, but which just seems to be out of my reach."

Katya drew his hand to her wet cheek where the tears had spilled over and begun to fall openly. "Jake, we've known each other for many years... don't you recognise me? From the forest? Where we used to play together as children. It's me, 'Kit' as you would call me, but a slimmer version, thank God, from that chubby little girl who just loved her naughty little playmate!"

Jake stared at her in astonishment. He gently wiped her tears away with his fingers. He felt as if he'd been hit in the stomach with a sledge-hammer. No wonder they had this extra-sensory connection. There was such a story behind that small child who, with her nanny, had run away from her abusive, aristocratic Russian father and sought refuge in the forest with Gunari. The gypsy had taken her in to hide them and had thereafter proclaimed her to be of his clan for her own safety. How could he have forgotten the girl who had been like a sister to him all those years ago and had kept up with him in all the adventures they'd shared.

"Great Heaven's above Katya! That's it. Of course! It's the way you smile and the way you move your hands. My darling little tomboy who I loved, now all grown up... look at you and with the heart of a lion as well." He let out a long sigh and drew her to him. Her intense black eyes shone and she was quivering.

"Do you remember what Gunari used to say about us, when we were children?"

"No what did he say?" he was kissing her neck, moving to her face.

"Just that we were 'two peas in a pod'. I always remember that; he must have learnt it from you. I never forgot you. When you walked onto the plane my heart did a huge lurch. I recognised you instantly."

"Really," he said, "well..." taking her hand and placing it under his shirt over his heart, "can you feel mine now? We have so many years to make up for. What an evening; but look what you helped us to accomplish.

"Katya. 'Kit' suits you no longer although you were the bravest and most fun child to be with; my darling Katya, now you are everything a woman could possibly be. Stay with me tonight, I can't let you go again," whispered Jake taking her in his arms. He couldn't think about anybody else or another person, in another far away country.

This was deeper than anything he'd ever felt before. He was overwhelmed as if by a giant tidal force.

✳ ✳ ✳

CHAPTER 34

Great Expectations
(The Swiss mountains)

IN that other far away country Alicia, in the hotel with Ollie and Rose, picked up a call from Emma. The twins had arrived early, in Scotland at Glencurrie, with Marc doing the honours! Emma told her that the babies didn't look in the least bit premature and Marc also had said that Adriana had admitted being intentionally vague about her due date. She had wanted them born in Scotland. Now both he and Alec were using their contacts to try to get word to Julian. It looked as though the mission in which he and Guy were participating, with Jake, had concluded and the men were imminently due home.

"How exciting! Oh! I can't wait to see them! Let's fly straight back to bonny Scotland then," Rose called out over Alicia's shoulder.

"Sssh Rose! I can't hear Emma. How is Arri?"

"She's delirious with happiness and Marc's tickled pink, because it all went so well, without a hitch, I think. Mrs H and I assisted!" Emma laughed. "Although we were glad to be up the top end most of the time, I can tell you that!" Alicia chuckled.

"I don't blame you. I wonder if we could fly direct from Geneva to Aberdeen and then get a train perhaps? But I don't suppose Alec would have room for us all?"

"Oh! I think it would be fine actually," Emma interrupted, "because the tenants due in the Lodge, have cancelled, so I'm sure Alec would love to have you all too. It would be such good fun, do come. Then Julian, Guy and Jake could come to Scotland also. We'll have a real party just like the last time we were here together." There was a slight pause, Emma noticed, at the other end of the phone.

"Well, as a matter of fact I suspect we might not have Ellie with us," Alicia continued a little hesitantly. "She might just want to stay out here in Switzerland a wee bit longer as she's loving the mountains. She's so much better." Alicia added rather lamely. Rose, perching on the arm of Alicia's chair, raised an eyebrow and made a face at Alicia who looked up from the phone, covering the mouthpiece with her hand.

"Don't say anything Rose, it might get back to Jake." Alicia warned.

"Oh alright, that sounds like a good idea," replied Emma slightly surprised. "Well then Jake must be due some leave by now, so he could probably fly out to the mountains to be with her for a few days."

"Yes, quite probably," Alicia answered, winking at Rose, who could hardly contain her excitement. She rushed off to find Olly in the bar to tell him about the babies' safe arrival.

*

When the others had left to ski down to the hotel, Zak and Ellie had stayed together at the middle-station bar. Alicia and Rose were both well aware that something was going on between their friends. It was obvious; you could feel the vibes emanating from the two young people. Oliver had picked up on it straight away.

What Zak and Ellie decided to do about it was, at present, anybody's guess, so the others had all agreed to give them some space and leave them to it.

*

Ellie fingered her glass of *glüwein*. They had all enjoyed an exhilarating day's skiing, but she and Zak could no longer hide their attraction to each other. Rose and Alicia, although very protective, had made it quite obvious that they had left her with Zak with their blessing. This made her feel happy and secure. At the back of her mind, all day, she had been deliberating what to do and what to say; when and how to tell Jake. But first things first.

She'd made up her mind and Zak was sitting waiting for her to speak. His brown hair was tussled, his skin such a healthy-looking colour from an all-weather outdoor existence. Outwardly he was perfectly calm but his deep dark eyes twinkled expectantly, betraying high emotion.

Ellie turned towards him. He took her free hand in his and squeezed it for encouragement.

"I've decided to delay going home," she said with a rush. "I'm not going back with the others. That is if you'll have me Zak?"

He grabbed her other hand letting out a huge sigh of relief.

"Ellie! Oh Ellie! That's just *wunderbar, es ist brillaint!*"

"Are you sure?" Ellie asked laughing shyly.

"I've never been so sure of anything." He leant forward and kissed her full on the mouth. They were oblivious to everybody until the barman appeared with two glasses of champagne.

"These are on the house!" he announced smiling at them both. "It seems you might have something to celebrate Zak. About time too, if I may say so." He laughed and went off to serve someone else.

* * *

CHAPTER 35

The Eyes Have It
(London, three months later)

THE twelve young people all sat around the table of the restaurant, chatting with each other and generally catching up. Guy and the blonde blue eyed Alicia, at one end, Julian and the voluptuous Adriana at the other. In between on one side sat Emma with Marc, then Jake and the beautiful Katya, so full of life and happiness as if they'd always been together. Opposite, holding hands, sat Zak with the shy and alluring Ellie, next to Olly and the vivacious Rose. Luckily the Londoners' favourite restaurant had given them a private room. The noisy atmosphere was loaded with happiness, as old friends and new, with so much in common, were brought together in one place. It was a celebration of everything good in life, after the successful end to a mission that could have evolved into a global crisis.

Katya, the newest addition to the group, was confident enough with her English to keep up with the conversation without hesitation. She seemed to have come alight, thought Jake: he could see that she was going to fit in with the others straight away. She kept reminding him of their earlier adventures in Irina's forests, when they were children. As she did so he recalled her gesticulations and facial expressions from those long ago days. How could he have known that child would become such a beautiful woman and that she would be here sitting beside him today. He glanced across at the brave and lovely Ellie; she was no longer his and she was her usual fairly quiet self but, looking happy and relaxed in Zak's company. They obviously had something extra special between them, you could tell by the way they gazed at each other.

Jake had known in his heart, way back, that he and Ellie weren't meant to be together long term; he had always sensed her to be slightly holding back from him; so she must have felt the same. How extraordinary that they should both have wished to end their relationship and had met their real soulmates at the same time in far-away contrasting countries. He hoped they would always remain close. He had liked Zak immediately.

Toasts were made to those involved in the successful conclusion of the recent operation; the courage of both Katya and Ellie was much applauded. Jake regaled them with graphic descriptions of Katya's dancing and the Russian reaction. Adriana and Julian were congratulated on the birth of their twins and the remarkably calm doctor was thanked yet again for delivering the babies so efficiently. As the evening wore on, Katya felt warmly welcomed into the group and everybody drank to the two new relationships.

Ellie asked if Adriana had any photos of the twins. Arri proudly produced her mobile and passed round the pictures of the two unidentical little boys who, now three months old, were staring wide eyed up at the photographer. Suitable comments were made, one was like one parent and vice versa, so sweet, so chubby... then Katya studied the pictures closely looking from Julian to Adriana: Emma noticed her glance at Marc before speaking.

"They are *frumos* Adriana," she said; "that's beautiful in Romanian, by the way. They will have red hair I think, no? Such interesting coloured eyes too. '*Binecuvânta i pruncii*'. That means bless the babies," Katya smiled at Julian and handed back the mobile. "You must be so proud." Julian was proud as punch and said that as he'd known that Adriana was in good capable hands; he'd been both delighted and relieved to have missed out on the drama of the actual births.

The pictures on the mobile, many of them, continued to circulate. Emma spent a long time looking at them as there were pictures of herself and Mrs H as well, up in Scotland holding the new-borns. They were adorable, then whilst the others continued their noisy chat and laughter, she studied the newest pictures more closely. Something untoward immediately came to mind. As Emma looked up and caught Adriana's eye, then glanced at Marc beside her and back again to Arri's flushed face, she knew... she'd always had a funny feeling and now she knew for sure.

"Whoops, sorry," Emma exclaimed, laughing to cover herself, as she got up too hurriedly nearly knocking over her chair. "Must just visit the ladies room, too much wine, won't be a tick."

Adriana gave it a minute then, after a quick glance in Marc's direction, followed Emma to the wash-room. The others were engrossed in hearing the fascinating details of how the incredible last mission had ended in Estonia, although Rose and Alicia exchanged the merest suggestion of a raised eyebrow as their two friends left the table.

Emma came out of the cubicle to wash her hands, Arri was waiting, sitting on a stool by the mirror, fiddling with a box of tissues. Emma said nothing and turned on the cold tap to hold her wrists underneath: something she'd learnt to do when on occasion she needed to steady her heart rate and clear her head. She must just hang in there and see what Arri had to say. Luckily, because they had a private dining room, the ladies room was exclusive too. They were alone. Her friend started to speak almost immediately.

"Julian was told he was unlikely to be able to father children," she said. "As you know we tried everything possible. I love him beyond everything and he was desperate for us to have a child. I did what I did for him... much, much more than for myself... and I never intended to hurt anyone else that I love either, especially you. No-one else is to blame, only me. For with Marc, it was entirely a practical arrangement... nothing else. Julian thinks the children are, by some miracle, his. But now that you know the truth Emma, you must do with it as you feel you must. But please just think of the affect on the children and on your husband if this becomes common knowledge. By the way the unusual coloured fleck in one twin's eye, similar to Marc's, is apparently much more usual than I realised and Julian's hair has an auburn tinge to it as well."

She stopped talking and let out a long, defeated-sounding sigh. Emma had never seen Adriana look so fearful. "Forgive me Emma: it is all my fault, I'm afraid I deliberately set out to seduce your husband, entirely for my own purposes," she murmured before quietly leaving the room.

Emma stared at her own shocked face in the mirror. He hands were clutching the basin edge, she felt cold, shaky and slightly sick. What must she do with this distressing and complicated revelation which concerned the people who she loved most in the whole world? What an appalling situation.

It was no use looking back, what had happened, had happened and what good would it do anybody if she made a fuss? She had no doubt Marc loved her. What he'd done that last time, when they were all up in Scotland together, with a lot going on around them, was to help somebody desperate. She wasn't even going to think about him making love to Adriana. No! No! She just couldn't and wouldn't go there.

The gift of children, even if created in a somewhat unconventional way and between friends, was something miraculous, however you looked at it. She knew that. Emma herself was involved. She had helped deliver her husband's babies. Although oblivious, at the time that they were his, she had actually found the whole event exciting and it left her feeling that she had a special connection to the twins, an extra special bond.

How to deal with the whole scenario now, Emma wasn't really sure. She herself was strong and would somehow have to come to accept the situation and get on with it, as otherwise this new knowledge, could destroy so much and so many. Adriana was right as first and foremost Emma must think of the babies and their future, but also she must consider Marc and Julian, as well as the twins. Would the children need to be told? If so when? At what age? How would that affect all of them? Would these new found facts remain undisclosed? What if the others guessed?

Emma stared into the mirror again noticing her worried eyes. She must pull herself together. There was no way she was going to upset the applecart; she had the girls to think about. She was overly protective of them already. These last conundrums weren't really for her to consider at present. What was to happen in the future would be down to Adriana and Julian, if and when she told him; Marc too of course, she supposed. She just hoped if all their friendships endured, that her own little girls and Adriana's twins, would also become friends. To begin with at least they would grow up unaware they were half-blood siblings.

This group of people were so dear to her. They had all been through so much together in the past. They meant everything to Emma. Time would move on; the men had a secret world with special rules by which they had to live.

So, she also could keep this unwelcome information to herself for now. What will be will be. If Marc wished to discuss the situation in private, then she would keep her head and deal with it at the time. All things considered she just hoped that, as time moved on, life would settle again so that the sweet babies would have a happy childhood and that all their lives would be made richer by their arrival.

Emma waited a few minutes more to calm her nerves. She brushed her hair, sprayed a little scent behind her ears and returned to her place beside her husband. The others were still chattering away nineteen to the dozen, hardly, it seemed, having noticed the time she'd been away. But Marc heard a gentle, almost resigned sigh, as she sat down. He knew that she had guessed and took her hand, understanding how his stoic wife must be feeling. He felt dreadful, he should have told Emma himself.

Marc squeezed Emma's hand and bent to whisper, "We'll talk later. I love you more than you will ever know."

She turned to look him in the eye, saw his deep love for her there. A lone tear leaked down one cheek. She brushed it quickly away and smiled gently. "I know." She whispered back. Marc released her hand and stood up.

"I want to make one more toast. Last but by no means least," he said looking down at his wife. "Before you all become completely legless, I just want to say that my darling Emma has to be the bravest and most remarkable person I know." He laid a supportive hand on her shoulder and squeezed it reassuringly. "Who on earth would be capable, or wish, to assist their husband, myself..." he bowed before continuing, "in helping deliver Adriana and Julian's delightful twins, in winter, miles from the nearest known medical facility, in the freezing, gloriously snow-laden Highlands of Scotland. What a task. I salute you Emma, you were and are simply the best!"

Emma jumped up to stand beside him and join in.

"Don't forget we had dear old Mrs H in her starched white apron assisting us. She was so down to earth and reassuring about it all, wasn't she Arri? I think she enjoyed every single minute almost as much as she does making her sauces and delicious puddings!" Emma giggled, herself once more.

"Well," answered Adriana, from across the table, a huge relieved smile transforming her beautiful face, "I had the best midwifery team you could possibly imagine and at least you didn't have to call in Hamish, Alec's game keeper to help; that might have been most interesting for all of us!"

"Hamish would most likely have been brilliant, actually" Marc chuckled, "he's used to birthing sheep! But seriously," as the laughter died down, he raised his glass, "to good health, family and friends. Emma and I wish you and your little boys all the luck in the world. May they thrive and have a happy, healthy and wonderful life full of love. We'll all spoil then rotten." He finished grinning widely.

Everybody laughed and clapped. Emma caught Adriana's slightly hesitant meaningful glance and raising her glass to her alone, nodded. The two friends both smiled deeply at each other. Somehow, they would come to accept the situation. A united front. All would be well. The sun, moon and the stars still retained their places in the spinning of the earth and life would settle and move on again, for them all.

✳   ✳   ✳

The author with her beloved little dachshund – Marmite

About The Author

GINNY Vere Nicoll was born and brought up in England. After leaving school she attended art college, continuing to study fine art both at West Dean College and privately in Italy. She exhibited in the West End of London, before turning her hand to writing.

Ginny has a large family and lives in a converted old barn in West Sussex. Some years ago, when the children were grown, Ginny began writing her books. She now also draws, paints and creates her Feel Good Cards, selling them both online and across the South of England. Some of the many cards relate to her children's book, I Can Fly, which all have a storyline on the back relevant to the pictures.

Passionate about travelling, particularly across Europe, by car, train, or even on foot, Ginny takes every opportunity to collect information and material for both her books and cards. The Silence Of Snow is her fifth novel: Her first, The Smile, is set mostly in Italy. Under The Olives spells romance and adventure in the Ionian Islands. The Coldest Night Of The Year is based in the majestic Swiss Alp's, while her last novel, Loch Island, reflects the wild remote parts of the Scottish Highlands and the alluring beauty of the Isle Of Skye. There is a subtle link between all five stories when the charismatic characters meet up again, revel in romance and unexpected action-packed holidays, in stunning locations.

'These last two years have been a challenge for us all, yet I am an eternal optimist. Writing is another life into which I disappear from the real world. My characters are mostly 'friends' whom I strive to introduce to you, so that you may feel the atmosphere and travel with them to both the real and the imagined places. My wish is that you will experience and enjoy a genuine 'feel good' escape; especially in troubled times.'

Also by Ginny Vere Nicoll

Novels
The Smile: ISBN 978-1-4251-7153-7
Under the Olives: ISBN 978-0-9563366-0-6
The Coldest Night Of The Year:
ISBN 978-0-9563366-1-3
Loch Island: ISBN 978-0-9563366-2-0

Short Story Collection
Feel Good Tales: ISBN 978-0-9563366-3-7

For Young Children
I Can Fly
ISBN: 978-0-9563366-4-4

All the author's books are available from bookstores
everywhere, via her website: **feelgoodbooksonline.com**
and on line at Amazon.

Feel Good Cards
Feel Good Cards are available online at
www.feelgoodbooksonline.com
Direct from **ginny@verenicoll.co.uk**
The cards also are sold at several shops local to the
author, in the South of England: in the Petworth,
Petersfield and Midhurst area.

'THE SMILE' 2008

ISBN 978-1-4251-7153-7

TWO women are thrown together through force of circumstance far beyond their control. With courage and determination they set forth to find out the truth and the whereabouts of the two men in their lives, suddenly disappeared, without trace, into thin air.

An unlikely boating accident in the South of France. A macabre funeral in Scotland. Unexpected and erotic happenings in Venice on the night of 'La Senza', the celebration of that city's marriage to the sea and a final, dramatic, scene on the island of Torcello, played out under the hot Italian sun.

'UNDER THE OLIVES' 2010

ISBN 978-0-9563366-0-6

EMMA Brook, vulnerable and fragile, leaves a bad situation behind in England to explore the possibilities of a painting holiday in Greece for her 'Island Hops' travel Agency.

Underneath the olives Emma does indeed discover a whole secret world, just as the stranger on the plane implied. Who was the shy goatherd who never came out into the light? Why was he hiding? Who was the beautiful reclusive woman? And who were the mysterious little gypsies playing amongst the trees?

At the Hotel Stavros Emma meets an intriguing mix of diverse, irrevocably linked characters. In the hypnotic atmosphere of the olive grove she encounters tenderness, tragedy and unexpected drama. She finds the answer to a gripping riddle from the past and a certain magic for herself never before experienced.

'THE COLDEST NIGHT OF THE YEAR' 2012

ISBN 978-0-9563366-1-3

AN idyllic winter holiday in a lovely hotel in the Swiss Alps becomes a nightmare. Early one morning a young woman finds suspicious and gruesome evidence in an otherwise beautiful winter wonderland.

Unwelcome strangers, 'grey men' of questionable intent, infiltrate the area and an atmosphere of veiled threat engulfs the village in the valley. As the heavy snow clothes the mountains in thick layers of silent white, it both hides and protects those that wish to take advantage of its camouflage.

A group of friends unwittingly becomes involved in unexpected events, when one of their party fails to finish a train journey and has to pit her wits against much more than the prevailing harsh weather.

Friendship and love blossom as six people take part in an adventure which demands enigmatic skills, courage, determination and for some endurance beyond all imagining. In the cold glorious surroundings of a land where few are brave enough to dare venture 'off piste', skiing becomes secondary to that most basic of instincts – survival.

'LOCH ISLAND' 2015

ISBN 978-0-9563366-2-0

A GROUP of friends head up to North Western Scotland for a late autumn break. Two of the men have a hidden agenda in Paris but are sworn to silence.

On previous holidays turmoil seems to have trailed in their footsteps, causing adventure, danger and romance in equal measure. This time they have organized to stay in a remote place, with spectacular scenery, where they all look forward to absolute peace and quiet.

But, at the onset of another harsh winter, in the beautiful Scottish Highlands, something shocking and unexpected happens. This threatens to disrupt the friends' perfect haven and fracture personal relationships – possibly beyond redemption.

'FEEL GOOD TALES' 2015

ISBN 978-0-9563366-3-7

A SELECTION of short stories set in special places: courage and heartache in the snow-laden Swiss mountains: an extraordinary dream come true: unexpected happenings on the beautiful Isle of Skye: unsettling romance in the hills above Rome: and exciting drama on an exotic island in the Indian Ocean.

Including magical festive stories for both adults and children, featuring Marmite, the brave, adventurous little dachshund.

'I CAN FLY' 2017
For all those who believe in magic

ISBN 978-0-9563366-4-4

AN enchanting feel good tale about a real-life puppy, her friend Marmite, a little girl and their animal and bird friends.

Wishing that she could fly high in the sky with the birds, spread happiness and help to those in trouble on the earth below, the little puppy Nutmeg sets out to make this magical dream come true.

Illustrated by the author.